Mary Wesley was born near Windsor in 1912. Her education took her to the London School of Economics and during the War she worked in the War Office. She has also worked part-time in the antiques trade. Mary Wesley has lived in London, France, Italy, Germany and several places in the West Country. She now lives 'rather a hermit's existence' in Devon. She has previously written for children and comments that her 'chief claim to fame is arrested development, getting my first novel published at the age of seventy'. That first novel, *Jumping the Queue*, is published by Black Swan, as are her later novels, *The Camomile Lawn, Second Fiddle, Harnessing Peacocks, The Vacillations of Poppy Carew, Not That Sort of Girl, A Sensible Life, A Dubious Legacy* and *An Imaginative Experience*.

An Imaginative Experience

Mary Wesley

BLACK SWAN

AN IMAGINATIVE EXPERIENCE
A BLACK SWAN BOOK : 0 552 14326 X

Originally published in Great Britain by Bantam Press,
a division of Transworld Publishers Ltd

PRINTING HISTORY
Bantam Press edition published 1994
Black Swan edition published 1994

Set in 11pt Linotype Melior by
County Typesetters, Margate, Kent.

Black Swan Books are published by Transworld Publishers Ltd,
61–63 Uxbridge Road, Ealing, London W5 5SA,
in Australia by Transworld Publishers (Australia) Pty Ltd,
15–25 Helles Avenue, Moorebank, NSW 2170,
and in New Zealand by Transworld Publishers (NZ) Ltd,
3 William Pickering Drive, Albany, Auckland.

Reproduced, printed and bound in Great Britain by
Cox & Wyman Ltd, Reading, Berks.

for Tessa Sayle

1

The sheep lay on its back in the centre of the field with its legs in the air. As the InterCity train ground to a halt an acrid smell from the brakes percolated through the First Class carriages; one of the passengers sneezed.

From his corner seat Sylvester Wykes could see the long line of carriages curve round the perimeter of a green field in the centre of which was posed the up-ended animal, and sense as the train settled to its stop the creaks and groans of protesting metal. Around him voices queried, 'Why are they stopping?'; hoped not to miss connections; voiced distrust of British Rail and made odious comparison with the incomparable train services of France, Germany, Switzerland and Italy. Then there came the abrupt slam of a train door and into his line of vision a figure came racing.

Sylvester pulled his reading glasses down his nose and reached for his bifocals. The figure, though trousered, was female. She reached the sheep, leaned down, gripped it by its fleece, heaved it to its feet and, still gripping, held it upright on tentative hooves.

'What's going on?' A passing passenger leaned familiarly across Sylvester from the aisle to squinny out of the window. He smelled of tobacco and alcohol. Sylvester drew back in his seat.

'Half a mo',' said the man, as though Sylvester had spoken. 'Let's focus the old binoculars. I've been bird-watching in the Scilly Isles,' he informed Sylvester. 'I'm what's known as a twitcher. Ah!' He adjusted the binoculars. 'Here we are, got it. A sheep was on its back. Want a look?'

'No thanks.' Sylvester pressed back in his seat.

'Saw it as we stopped,' said the man, leaning his elbows on the table and thrusting his rump into the aisle. 'Pretty girl!' he said appreciatively. 'Want a look?' He again offered his binoculars.

Sylvester said, 'No.'

'What was it doing on its back, I wonder?'

'They get stuck,' Sylvester said tersely.

'Oh?'

'And die.'

'Rush of blood to the head? That it?'

'This is a non-smoker,' said Sylvester.

'I know,' said the twitcher. 'I'm in the next carriage, passing by from the buffet. Ah!' he exclaimed. 'Here comes the guard! Fireworks, d'you think? Naughty, naughty? An Asian, you must have noticed when he took our tickets. Sticklers for the rules, that lot. Revel in a spot of authority. Oh! He's shouting and she's shouting back. It must be she who stopped the train. Looks a bit crazy. D'you think she's mad?'

Sylvester did not reply.

'There will be trouble,' said the man. 'She'll get a summons. Costs a bomb to stop a train. Oho! She's let the sheep go. It's lolloping away and now the guard is bringing her back to the train. Sure you don't want a look?'

'Go away,' said Sylvester.

'All right, all right,' said the man. 'Keep your cool.' He drew himself upright, letting the binoculars thump against his upper stomach. The communicating doors swished at his passing.

Sylvester straightened legs which had winced away from the man and looked ruefully at his bifocals, which had snapped in his hand.

But his tormentor was back. 'Think I'll see if I can have a word with her,' he said. 'Want to come? There

8

might be a story there. She's in the Second Class. What do you think?'

'Oh, leave her alone,' said Sylvester, regretting the words as he spoke.

'She a friend of yours or something? Didn't leave the sheep alone, did she? Didn't consider her fellow passengers much. Some of us have business to attend to. Leave her alone. That's rich!'

The man, Sylvester realized, was partially drunk. He closed his eyes and listened for the swish of the communicating door.

'You've cut your hand,' said the man, still hovering close. 'Broken your glasses. However did you do that?' When Sylvester did not answer he moved away and the communicating doors closed at last.

The train began to move. As it gathered speed Sylvester put the broken bifocals in his pocket and wiped blood from his cut palm. Rage had made him prickle with sweat. He wanted a drink but feared meeting his tormentor in the buffet. He had not seen the girl clearly, but was left with the impression of a white face, black eyes, squared mouth shouting at the guard, and brown hair ruffled by the wind. She had seemed a creature more vulnerable than the sheep she was rescuing. She looked bogged down in despair.

Would the guard be rude to her? He had seemed a quiet and courteous man when he asked for the passengers' tickets; his turban was beautiful, furled round the contours of his head like an exotic shell. No, the guard would be polite, stick to the rules; he would not bully. But that foul-smelling bird-watcher was another matter. Was he perhaps a journalist? 'There might be a story there' were ominous words. If he was a journalist, he would be employed by the gutter press. Would the guard protect the girl? Would she perhaps take shelter in the lavatory? Lock herself in? Sylvester visualized the girl crouched miserably in confined and possibly malodorous space for the rest of the journey.

Should he follow the twitcher and prevent him imposing himself, demanding a story, not listening to a word she might say while he fabricated his own? 'Communication cord drama on InterCity train'. 'Shepherdess leaps to rescue lamb', or, worse, 'Little Bo-peep in Lamb Chop drama'. Furious, Sylvester rose to his feet, but instantly sat down again; rushing to the rescue would make things worse.

When the train stopped at Reading he scanned the crowds. Would she get off? If she had not got off the train, Sylvester thought as the train moved on, and he was almost sure she had not, the intelligent thing for her to do would be to pick up her bag and make her way forward so that at Paddington she would have a head start for the taxi-rank or the Underground. If she comes through here and that fellow follows her I shall bar his way while she escapes, he decided.

The girl did not materialize.

In any case, Sylvester thought as the train jostled into Paddington, how do I imagine I would recognize her? I bust my glasses, I did not see her clearly; it was the impression that was clear. He got to his feet and, heaving his bag off the rack, joined the queue by the carriage door.

When he saw the girl threading her way through the hurrying crowd he was reminded of Greta Garbo in the film *Ninotchka*, seen long ago in black and white. She was wearing a long black coat which reached her ankles and a big black hat pulled low over her nose. He could not be sure it was the right girl until he glimpsed the twitcher hunting through the crowd, dodging like a rugby player to get ahead and confront her. As the black coat brushed past him Sylvester stepped in her wake and the twitcher, recoiling, cannoned backwards into a trolley piled high with mailbags to fall on his back while the girl disappeared.

Affecting not to notice the twitcher's plight,

Sylvester sauntered on to join the queue waiting for taxis.

It had not been necessary to trip the man, Sylvester thought, but if it had been necessary he would not have hesitated to do so.

2

At about the time Julia Piper was stopping the InterCity train to succour a sheep, her mother, Mrs Clodagh May, was bracing herself to clear up the mess left in her house by a variety of people who had come to sympathize and mourn with her after her son-in-law Giles and grandson Christy's joint funeral. Their kindness was such a solace, she told her friend and gossip Madge Brownlow, who had volunteered to help. 'I did what he would have liked, what he would have chosen if he had been here,' she said.

Madge said, 'Yes, of course.' I am used to sherry and perhaps whisky at funerals, she thought, not smoked-salmon sandwiches and champagne. Out loud she said, 'Shall I stack the dishwasher?' And, removing the coat of the black suit she jokingly referred to as her *tailleur*, she pushed up the sleeves of her white silk shirt.

'The dishwasher is out of order,' said Clodagh.

'So the plumber did not come?' Madge, who had opened the dishwasher, closed it. 'Useless!'

'The plumber,' said Clodagh, enunciating carefully, 'is on holiday.'

'But he has a partner,' suggested Madge.

'Gone to a football match.'

'Shall we leave it then?' ventured Madge, unrolling a sleeve, feeling pusillanimous. Her friend eyed the disorder with distaste. 'Oh, if only Giles—' she said. 'He was such a—' She choked.

Madge, searching for the right appellation, supplied: 'Handyman?' Then, seeing her friend's eyes begin to swim, she added, 'And so much more.'

12

'Oh, so much, so much.' Clodagh wiped her eyes. 'He was – oh – he – oh—'

Madge said quickly, 'Yes,' and, 'Of course he was. Well then, let's get cracking.' She rolled up her sleeves for the second time. No use waiting for handyman Giles, she told herself ironically; he had kept people waiting even when he was alive. Wrapping an apron round her waist, she said, 'I'll wash, you dry,' turned on the hot tap and squirted washing-up liquid into the sink. 'You'll feel a lot better,' she said bracingly, 'when the house is tidy. Shall we clear the living-room first?'

Clodagh May did not answer but picked up a tray and went to collect plates and glasses. I wish Madge would not call my drawing-room a living-room, she thought. Giles never called it a living-room, though sometimes he called it 'your parlour'. Joking, of course. His dear jokes. 'Shall we go into your parlour?' She could hear his voice.

'Phew! What a stink! I wish people would not smoke, it's a disgusting habit.' Madge threw open the windows. 'Let's get a through draught,' she said, opening the door into the garden to let in the chill blast of autumn.

She forgets he smoked, thought Clodagh. Then she smiled, remembering his voice. 'Dear old Madge, not strong on tact.' She followed her friend and quietly closed the garden door.

But Madge opened it again and stepped on to the terrace. 'Gosh,' she said, 'empty bottles. Glasses, too. Whoever was out here punished these bottles.' Then she remembered that the vicar who had officiated and the doctor had been out here, talking to Julia while she waited for the taxi to take her to the station; both men chatted kindly as they gulped their drinks and tactfully chewed their sandwiches. Julia had stayed mute, neither drinking nor eating, just standing.

The two men had remained out here after the taxi had driven away. Had they come in to say goodbye and thank you to Clodagh? People, even doctors and priests, had such casual manners these days. She eyed the empty bottles. One heard doctors took to the bottle, their life was such a strain, but priests? 'You would think,' she said to Clodagh as she clattered glasses into the foaming sink, 'that Julia would have stayed to help. It would have been considerate.'

'Julia only considers herself,' said Clodagh. 'Mind those glasses don't break. Oh!' she wailed. 'Why must this happen to me? I was relying on Giles. I didn't ring the plumber until yesterday. Giles had said – so of course—'

Madge said, 'Oh,' rinsing a glass under the tap.

'She didn't even wear black,' said Clodagh bitterly.

'Be fair, she did. A black hat and black coat.'

'Not *underneath*,' said Julia's mother. 'She was wearing jeans and a sweater. Imagine wearing jeans and a sweater at Giles and little Christy's funeral.' I wish, she thought, that Madge would not be so particular; it grates.

'True, and he her husband,' said Madge thoughtfully, rinsing another glass. 'And *she* his widow. Are you the widow of a divorced husband?'

'Don't start splitting hairs,' exclaimed her friend. 'Little Christy was her child!'

'So he was.'

'And *my* precious grandchild.'

'She probably had no black clothes with her wherever she was when she got the message,' said Madge tolerantly. 'She looked as though she was wearing black even if she was not. One did not notice the jeans.'

'I did,' said Clodagh.

'You are such a perfectionist,' said Madge.

'Whose side are you on?' Julia's mother raised her voice to a shout. 'It was all her fault, that accident; everyone knows Giles was a terrible driver. She always did the driving when they were together. She should never have divorced him.'

14

'Did she ever give a reason?' Noticing that her friend stood idle, Madge took the cloth from her and began polishing the glasses. 'You never told me the real reasons. We all heard the reasons in court, of course, but— Where do these go?' She held up a glass.

'On that shelf, no, not that one, the one on the left. Julia's reasons were outrageous.'

'Oh?' Madge set the glass on the shelf indicated. Damn, I've cracked one, she thought. Better say nothing, old Clodagh's such a fusspot. She turned the glass so that the crack faced inward.

'One reason was that Giles – no, I can't tell you, it's too—'

'Go on,' said Madge, 'nothing shocks me.'

'What was shocking,' said Julia's mother, 'was the utter frivolity of her reasons. Hey! Madge, you've cracked a glass.'

'It's a very small crack. What do you mean by frivolous reasons? Give me an example.'

Ignoring Madge's request, Clodagh said, 'Giles gave me those glasses. You have spoiled the set.'

Madge said, 'Oh dear, sorry.'

Clodagh, harking back, said, 'Their divorce was not yet absolute so she would be his widow, and the divorce was making no difference to Christy.'

'Julia had custody,' said Madge.

'Yes.'

'If my child was killed in a car smash I would be stricken, absolutely stricken. Perhaps Julia is stricken,' said Madge.

'She doesn't look it, does she?' Clodagh snorted. 'Julia is not stricken. If you ask me, the judge who gave Julia custody wanted his head examined. Dreadful old man.'

'Then would you have wanted Giles to have custody?' Madge raised astonished eyebrows. 'Surely everybody—' Surely everybody knew that Giles was to all intents and purposes an alcoholic? Charming, of course, but an alcoholic.

'Of course I would,' said Clodagh. 'Christy would have lived with *me*, that's what Giles would have wanted.'

Madge said, 'Gosh, Clodagh, what honesty.'

3

Leaning forward to read the meter, Sylvester Wykes noticed that there was another taxi outside his house and, standing by it, his wife Celia. 'Drive on a bit, please,' he said to the driver. 'Stop at the next corner by the pillar-box.'

The man drove on. At the corner Sylvester got out, paid his fare and waited while it drove away. Then, sheltered by the pillar-box, he looked back.

His wife, watched by her driver, was loading suitcases and packages into the cab. 'You might give me a hand.' Her voice, high and whining, carried in the quiet street.

'Got a bad back,' said the driver.

'Bet you haven't.' She heaved a large cardboard box into the taxi.

'That the lot, then?' asked the driver.

'No, it is not the lot.'

Sylvester smiled.

Celia went back into the house to reappear with two outsize carrier bags which she threw on to the seat of the cab, followed next by a cardboard container.

The driver produced an evening paper and began studying the form.

Sylvester waited.

Five and a half, six years ago, he thought, I looked across the room at a party and saw that woman, caught her eye. We nodded, I wove through the crowd and took her arm. As we left the party I told her my name and she told me hers. I took her out to dinner, she confided her troubles. We ended the evening in bed and were married six weeks later. I loved her, he thought. I supposed it to be a grand passion.

His wife had gone back into the house. Sylvester shifted his weight from foot to foot.

Now Celia emerged from the house dwarfed by the television in her arms. She negotiated the steps with care, biting her lip in concentration.

The cab driver half-folded his paper, but thinking better of it opened it out while watching his fare in the driving mirror as she placed the television on the floor of the cab.

Sylvester thought admiringly: she took the small television from the bedroom on her first raid, bravo, full marks for thoroughness. Finally Celia went back into the house, but only to fetch her bag; she slammed the door shut and got into the cab, shouting, 'Drive on, then.'

Did I confuse love with lust? Sylvester wondered. Time was when I would have raced after that taxi, stopped it, dragged her out, prevented her going. 'It was lust,' he said out loud to the pillar-box.

The taxi diminished down the street and turned out into the King's Road. Sylvester walked back and inserted his key in the lock. Inside the house he sniffed, let the bag he was carrying drop and, breaking into a run, rushed round the house opening windows. Cold air streamed through french windows opening on to the garden from the sitting-room, and upstairs through bath and bedroom. Hurrying to the basement, he heard the door-bell ring. He threw open the kitchen window and squinted up to catch a glimpse of his visitor.

Recognizing stout calves above neat ankles and extremely high-heeled shoes, he said, 'Rebecca! I'll come up.' He wedged the area door open with an empty milk bottle.

'What's going on?' Rebecca leaned to peer through the area railing. She had immense black eyes popping

18

either side of a handsome nose and sensual lips parted over large competent teeth.

'I'll let you in.' Sylvester retreated from the area to hurry upstairs and open the front door.

'Are you aiming to catch pneumonia?' Rebecca stepped into the house. 'It's freezing.'

'Celia has been here.' Sylvester closed the door behind her.

'Oh?'

'Removing the last of her clobber.'

'I *see*.' Rebecca moved into the sitting-room. 'But why the howling gale?' she enquired.

'Can't you smell it?'

Rebecca sniffed. 'M-m. How long was she here?'

'Long enough. I don't know.'

'It won't linger,' said Rebecca. '"Emotion" doesn't. I thought you were still away,' she said. 'I brought a note asking you to telephone when you got back, thought you might like a meal or something, thought you might be lonely.'

'I am,' said Sylvester. 'It's lovely. Great.'

Rebecca laughed. 'If you are going to keep all the windows open I'll borrow a coat,' she said.

'Just a few more minutes,' said Sylvester. 'I'll put the kettle on and give you tea.'

'Coffee, please,' said Rebecca, 'and I shall shut the windows now. You are imagining the smell.'

'I saw her from a distance,' said Sylvester. 'She was piling her stuff into a taxi as I got back.'

'You talked to her?'

'I dodged.'

'Coward,' said Rebecca. 'I wonder what else she took.'

'She's taken everything floggable already, probably sold it to pay for her new outfits.'

'Don't you mind? The house looks dreadfully bare.'

'No.'

Rebecca closed the french windows and followed

19

Sylvester down to the kitchen. 'Has she left you a kettle?'

'I bought a new one. Oh, confound it, she's taken it!'

'Come round to my place,' said Rebecca, laughing. 'I'll make you tea.'

Sylvester said, 'I'll boil a saucepan.'

'Get the locks changed,' said Rebecca, 'or you will come home one day to a completely stripped house.'

Not fond of unsought advice, Sylvester boiled water in a saucepan and made coffee for Rebecca and strong Indian tea for himself.

'That stuff will rot your guts. Celia was right there,' said Rebecca.

'Coming up in the train,' said Sylvester, putting their cups on a tray and setting off up the stairs, 'I saw the most extraordinary thing.'

'What?' Rebecca sat on the sofa with her legs apart.

About to sit in an armchair opposite, Sylvester changed tack to sit next to her on the sofa. The brevity of Rebecca's skirts unnerved him. 'I am easily unnerved,' he said.

'You are too easily unnerved. What was this thing?' Rebecca reached for her cup.

'A sheep.'

'A sheep?'

'On its back.' Sylvester explained the sheep, the rescuing girl, the drama, the guard, the twitcher, the broken glasses.

'The train must have been going very slowly,' said Rebecca.

'InterCity trains go very fast, at least a hundred miles an hour.' Sylvester gulped his tea, hot, strong, just as he liked it.

'Not on Sundays. On Sundays they mend the track, the trains go slow. The train must have been going very slowly or it would not have been able to stop still within reach of the sheep. The girl would have had to run back miles to reach it if the train had been going fast.' Rebecca, knowing best, gripped her saucer. 'I expect you were asleep when she stopped the train,' she said.

'I smelled the brakes,' said Sylvester.

'You and your sense of smell! Did you speak to her?'

'No. I told you.'

'You wanted to, but you hesitated. You are a terrible hesitator,' accused Rebecca.

Once, for a brief moment, I was tempted to make love to you but I hesitated, thought Sylvester, and laughed.

'What's the joke?' asked Rebecca. 'The way you tell it, it's a sad story. You said the girl looked mad.'

'No. The oafish bird-watcher suggested she was mad – she looked terribly sad, not mad at all. I should say she was perfectly sane.'

'How could you see all this without your glasses? You say you broke them. Let me see your hand.' Rebecca took Sylvester's hand. 'Gosh, Sylvester, that's a nasty cut. Shouldn't it be stitched? Let me get you a plaster.'

'No.' Sylvester withdrew his hand. 'Thanks, but no. It's OK.'

'And you must get new bifocals. Shall I make an appointment for you?'

'You are no longer my secretary,' said Sylvester.

'I'll ring your oculist tomorrow.'

'No thanks,' said Sylvester and thought: mustn't tell her I no longer go to him.

'Have it your own way, I'm only trying to help.' Rebecca pursed her lips. 'Anyway,' she said, 'sad story, poor little sheep.'

'It was a very large sheep, probably a Texel. They are the largest breed.'

'Does it matter?' Rebecca was tiring of the sheep.

Sylvester said, 'No.'

'So what else did Celia take?' Rebecca's eyes probed the room. 'Books?'

'She hardly reads.'

'I see she has taken the Meissen pugs and the Chelsea bowl, oh, and the Capo di Monte snuff boxes.'

'She gave them to me. She's taken everything she ever gave me. And her furniture, of course.'

Rebecca said, 'Oh my!'

'She never gave me anything unless she wanted it herself.' Sylvester stretched his legs and looked round the room, savouring the lack of clutter.

'I think Celia has been utterly outrageous,' said Rebecca, 'and I am a feminist. Has she left you any sheets? I remember when you married, it was she who brought the bed linen. If she has purloined the sheets I can lend you some. Bath towels, too. She's probably taken those. I'd better go and look.' Rebecca rose, stabbing a sharp heel into the parquet, raising her bulk from the sofa in a surprisingly spry movement.

Sylvester said, 'No, no. Please don't bother, Rebecca. Everything is fine. I'll see you out,' he said, assuming she would go, thinking that there would be another carry-on if she saw all the new stuff he had bought at Habitat.

'I'll just wash our cups,' said Rebecca, gripping the tray. 'I gave you these cups when you married,' she said. 'I'm glad Celia left them with you.'

'So you did. No, Rebecca, please leave it. I am capable of washing a teacup.' Sylvester inclined his torso towards the door.

'Promise me you will let me know if there is anything I can do,' Rebecca relinquished the tray but stood her ground. 'I'm glad she left you the sofa,' she said, her eyes making an inventory of the room. 'Did she leave you the bed?'

Sylvester said, 'Yes.'

'M-m. That figures, yes. You will need somebody to come in and clean. I'll ring the agency I deal with and get you a cleaner.'

'Please don't bother,' said Sylvester. 'I propose to manage without.'

'You can't possibly manage, I—'

'I don't want a cleaner. I don't want the noise of Hoovers. I cannot cope with all the talk.'

'Talk is part of the wage, you have to talk. You learn a lot, it's interesting.'

'No, thank you. I shall manage, Rebecca.'

'The house will be a shambles within a week, unwashed dishes, soggy bath towels on the floor and you will run out of loo paper. Marriage has not changed you.'

'Rebecca, please stop bossing me. You are no longer my—'

'Secretary. I know, but I will get you a cleaner who comes when you are out, and while I am about it I will get the locks changed. You will live to thank me and be properly grateful.'

Sylvester laughed. 'You are a bossy lady.'

Rebecca said, 'I am. I should not tell you this,' she said, moving at last towards the door, 'but Celia once told me that you bored her.'

'I bored her because she bored me,' said Sylvester equably and pecked Rebecca's cheek. 'Goodbye.'

Closing the door on Rebecca's departing back Sylvester Wykes sniffed the air of his empty house and, sensing no lingering trace of 'Emotion', let out a whoop.

4

The twitcher, whose name was Maurice Benson, assumed he would have little difficulty in locating Julia Piper. He had what he liked to think of as flair, a talent developed during a brief career in the police and a slightly longer period snooping for a private detective agency. Neither career had remotely satisfied those who employed him and in consequence had given him small job satisfaction. So when his widowed mother died, leaving him a small but adequate income, he turned bird-watching, which had previously been a hobby, into a way of life. He was not married; he was as free as the birds which were his passion to travel wherever and whenever he pleased.

One pleasure was getting into conversation with strangers. He would tell those who would listen that he was writing a book, although this was not strictly true, his writing having got no further than an article or two in his local paper and a paragraph promised in the RSPB magazine. Returning from an autumnal trip to the Scilly Isles and observing from his seat near the buffet the wading birds on the Exe estuary, the swans and heron further up the line, and with binoculars focused on a kestrel hovering above a field mouse on the railway embankment, he was able to get a sighting of Julia when she leapt from the train and later exchanged words with the guard.

If Sylvester had not been so withdrawn and toffee-nosed Maurice might not have bothered to do more than tease; as it was, his stuffy and protective attitude annoyed him and aroused his curiosity; he resolved to include Julia and the sheep in an article he might write on 'Autumn Birdlife as Viewed from a Train', or some such guff.

Banned as Sylvester had hoped he would be from contact with Julia by the guard, he had yet managed to read her name on an overnight bag a fellow traveller identified as hers by the seat she had vacated when she leapt on her errand. The traveller volunteered, too, that Julia had joined the train at Tiverton Parkway.

Irritated by Sylvester's attitude, Maurice thought he would find out what the girl was about and what had roused the interest of a bloke like Sylvester who, smelling of expensive soap, had visibly and offensively reared away from his own well-worn and pub-scented Barbour. It would serve Sylvester right, Maurice told himself, if he located Julia; for already he linked the two in his mind, just as he would the hen when he spied a cock bird; there might be a place for Julia in his notebook marked 'useful contacts'. It would be agreeable, too, to queer Sylvester's pitch in some revengeful way.

On arrival at Paddington, Maurice became convinced of Sylvester's interest in Julia when, on seeing him hunting for her through the crowd, he had barred his way and, watching him stumble and fall, had done nothing to help. Then, obviously thinking he would have lost the girl, he stalked on towards the cab rank not noticing that, rather than pursue Julia, Maurice had followed to listen for and note the address he called out to the driver.

This done, Maurice Benson wandered back along the concourse to fortify himself with a beer before chatting with old friends in the police and people he had formerly known in the station hierarchy. While drinking his beer, he decided it would be better to leave the police out of his quest and confine his enquiries to old associates among the railway staff. But he was disappointed to find most useful contacts he

25

had known had moved on and the two who were left were less than co-operative. True, they were willing to tell him Julia Piper's name, since he knew it already, and they agreed that she might be charged for stopping the train. And, should she be charged, she might be fined.

'Then again, she might not,' said a man called Bates. 'So much gets dealt with by post these days.'

He occupied a far more senior post than Maurice remembered and was viewing him now without much friendship.

'Why do you want to know?' he enquired, but before Maurice could think of an answer his colleague, whose name was Smith, volunteered the suggestion that since the train had scarcely been delayed and unless somebody lodged a complaint, the whole episode would most likely be overlooked, since stopping a train to rescue a sheep was a trivial and laughable matter which did little to enhance British Rail's image.

'You wouldn't be in the business of writing for the newspapers, would you?' asked the man called Bates, beginning to scowl. 'Because if—'

Remembering belatedly the terms he had once been on with Bates, and that Bates owed him no favours, Maurice voiced a hasty denial and said quite humbly that he 'only wanted the lady's address'.

To which Bates riposted, 'We are not in the business of giving ladies' addresses to casual enquirers.' Enjoying himself, for he too remembered Benson, he added, 'And now, if there is no more we can do to help, we have other, more urgent matters to attend to.'

Feeling that he now had nothing to lose, Maurice said, 'Like what?'

'Like IRA bombs,' said Bates. 'Didn't you once have Irish connections? Have you any contacts with your boggy cousins? 'Cos if you have, we might be interested.'

Maurice, feeling bullied, denied any Irish cousins or

knowledge of that country. 'Look here,' he said, 'all I wanted was—'

'A bird's address,' said Bates.

'Which you won't give?'

'Didn't we say?' Smith picked up a folder.

'Well then,' said Bates.

Maurice Benson said, 'Goodbye, then,' and muttering, 'Thanks for nothing,' left the office. As he left he heard Smith laugh and Bates ask, 'What was his interest, anyway?'

Smith replied, 'Search me. The birds he takes an interest in are of the tweet-tweet variety.'

Solacing himself with another beer in the station buffet, Maurice Benson comforted himself with the thought that he had Sylvester's address in London and the knowledge of where Julia Piper had joined the train. There was plenty of time, no hurry at all. It might some time be amusing, when in that part of the country, to hunt tail, snuffle round the region of Tiverton Parkway.

5

In late afternoon Julia Piper, having walked from Paddington, shuffled through a pile of letters and circulars which had dropped through the letter-box during the preceding week; she did not pick them up, but climbed the stairs to the flat she and Giles had occupied during the years of their marriage. On the top floor she fumbled for her key, unlocked the door, stumbled in and, without taking off her coat, lurched forward to lie face down on the divan which served as sofa and occasional bed in the room that was her sitting-room. As she fell her hat slid off, and she lay inert, spent.

In the flats below people came in from work, turned on their televisions, cooked their suppers, talked loudly, slammed doors, ran baths and subsided into bed as night closed in not to silence but the muted roar of a vast city interrupted by occasional police sirens and the distant sound of tugs hooting on the river. Some time in the night an ambulance raced fast through the street, bell ringing. Half-conscious, Julia eased her shoes off, pressing one foot against the other in a state between sleeping and waking.

In the early hours the sound of rain lashing against the window roused her. She got up stiffly, pulled off her coat and went to the window. A wild wind was blowing the rain in slanting lines into a river which was the street, as though a million fishermen cast for trout in the pools forming among the parked cars whose humped roofs resembled rocks. So she had once described them to her child, holding him in her arms warmly wrapped in a towel after his bath, nuzzling his neck where his hair was damp from soapy water. 'Look,' she had said, 'a rushing river, darling. If we look hard we may see a fish.'

'A trout?' He had jogged in her arms. 'A salmon? A shark?'

'No, no, my love, a dolphin! You shall ride on its back.'

She had held him tight, kissed the nape of his neck, rolled him into his pyjamas, put him into his cot, promised to show him a real river, a real dolphin, yes, soon.

Cramp seized her tired feet, knotting her toes into twisted shapes, moving up to her calves until she gasped with pain. Stamping and trying to tread away the agony, she drew the curtains, switched on the light. There was no river, no fish, no child. In bleak desolation she padded to the kitchen, poured water from the tap and drank the chlorinated stuff in thirsty gulps until, surfeited, she gagged.

In the bathroom she filled the basin and splashed icy water over her face and ran wet hands through her hair. Doing so, she was aware of a tang of sheep dung and lanolin and briefly remembered her train journey. Moving back to the kitchen she found stale bread, made toast and tried to eat. She was ragingly hungry but could not swallow. She put the toast into the garbage-can.

In the cupboard under the sink, searching for the plastic bin-bags she used for rubbish, she remembered that she had run out. Taking her purse she let herself out of the flat and ran down to the street, hurrying through the rain to the Corner Shop, which was just opening ready for its first customer.

'I need bin-bags, Mr Patel.'

'A packet of three, Mrs Piper? You have been on holiday?'

'A lot of packets, please, Mr Patel.'

'Three packets, Mrs Piper?'

'At least six, Mr Patel.'

'So we are having a grand after-the-holiday spring clean, Mrs Piper, an autumn clear-out, I'm thinking.'

'A clear-out, yes.'

'They come cheaper, I tell you, in fives, Mrs Piper.'

'Two fives then, please—'

'And how is little Christy, Mrs Piper?'

'Dead.'

'*Dead*, Mrs Piper?'

'Dead.'

'???'

'In a crash, Mr Patel. Please don't cry.' She avoided his eyes.

'But he was with his daddy! You told me!' Mr Patel protested.

'Dead, too. Please, Mr Patel, how much are the bin-bags?' She was afraid he would not let her pay.

'Fifty-three pee a packet. They are old stock, a discount for quantity would not help, I think.' Mr Patel wept as he took her money. He put the bin-bags in a carrier bag and surreptitiously added a ball of string. She had often forgotten to tie up the bags and the neighbourhood cats, filthy things, scattered refuse on the doorsteps.

Back in the flat, aware of the stale air, Julia flung open the windows, then, bin-bag in hand, she worked her way through the rooms. Into the bags went remnants of Giles: clothes he had not bothered to take, confident that she would send them on and she had not. Socks hardened by wear and sweat, several old T-shirts, a sweater, a pair of jeans, the trainers he had bought a size too small, an anorak, a tweed jacket, a drawer full of grotty underwear, snapshots of happier days and a few books. She tied the necks of the bags and heaved them on to the landing.

In the kitchen she drank more water and again tried to eat, but could not.

Christy's possessions were harder. Bundling his clothes into the bags she averted her eyes, held her breath to avoid his scent. When the bags were full she tied the tops as though some vicious animal might escape from them. His toys were scattered about the flat. Plastic duck, comic, sponge and flannel in the bathroom, soft toy in his cot. What had he taken with him? What favourite toy? Why could she not remember? She sat back on her heels, her mind a blank.

At last, every toy, every garment safely bagged, she dismantled the cot. It was large and heavy. She had put off buying him a bed; she manhandled it out and down the stairs. When all the bags were grouped on the doorstep, she found a taxi and, helped by the driver, loaded it and drove to the Oxfam shop. Walking back through the rain she felt strangely light-headed and had difficulty climbing the stairs.

Some time in the late afternoon she woke shivering from an exhausted sleep, got up, made strong tea and drank it scalding hot, so that it left a metallic taste on her palate. Then, using soap and ammonia, she set to work scrubbing shelves and drawers, the insides of cupboards, pulling the furniture out and washing the spaces behind; she moved the divan, surprising eddies of dust which soaked into balls of felt. When all was clean she got out the Hoover and siphoned unreachable detritus from behind the radiators and gas fire. She had nearly finished when the Hoover stalled with a metallic clang and regurgitated a whistle. A whistle, a police whistle, a loud and dreadful whistle.

Mr and Mrs Patel stood on the doorstep. Mrs Patel held a bundle against her chest. Tim Fellowes, tenant of the ground-floor flat, answered the bell, listened to Mr Patel's query.

'Yes, she's up there, she must be.' He looked up. 'All her windows are open— What? Oh no, we haven't actually spoken, we don't know her that well. We've passed on the stairs, that sort of thing. We are new here as you – you'd think she'd be cold,' he said, looking up. 'Wouldn't you?'

Mrs Patel murmured indistinguishably in her native tongue. Her husband translated, 'Has some friend perhaps? Anybody else?'

'Not to my knowledge,' said Tim Fellowes, 'I've been working late. Only just got back, as a matter of fact.' He looked doubtfully at the Asian pair. What could they want? What were they on about? How could one tell with these people? He caught the woman's eye, looked hastily away. 'Tell you what,' he said, 'I'll ask my girlfriend, she may know. Wait here.' He went back into the ground-floor flat, not quite closing the door. The Patels took note of his scrubbed appearance, pink face, hair receding from high forehead, Marks & Spencer suit. Through the half-open door they heard colloquy punctuated by a laugh, then a burst of giggles. They waited patiently.

Tim Fellowes came back, grinning. He had caught Janet half-undressed; she was ticklish.

'She says she supposes she's up there because earlier on she put out her rubbish in a lot of bin-bags, but she hasn't spoken. As I said, we are new but Janet, who's not just a pretty face, suggests your Piper lady wouldn't go out leaving all her windows open, would she? And apparently she's on her own since – oh, here she is,' he said as Janet, tying the belt of a towelling robe round her waist, joined him in the doorway.

Pink from a bath and smelling of shampoo, she smiled and said, 'Hi. As I told Tim, she put the trash out but she's up there now.'

Mrs Patel murmured again. Her husband translated, 'The other flat people?'

'The Eddisons? Oh, they are away, they're on holiday.'

Still the Patels stood in the hall.

'Well,' said Tim, 'I need my sleep, have to be at the

office by eight. Why don't you try again tomorrow? Oh, by the way, we are away this weekend. Could you cancel our papers?'

Yet again Mrs Patel murmured. Her husband said, 'May we go up, please?'

'Oh? Go up? I suppose you may. I suppose it's all right. But shut the street door when you leave, there's a good— I say,' he said to his girlfriend as the Patels vanished up the stairs, 'what a peculiar hour to call, what an odd sort of visit. I suppose it's all right? D'you suppose I shouldn't have told them the Eddisons are away?'

'They must know the Eddisons are away,' said Janet, 'Angie shops there. They get their papers there, as we do. Are you imagining those two will tip off a burglar?' she said, laughing.

'Of course not,' said Tim, to whom this thought had occurred. 'It's just that one can't be too careful with those sorts of—'

'Oh, come on, you old racist.' The girl drew him into their flat. 'That sari Mrs P is wearing is the most gorgeous colour; d'you think it would suit me?'

'No, I don't,' said her lover, discomfited by her tone. 'You'd look a freak,' he said. 'You are sallow.'

When eventually Julia answered the Patels' gentle but insistent knocking it was nearly midnight and the curry, well wrapped though it was in its covered dish, had grown cold in Mrs Patel's arms. Entering as Julia stood back, Mrs Patel handed her burden to her husband and gestured towards the kitchen. Taking in Julia's appearance with a slanting glance, Mr Patel took the curry, went into the kitchen and closed the door.

What followed blurred in Julia's memory. Extraordinary though it was to seem in retrospect, Mrs Patel had bathed her and washed and dried her hair. What she did remember clearly was that not once did Mrs

33

Patel try to remove the whistle from her clenched fist but with soapy sleight of hand transferred it from one hand to the other as she worked. Then she was back in the sitting-room wrapped in her bathrobe, sitting by the fire which Mr Patel had lighted, cosily in the half-dark of one lamp with the night shut out behind drawn curtains.

Now the Patels brought the dish of hot vegetable curry and rice from the kitchen and steaming tea. Unwilling to hurt the Patels' feelings, Julia ate, hesitant at first, then ravenously, and as she ate tears coursed down her cheeks.

She said, 'It's delicious, thank you, and so hot the chillis are making me cry—'

And the Patels nodded and wiped tears from their sympathetic eyes. Then she was in bed, still clutching the whistle, knees drawn up to her chin with the duvet pulled up to her ears.

Waking once in the night and crying out, she had the impression that Mrs Patel, crouched at the foot of the bed, rose and laid a cool hand on her forehead and spoke in her own language, but when, late the next day, she woke, the Patels were gone.

6

Returning from work, Sylvester was irritated but not surprised to see his one-time secretary standing on his doorstep in the company of a stranger.

'Hallo, Rebecca, what brings you here?' he pecked her cheek.

'This is the man from Chubb,' said Rebecca. 'He has fixed your new locks. Since you are here, it will save me posting you the new keys.'

Sylvester said, 'Ah,' and wondered how she had imagined he would get in. (Waited for me on the doorstep, no doubt; she knows my habits all too well!)

The man from Chubb introduced himself. 'Somers. I think you will find everything in order now.'

Sylvester said, 'It was in order before.'

'So here are your keys, sir, the three lots your secretary ordered. If you could just sign here, I'll be on my way; our invoice will follow in the post.' The man handed Sylvester three sets of keys, made an abbreviated gesture indicating that had he been wearing a hat he would have touched it, and walked briskly off.

Sylvester said, 'Bloody cheek.'

Rebecca laughed. 'Don't be silly, Sylvester. You needed the locks changed, you can't run the risk of Celia forever popping in and out.'

Sylvester said, 'God!'

'And if you just give me my set,' Rebecca went on, 'I'll see that the cleaning woman gets it. She's called Andrews. She's coming Mondays from eleven till one to tidy after the weekend, and Fridays from twelve to two to tidy ready for the next. All arranged.'

Sylvester said, 'Unarrange it.'

Rebecca said, 'What?'

Sylvester said, 'I do not want a cleaning lady.'

'Oh, but you *do*. It's fixed with the Sloane Agency. They are totally reliable. If Mrs Andrews can't come for any reason, they send a substitute. You cannot live in a mess, Sylvester.' She held out her hand for the keys. 'I'll take the keys now, it's on my way. And by the way, Sylvester, I've made you an appointment with your optician.'

Sylvester said, 'Now I know why I sacked you.'

Rebecca smiled. 'Aren't you going to ask me in for a drink?'

Sylvester said, 'No.'

Rebecca said, 'Come on, Sylvester, don't be such an old—'

'If I want a cleaner, I'll get one myself.' Sylvester thrust one of the new keys in the lock and half-opened the door.

'Where from?' asked Rebecca. 'Where do you imagine you'll find a cleaner? Good cleaners are rare as gold. You don't want an out-of-work actress, or some young thing who will bring her child to pee all over your— Oh, come on, Sylvester!'

'Should I want a cleaner, which I don't, I would put a card in the Corner Shop.'

Rebecca said, 'What corner shop? You can't do that, not nowadays. You—'

Sylvester opened the door. 'And you can cancel the appointment with the optician.' He stepped across the threshold, just managing to block access without appearing deliberately rude.

'Sylvester, your eyes!' Rebecca exclaimed. 'You must be careful of your eyesight, you need bifocals. You—'

'Mind your own business, leave mine to me.' Sylvester began closing the door. 'If you must know,' he said more kindly, 'I've been to my oculist and he says the last thing I need are bifocals. My long sight is remarkably good. I only need to use reading glasses if I get over-tired. Good night, Rebecca. It's good of you to be so interfering and bossy, but I can manage without it. I won't ask you in for a drink. I've been dealing with nitwits all day and look forward to my own company. Bye,' and he closed the door.

'Whew!' he said, standing alone in his sitting-room. 'Was I too strong?' He mixed himself a drink and took a revivifying gulp. 'What do I need with a cleaning lady? I'm quite able to dust and hoover. Gosh, look at *that*.' He drew a line with his finger across the dust on a side-table; then, grinning, he wrote 'Free!' tracing the word in joyful loops, swallowed his whisky, refilled the glass and sat back on his sofa. 'Great!' he said. 'Great.' And then, 'Oh, curse it, I forgot to order the Sunday papers.' Sipping his drink, he ruminated: should he wait until the morning and go out and buy them, or should he go now and arrange for them to be delivered? Were they delivered he would hear that wonderful Sabbath plop of papers on doormat, wander downstairs – naked if he wished – gather them up and trail back to bed to the sound of church bells, as he had not done since his marriage to Celia. Oh, Sundays, blessed Sundays, to waste again in snooze and idleness in one's own bed, solo!

Reminded of this item of furniture Sylvester got up and went upstairs. There was something wrong with the bed. The pillows, of course. 'Fool,' Sylvester exclaimed, 'fool.' Swiftly he rearranged the pillows, smacking and punching, stacking them dead centre so that propped against pillows, meagre for two, just right for one, a man could read in comfort, stretch his legs without fear of encounter. (Oh Christ! Why can't you cut your toenails? You've scratched my ankle.)

On impulse Sylvester ran downstairs and out of the house. He was no longer bound by marital practice to ask what paper Celia would enjoy, nor bound to buy her flowers – how had that placatory act grown into habit? – nor add to the flowers *Harpers, Marie Claire* or *Hello!* depending on her mood, all of which entailed walking as far as Sloane Square – one did not dare take the car for fear of losing one's – Celia's to be exact – parking space. Now, if he doubled back towards World's End, he could sample a corner shop sometimes sighted in passing but never entered.

Waiting to be served, Sylvester eyed the display of goods. All the usual breakfast foods and tinned meats were there, baked beans, pastas, jams, marmalades and honeys, but somehow they took back place to a truly splendid display of rice, brown, white and wild, spices, chutneys, herbs and poppadams. Jingling the change in his pocket, Sylvester hummed, 'Poppadam, poppadam, a preponderance of poppadam—'

'Sir?' Mr Patel was ready to serve him.

'Oh!'

'?' Mr Patel's eyes were large and thoughtful.

'Oh,' Sylvester said again. 'Um – do you deliver newspapers? Sunday newspapers?'

'We deliver, certainly, yes, Sundays too.' Mr Patel indicated a newspaper rack presently occupied by a solitary *Evening Standard.* 'Gone tonight,' he said. 'Sold out.'

'Ah, yes. Could I open an account?'

'Address?' Mr Patel picked up a pen.

'Not far.' Sylvester named his street and watched Mr Patel write it in a ledger.

'Which?' said Mr Patel.

'No, no, I don't want *Which?*, I'd like the *Independent* on weekdays and on Sundays the *Observer* and *The Sunday Times,* please.'

'And smellies?'

'Smellies? You have me foxed.'

'One moment.' The man disappeared through a door behind the counter. 'Smellies,' he said, returning with a colour magazine of the previous week and indicating with deprecating finger a scented sachet attached to an advertisement for aftershave. 'We remove or leave in to customer's taste.'

'Now that's what I call service,' said Sylvester. 'What a splendid business you run. No smellies, please.'

Mr Patel smiled.

'Why don't I pay a month in advance?' Sylvester suggested.

Mr Patel was agreeable, and while he wrote a receipt Sylvester, renewing his inventory of goods on offer, noticed a small board on which were pinned ads and requests: *Violin Lessons, Massage, Home needed for Tabby Kitten (neutered), Wanted Child's Cot in good condition, Ski boots size 12.* On impulse he asked, 'Would you stick up a notice for me?'

'One pound a week,' said Mr Patel and handed Sylvester a blank card.

Sylvester wrote: *Cleaner wanted four hours a week, usual rates, while owner out at work,* and added his address.

'Better not give address, burglars,' said Mr Patel. 'I write it again with telephone number and I go-between.'

'Fine,' said Sylvester. 'I leave it to you.' But on his way home he regretted his impulse and blamed Rebecca for her pervasive though waning influence; then, rendered optimistic by the delightful solitude in his house, he consoled himself as he mixed himself a drink with the thought that nothing would come of it. Should some person apply, it would be simple to rebuff her.

Sitting back on the sofa and stretching his legs, Sylvester relished Rebecca's departure as he gazed appreciatively at his almost empty sitting-room. Celia had been a great one for clutter. He sipped his drink and eyed the mantelshelf denuded of Capo di Monte snuff boxes, Meissen pugs and the fussy French carriage-clock which had been her pride and joy.

Contentedly he savoured his whisky, considering without rancour his errant wife, and began to laugh out loud at the thought that, had the house not belonged to him as it had before their marriage, Celia would have that, too. Or perhaps not, he thought. A tiny house in a Chelsea cul-de-sac was not comparable to the establishment on Barnes Common owned by Andrew Battersby into which Celia was planning to move next. There was, too, a house in Gloucestershire. How meteoric had been Andrew Battersby's rise in the City since Celia divorced him. From 'something or other in insurance' the name of Battersby had grown to giant proportions in the financial world. She won't divorce him a second time, Sylvester thought, sipping his whisky; she will turn a blind eye to pretty secretaries. She won't want to stay long in that new flat; she has to remarry before some other girl catches him. She should have stuck to Battersby; I was never more than an inadequate safety net, a five-year stop-gap. Five long years. Phew!

How quickly, he wondered, would she get around to asking for a divorce? How would she word it? Would she expect him to divorce her? Unlikely. Would she want to divorce him? What grounds would she find? Sylvester pondered. He had not been unfaithful; he had not been cruel or violent, rather the contrary. Celia was not a woman to inspire crimes of passion; he had let her go taking most of the contents of their home with her without a bleat of protest. 'Good luck to you, Celia,' he said out loud, 'first and about to be third wife of Andrew Battersby.'

7

Janet heaved her bags of shopping into the ground-floor flat and kicked the door shut.

Sorting out groceries in the kitchen, she pondered over the growing pile of letters lying in the communal hall addressed to Piper.

She knew her lover Tim would say, 'Leave well alone, don't interfere. It's not as though she was a friend. We are new here, we don't know the situation,' and so on and on. She popped a fresh loaf into her Provençal bread pot and consigned the residue of last week's loaf to the litter bin. Then she switched on the kettle and brewed herself a mug of instant coffee, which she drank standing. As she drank, she thought of the Piper woman in the top-floor flat. Divorced, one had gathered, but visited rather often by her ex. Presumably he had access to the child? Access night or day, if one went by the shouts and thumps one could not help hearing even two floors down. There had been no disturbances lately, though, and a perceptible absence of noise from the child. Nor had she seen the Piper woman passing through the hall. She couldn't be away, not if the Indians from the corner shop had been up to see her. Funny, that. Lovely colour that sari – sallow? I am not sallow! Frowning, she scrutinized her face in the glass. It's the autumn light, must be. Why not be neighbourly? Take her some of Tim's aunt's apples. Hard to know whether they were cookers or eaters. She'd brought far too many; sitting there, they'd turn to cider before one found out. Janet picked out half a dozen fruits which looked all right and put them in a plastic bag. In the hall she gathered up the pile of letters, mounted the stairs and knocked on the door of the top flat.

When Julia opened the door, Janet said, 'I am Janet. I live with Tim Fellowes on the ground floor. I wondered whether you would like some of the apples Tim's old aunt brought us from the country? She didn't say whether they are cookers or eaters, but they smell quite nice.' So saying, and gaining impetus from good intentions and curiosity, she pressed forward so that Julia willy-nilly stepped back and, peering over her shoulder, Janet could see into the room.

'Oh!' she said. 'Oh! How squeaky clean! Oh, gosh, am I interrupting something?' she said as she sighted a bottle of vodka on an otherwise bare table, flanked by a bottle of aspirin. 'You are going to have a party or oh, God, I am inept, you were going to— Oh,' she whispered, covering her mouth with her hand. 'Suicide.'

Julia said, 'You've brought my letters,' and took them from Janet. 'Thanks.'

Janet said, 'May I sit down?' She was feeling, as she would tell Tim, a bit weak.

Julia gestured towards a chair. Janet sat. Julia subsided cross-legged on the floor, letting the letters fall in a heap beside her.

Minutes passed; an age, Janet later told Tim.

'Aren't you going to read them?' she presently ventured.

Julia said, 'What's the point? They will all say the same thing.'

'Same thing? I don't get—'

'They will say how terribly sorry they are to hear that Giles and Christy are dead.'

I must have looked like a stranded fish, Janet would tell Tim. My jaw dropped.

'And they are not, of course, terribly sorry. Sorry, but not "terribly" and in most cases, apropos Giles, not sorry at all but positively pleased, as I am.'

Janet said, 'Oh my God!'

Julia said, 'Is he *yours*? Are you *sure*? How do you *know*?' So viciously that Janet pressed back in her chair, affronted.

Julia said, 'Like a drink? Vodka and tonic? That's all I've got. I'll get a lemon,' and sprang to her feet in an alarmingly agile manner. Janet, watching her go into the kitchen, thought: I could hop it, but Julia was back carrying glasses, tonic and a lemon before she could make up her mind to go. Julia said, 'Say when,' and sloshed vodka liberally into the glasses.

Watching her add lemon and tonic, Janet said, 'But I thought you were—' and stopped herself.

Julia smiled slightly. 'No,' she said. 'No, I was not,' and she took a gulp of vodka. 'The aspirin,' she said, 'is a dodge I learned long ago. Take a couple before drinks and it helps with the hangover. Drink up,' she said. 'As you *are* here, you can keep me company.'

Janet took a large swallow of her drink and, choking at its strength, said, 'Do you think I am sallow?'

Julia said, 'Sallow? Why?'

'Something Tim—'

Julia said, 'It suits you. You're pretty.'

Janet said, 'Thanks,' and swallowed some more vodka and tonic. 'Not an awful lot of tonic,' she said. Then she said, 'So you weren't – er – going to – er – well, no, obviously, but why alone?'

'You don't think I look like a lonely drinker?'

'Lonely, yes. Well, you must be lonely if your Giles is, you did say Giles? Your husband?'

'Yes.'

'Is dead and Christy, too. Oh my God, that's why it's been so quiet lately. Oh! What a dumb chum I am!'

Julia refilled Janet's glass and topped up her own, adding a slight amount of tonic.

Janet said, 'You were going to celebrate, not—'

Julia said, 'That's right; celebrate the one and blot out the other. Or is that too complex for you?'

Janet said, 'You are making me drunk; it's all too complex for me.'

Julia said, 'Lucky you.' Later, she said, 'Come along, time to go. I'll help you downstairs.'

'And she did,' Janet told Tim. 'She gave me two aspirin and tucked me into bed. Oh, Tim, I've never seen anyone so terrifyingly unhappy in my life. It's appalling.'

And Tim said, 'Darling, you are pissed, it can't be as bad as that,' and held her in his arms for a few minutes. Then, hesitantly, he said, 'Are we going to have any supper? I'm starving.'

At this Janet jerked upright, only to lie down again with a groan. 'I'm still on a merry-go-round. I'm sorry, Tim, but I'm better lying flat.'

Tim said, 'Oh,' and then, because he really was very hungry, he volunteered to go and buy fish and chips or a take-away.

Gratefully Janet closed her eyes, saying, 'I might be able to sleep but leave the light on, please.' Tim left the flat, shrugging his shoulders.

Returning presently with two lots of fish and chips he found Peter and Angie Eddison, tenants of the flat immediately below Julia Piper's, unpacking luggage from their car. 'Hi,' he said. 'Back from your hols? Had a good time?'

Peter Eddison said, 'Super. We drove right across Eastern Europe; fascinating.'

Tim said, 'What was the food like?' He picked some chips from his package and put them in his mouth. 'I'm on my way home with our supper,' he said. 'Janet's not – like a chip?' He offered the package. 'Janet's not feeling very grand.'

Peter Eddison said, 'Oh, thanks,' and, pushing the greaseproof paper open, extracted a lump of cod. 'It's great to be home,' he said. 'We got sick of dumplings and sauerkraut and God-knows-who's in the saus-ages.'

Her arms full of bulging packages, Angie Eddison came up the steps. 'How mouth-watering,' she said. She opened her mouth and her husband popped in some chips from Tim's parcel. 'Sure you can spare them?' she asked, munching. 'Oh! Could I just taste the fish?'

Tim obligingly opened out the packet and Peter chose her a piece of cod which, since her hands were full, he fed her. 'Has anything happened while we've been on our travels?' Angie Eddison asked. 'Prague was simply—'

'I'll say it has!' Tim interrupted her. 'There's been a drama. The girl on the top floor, the one with the ex-husband and the noisy little boy, oh, I'd better not shout, she's up there.' He opened his package wider to expose the golden chips and battered cod. 'Come closer,' he said. 'Help yourselves.'

Angie put her burdens on the ground and reached for a chip. 'What happened? What sort of drama? Did you send for the police? We've had to before now,' she said.

Lowering his voice, Tim said, 'The ex-husband had a smash, wrote himself off and the child.'

Huddling round the fish and chips, fingers ready to help themselves to more, the Eddisons said, 'No!' and 'Oh my God!' and 'But he'd lost his licence!' and 'Where did it happen?' and 'How *is* she, does anybody know?' as they reached for the comforting chips.

Tim said, 'It was in the papers. She's been up there for days; the paper-shop people went up. She let *them* in, we saw them. Then, this afternoon, Janet *finally* nerved herself, went up with the girl's letters. She'd not collected them so Janet thought— Well, she went up to see if she could help. Well, I suppose she wanted to find out what was going on; it's been so quiet.'

'It's never quiet,' said the Eddisons.

'It is *now*,' said Tim. 'Janet found her sitting with a

bottle of vodka and bottles of pills and naturally thought suicide, but apparently not.'

'We are eating all your chips,' said Angie.

'Go ahead,' said Tim, 'before they get cold.'

'What did she tell Janet?' asked Angie. 'If it wasn't suicide? If she didn't mean—'

'Bugger all. Oh, she told her about the ex-husband and the child being dead, she told her *that*; Janet is terribly upset.'

'But the Piper woman – what about her?'

'She seems to have questioned Janet's belief in God.'

'Is Janet religious?'

'No, of course not. Well, apparently, when Janet said, "Oh my God", the Piper girl flew off the handle.'

'Why?'

'I don't know, but she did; and then she made Janet drunk – she's paralytic, she's in bed. That's why I was buying fish and chips.'

'Which we've eaten,' said Peter.

'What d'you suppose we ought to do?' asked Angie.

'I think we should mind our own business and get the car unpacked,' said her husband. 'I have to work tomorrow and my experience of the Piper woman is that she keeps herself to herself. The one time I tried to interfere between her and that husband, I got my head bitten off.'

'So leave well alone,' said Angie. 'Thanks for telling us, Tim.'

Tim watched them go back to their car to collect the rest of their luggage, then let himself into the flat. Janet was asleep on her back, snoring; he finished what was left of the fish and chips, undressed disconsolately and got into bed beside her.

In the flat above them Peter and Angie Eddison finished their unpacking and went to bed. Comfortably settled, Angie said, 'Oh dear, do you suppose I should have gone up and seen the Piper woman?'

'Tomorrow will do, surely,' said Peter. 'It isn't as though we've ever been friends.'

Angie said, 'That's true; she's always been stand-offish. What heaven to be back in our own bed. I think it's the best part of a holiday.'

Some time in the night, Julia Piper walked quietly down the stairs and let herself out into the street.

8

Maurice Benson strolled out of the village keeping his eyes open, taking things in. He had left his car in the pub yard after a beer and sandwich at the bar, chatting with the landlord and a loquacious local. As he walked his binoculars swung across his chest, working a felty patch on the sweater worn under his Barbour jacket. Digesting his lunch and information gained, he paused from time to time to quiz the fields and hedges. This was not good bird country but as an inveterate twitcher he knew that the most improbable birds turned up in unlikely locations. There had, for instance, been a kingfisher in the pond near the railway station. But today birds were not his priority; his interest lay in Mrs May, mother of recently widowed Julia Piper.

'Two cottages a bit on from the cemetery. The one with the privet hedge is Madge Brownlow's, Mrs May's friend, and soon after that, with a camellia hedge, that's Julia's mum. Cost a packet when she planted it. Her son-in-law, the one that was killed, put her up to it. That was before he married. They said he got a discount on the shrubs, he was that sort.' The landlord's laughter had contained a snort.

A pair of magpies were at play in the cemetery, chattering and swooping among the headstones; Maurice paused to watch. Who was it had said they looked like croupiers?

A woman tending a recent grave straightened her back and, brushing detritus from her hands, shouted, 'Shoo, you horrors, shoo!'

Maurice called out, 'Two for joy!'

She was in her fifties, square with a fussy beige blouse under a sensible beige cardigan, corduroy trousers of beige also, a good fit when bought, tightish now, and green wellington boots. Her hair, rather mannishly cut, toned with her clothes. Staring at Maurice across the cemetery wall, she said, 'Fat lot of joy,' and briskly brushed her hands against each other.

Maurice said, 'Are you Mrs May?'

She said, 'I am Madge Brownlow. Who are you?'

'A friend, an acquaintance really of – well – what a tragedy.' He let his eyes rest on the grave (gravelly earth, awful stuff to work in for the gravediggers) under heaps of wreaths and bouquets of chrysanthemums tied with white ribbon, the words on the cards blurred by condensation under their Cellophane wrappings.

Madge Brownlow said, 'Thought you might be Press. Clodagh's had them up to here. Go away!' she shouted at the magpies, who had fluttered closer. 'Shoo!' She clapped her hands. 'Birds of ill omen.'

'They are like croupiers in a casino.' Maurice watched Madge Brownlow. 'Evening dress in the afternoon,' he laboured. 'Dinner jackets, tuxedos.'

'I have never been in a casino.' She left his joke stillborn and bent to collect a trowel and fork which she put in a basket half full of dead flora. 'Didn't see you at the funeral,' she said. 'Were you a London friend?'

'Scissors.' Maurice pointed at the ground. 'They might rust.'

Madge said, 'Thanks,' and retrieved the scissors. Maurice held the cemetery gate open. 'I'm doing this for Clodagh.' Madge made sure the gate was latched. 'She is still too upset, too utterly—'

Glancing sidelong, Maurice fell into step beside her.

'I tried to see Julia in London,' he said.

'Oh,' said Madge, 'Julia.'

'She was out.' Maurice persisted. 'They said she is out all the time,' he lied.

Madge said, 'I wouldn't know. They were divorced, on the point of absolution. Oh, wrong word. I mean, the divorce was almost absolute. Of course they should never have married.'

Maurice thought of the girl running, long legs, scissoring towards the sheep. 'Wasn't there a child?' he murmured, collating information gleaned at the pub.

'Of *course* there was a child – Christy. It's so terrible for Clodagh, devastating, dreadful. How will she ever—? This is my cottage. Why don't you come in? Like a cup of tea?'

Maurice said, 'Thank you very much,' and followed her in. Hollyhocks and roses, clematis and honey-suckle, traces of these in late autumn, converted workman's cottage, pricey, very *Homes and Gardens,* mind the beams. He ducked his head.

Madge said, 'Mind the beams. Go in there, I'll put the kettle on. Won't be a minute,' and, waving him into a sitting-room, turned right into a kitchen, leaving the door open.

'I did try and telephone.' Maurice raised his voice. 'But no luck from the number in the book.'

'It's ex-directory,' Madge shouted. 'Julia pretended Giles rang up at all hours and why not? He was Christy's daddy, wasn't he? Had been her husband. I've got the number somewhere, we got it from the police. I'll give it to you.'

'That would be kind.' Maurice examined the room. Chintzy covers, fussy curtains, plethora of china ornaments, women's magazines, a bag of knitting, large television, open fire, nutbags hanging outside the window, tits feeding, greenfinches fluttering near by and a tree creeper on the oak across the lawn, nice.

A set of photos on the mantelpiece. Let's have a dekko. Madge Brownlow with a younger woman. Clodagh May? The same with a young man, and again but with a child in her arms, the child in the man's arms, child alone. Child looks exactly like the man, ergo must be its father. There was a clatter in the kitchen. Maurice called, 'Can I help?'

'Oh, could you? I've put too much on the tray. Cracked a cup, butter-fingers. I thought a whisky in our tea would be in order, I need cheering up.'

Maurice said, 'Let me carry it. You carry the whisky,' (nice kitchen, Raeburn, Welsh dresser, blue plates, pine cupboards, *Homes and Gardens* again but awful tile floor) and led the way back into the sitting-room where, solicitous, he said, 'You must be chilled. Shall I put a log on your fire?'

Madge said, 'Oh, do, thank you,' and began pouring tea. 'I brought a large cup,' she said. 'Men like large cups, Clodagh always had a large cup for Giles. Help yourself to whisky, it was a present from Giles. He was so thoughtful—'

Maurice said, 'Later, perhaps. Just tea would be lovely, milk, no sugar.' Watching her pour (Edwardian silver teapot, common, but even so can fetch a lot these days), he took the cup from her and sat back in his chair.

Madge dolloped whisky into her cup, drank, sighed, said, 'That's good, that's better,' and stared into the fire.

Maurice said, 'Interesting photographs,' nodding up at the mantelpiece. 'Your family?'

'Oh! Oh *yes*. I think of them as my family. I have no blood relations except some sort of cousin in Canada. Clodagh has always— and Giles, of course, and little Christy. Oh, I can hardly bear— Oh! That's Clodagh, and that's Clodagh with Giles, and Clodagh and Christy, and little Christy alone. Such a darling— Clodagh's younger than me but we've been so close so long and then Giles— That's a very good one of Giles, the one with his head thrown back, and his hair all— Taken before Julia broke his nose, of course.'

'Broke his nose?'

'Of course! Didn't you know?'

'Um, I'd forgotten. Um – er – how?'

'With a frying-pan. The plastic surgeon had the devil of a job; the cartilage was pulped.' Madge stopped speaking and closed her eyes.

'The little boy is like his father, isn't he?' Maurice gave a gentle lead, watching his hostess drink her tea, refill her cup, add whisky. 'Little Christy was very like his father.' Maurice raised his voice slightly. 'Took after him, wouldn't you say?' He stood up to re-examine the photographs. What was it they'd said in the pub? Bit of a lad, very matey with his mother-in-law, dodgy with money, liked the girls. Temper? Oh yes, bit dodgy there too, but flash, and charm the birds off the trees. 'Very pretty little boy. Not like his mother. Funny,' he ventured.

Madge said, 'He was Giles's son and Clodagh's grandson. Why should he be like Julia? She was only a vehicle.'

'A what?' Maurice was startled.

'You heard.' Madge swallowed her tea, sniffed and added inconsequentially, 'She was barely in time for the funeral.'

'Oh?'

'She wasn't here, never *was* here once she grew up, left home at sixteen. Giles was here with Christy, staying with Clodagh. It was ridiculous that Julia had custody; Clodagh thinks the judge was bribed. Oh, not money, words, sweet talk, lies. Then Giles had this dreadful crash with the child in his car—'

'And they were both killed.' (The pub had provided details: car a write-off, father and child killed instantly, child's head practically severed at the neck, lorry driver in hospital with shock.) 'How very sad.'

'And *that's* the understatement of the year. That accident was wholly preventable.'

'Oh.' Maurice sipped his tea, wishing he had not refused whisky. Too late now. 'How—?' What was it that fellow had said in the pub? Kamikaze? 'How,' he repeated, speaking clearly, 'did it happen?'

'How indeed.' Madge raised her voice. 'Julia always did the driving when they were married. Giles was a bit adventurous, you might call it, yes, adventurous will do. Julia put him down, said he was a hopeless driver. He may have been; some people are. Anyway, she drove. You must have noticed she always drove.'

'Well, I, well, I'd for—'

'Well, she *did*. Then there was— Oh, I think the police were mistaken, but for some time I believe he had no licence.'

'Banned from driving?'

'That's what they call it, yes.' Madge looked ruffled. 'Too silly.'

'Ah.'

'Clodagh says they were over-zealous. Anyway, the point I am trying to make is that if Julia had been driving, there would not have been an accident. *That* is the point I am making and Clodagh is making. *If* Julia had been at the wheel Giles and Christy would be alive today.'

Maurice said, 'But forgive me, I understood Julia was not here when—'

Madge snapped, 'Of course she wasn't. Clodagh liked to have Giles and Christy on their own. Julia never fitted.'

Pondering this inconsistency, Maurice watched his hostess swallow her euphemistic tea and put up a hand to hide a smile as he tried to fit the girl who had raced across the field into the picture presently being painted by her mother's friend. 'So she did not fit in,' he said.

Madge said, 'Come to think of it, she never did.' Then she said, 'Fit or no fit, she's responsible, it's obvious.'

'You are making her out a murderess,' said Maurice. I usually watch birds, he thought. I am only here because the girl intrigued me slightly. And she would not have done that if that stuck-up bloke in the First

Class carriage had not tried to prevent me talking to her. He practically forced me to take an interest. 'I wouldn't hold her responsible,' he said. 'I wouldn't blame her.'

'Oh,' said Madge, 'maybe *you* wouldn't, but her mother does, and so do I. Are you sure,' she asked, suddenly belligerent, 'that you are not Press? You haven't really said what you are here for. Are you sure you are not a journalist? I thought for a moment you might be Police, plain clothes, but you don't look—'

'No, no,' Maurice said. 'Just a friend. I was hoping to get in touch with Julia; there was something Giles had asked me to do.' Less risky, since he was dead, to claim friendship with Giles than acquaintance with Julia. 'It was to do with her interest in sheep,' he said.

'Sheep?' The woman gaped. 'Sheep? What would Julia want with sheep?'

Maurice fumbled, 'Giles suggested I—'

'That girl wouldn't know anything about sheep. She's a murderess. Giles must have been pulling your leg.' She stared, unfocused by whisky, at her visitor. 'I will give you her telephone number. You can tell her from her mother, and from me if you like, that she is a murderess. We don't talk, of course; it would be wrong.' She got up and, moving to a bureau, began rummaging into pigeonholes. 'I know I have it somewhere,' she said.

Maurice, too, rose and studied the photographs, the girl's mother, husband and child, searching for some likeness to the figure seen fleetingly from the train. 'I was out of the country,' he improvised 'What was the reason for the divorce?' The pub had provided snide hints of something other than mere adultery and violence.

Madge spoke with her back to him. 'It was a put-up job. The real reason, the reason she gave her mother, was too piffling for words.'

Encouragingly, Maurice said, 'Oh?'

Madge said, 'I know I have put that number somewhere, I refuse to be defeated. Do smoke if you want and help yourself to whisky, and do please sit down. You are making me nervous.'

Maurice sat. 'I'm a bird-watcher,' he said. 'You have to keep very still watching birds.' He reached for his cigarettes and lit up, then poured a tot of whisky into his empty cup. 'Sometimes,' he said, 'the piffling comes close to the truth.'

'Well, if you *must* know,' said his hostess, still searching, 'when pressed by her mother, Julia said Giles's feet smelled, his pits smelled, and his breath reeked of tobacco. Her words.'

Maurice, inhaling, felt sympathy for Giles. 'She must have known he smoked when she married him,' he suggested.

'He had given it up but he took to it again, and I dare say before they married he did not take off his socks.' Madge let out a harsh laugh. 'Eureka!' she exclaimed. 'Here we are, I've found it. I'll write it down for you. Then,' she said, 'I'll join you in a cigarette, mention of Julia brings on the urge. And you,' she said, writing, 'can tell me what brings you to these parts, besides friendship with Giles. Here's the number,' she said. 'I wonder what you are really after?'

Maurice pocketed the piece of paper. Her tone was growing suspicious; the whisky was at work. It was inconceivable that he should tell this woman that the sight of Julia from the train window had briefly roused in him an erotic twinge; stubbing out his cigarette, he was conscious that like the defunct Giles he, too, smelled of stale tobacco. The woman's remark put a damper on lust, yet reminded him irritatingly of the fellow in the First Class carriage who had recoiled from him and snubbed his friendly overture. Would it be possible to get back at him through the girl? Maurice drained the last of the whisky and lit another cigarette. 'You have been very kind,' he said. 'I should be on my way. I suppose,' he said casually, 'that she had another chap handy when she divorced.'

'Absolutely *not*,' said Madge. 'Nobody who had been married to Giles would want anyone else.'

Maurice savoured this ambiguous statement and rose to leave. 'When Julia left home at sixteen, as you say, what did she do?' he asked.

'She moved out of Clodagh's orbit.'

'Oh.'

Madge lowered her voice. 'Out of Clodagh's class.'

Maurice again said, 'Oh,' and then, 'How was that?'

'She became some sort of domestic, I mean, really!' Madge almost whispered.

'Ah.'

'Clodagh says, and I am inclined to agree, that she found her proper level and that Giles should have left her there.'

'Indeed.' Maurice moved towards the door.

'Shall you go and see Clodagh?' Madge tried to delay him.

'Another time. I don't want to intrude.'

'What shall I tell her?'

'A friend' – he had reached the door – 'and my deepest sympathy.' He made his escape.

Walking back to his car, Maurice mulled over information gained and wondered to what possible use he could put it.

He drove slowly out of the village. He would go west to the Exe estuary, see whether the avocets had arrived, put up at the pub at Starcross, eat some oysters. He passed the cemetery and Madge Brownlow's cottage; the front door was closed and the curtains drawn, though the sun was not yet set. By contrast there was activity in the garden of the cottage next door. Clodagh May was piling weeds into a barrow.

Maurice slowed to a stop, rolled down his window and said, 'Good afternoon.'

56

Clodagh May was as tall as her daughter but there the resemblance ended; her hair was auburn, she had heavily lidded pale blue eyes, a Grecian nose and a large mouth turning down at the corners from the effort of heaving wet weeds into a barrow already overloaded. She looked, Maurice thought, a bit of all right. She said, 'You have been visiting Madge Brownlow.'

Maurice said, 'Yes,' and switched off his engine.

'She's watching *Neighbours*.' Clodagh May nodded towards the drawn curtains. 'She's addicted to soaps.'

Maurice got out of his car. 'Could I give you a hand with that barrow?' He put a hand on the garden gate.

'Are you the man from the Pru?' Clodagh May dropped her forkful of weeds on to an ill-balanced load.

'I was a friend of Giles,' said Maurice. 'My name is Maurice Benson.'

'I never heard him mention you.' Clodagh May pushed the prongs of her fork hard into the pile of weeds. 'Weeds!'

'Long ago. We rather lost touch. I only heard the other day that—'

'It was all in the papers. Ghastly, absolutely ghastly.'

'Yes.'

'He always did the heavy work for me.' She gripped the handles of the barrow.

'Please. Let me.' Maurice pushed the gate open. 'Where do you want it to go?'

Clodagh May stood aside. 'Round the back on to the compost heap. Thanks.' She led the way. Maurice followed pushing the barrow, which was extremely heavy.

'You should not do this, you might strain your back,' he said.

The woman gave a short laugh and, pointing, said, 'The compost heap is down there. Don't let the barrow run away with you, it always did with Giles.' She stood

57

watching while he trundled the barrow down a steep incline, tipped its contents on to the compost heap and then forked them evenly into place.

'You can leave the barrow there.' Clodagh May raised her voice.

'Right.' Maurice tipped the barrow on its side and walked back up the path.

'So you know about compost.' She took the fork from him and leaned it against the house. 'You've earned yourself a drink. How did you come to know Giles?'

'It was before his marriage – er – quite some time ago,' Maurice murmured.

'Oh,' she said, the Oh sounding like Ugh!

'Could you – um – could you tell me – er – if it's not too – er – put me in the picture? As a friend, I'd like to be up to date.'

'A disaster.' She opened a french window. 'Come in, wipe your feet.'

'Such an—'

'I mean the marriage. Come in. I don't know what Madge told you, she has been known to be discreet.'

So that's discretion. Maurice followed Clodagh May into the house. 'What a pretty room—'

'Yes. Giles had such taste.'

'She told me the bare facts, that Giles married your daughter—'

'That girl—' Clodagh May curdled the word girl into an epithet. 'You'd better sit down,' she said. 'No, not that chair, that's Giles's. Sit there, in that one.'

Shying from the comfortable chair he had aimed for, Maurice sat in the one indicated. His hostess moved towards a drinks table. 'Whisky?' she offered.

'Thank you. Weak, I'm driving.'

'And I am not.' Mrs May measured a small whisky for her guest and a generous one for herself. 'Help yourself to water.'

Maurice sloshed a little water into his miserly portion and resumed his seat. 'You were saying?'

58

'I was not saying anything.'

She was a handsome woman, Maurice thought, long legs, deep bosom, sexy, eat you alive. She would have been his cup of tea a few years ago but was now rather alarming. He searched the room for inspiration. 'No photos,' he said.

'Who needs photos?'

'Your friend – um – your neighbour Mrs Brownlow.'

'Miss.'

'Oh? Not married?'

'Old maid.'

'Sentimental?'

'Never experienced passion.'

'I see.'

'You don't see anything.'

'I don't?'

'Not a thing.'

Maurice Benson said, 'Then tell me.'

'Why not?' She stretched her legs out, quizzed him over her glass. 'If I don't, you will get a garbled version and I will not have my Christy and Giles garbled. Those, by the way,' she said, pointing to a recess behind Maurice, 'are my grandson's toys.'

Maurice swivelled round to find himself staring at a row of grossly outsized toys. Crushed together on a sofa like rush-hour travellers were a pink bear, a life-size clown, a blue tiger and a green elephant with a sort of boa constrictor round its neck. They looked pristine, new; he almost expected to see their price tickets. He said 'Oh!' and gulped his whisky. 'Was little Christy very fond of them?'

'Of course. Not that *she*— She would not have them in London. Not that it mattered, of course. This, *this* was his home. Their home.'

'So—'

'I mean Giles and Christy's home.'

'Ah.'

'Got that straight?'

'Mrs, I mean Miss Brownlow did indicate – suggest—'

'What?'

'That you – er – that your daughter—'

'I do not regard her as my daughter.' Clodagh May gulped her whisky and rose to refill her glass. She had splendid legs, Maurice thought, and the arse of a young woman.

'Miss Brownlow called her a vehicle,' he said, venturing into jocosity.

Clodagh May's smile was sardonic. 'That's just what she was. Excellent. Quite clever of Madge. So,' she said, 'd'you want the truth?'

Maurice said, 'Please,' and waited.

Clodagh May arranged her thoughts, gazing past her visitor into the garden hedged round with camellias planted by Giles. 'I married an architect,' she began. 'He impregnated me with his sperm. You're shocked by the word sperm? Some men are. The regrettable result was the girl. He left quite soon. I kicked him out actually, I can't live with my mistakes. And the girl left too, eventually. One day she was at school as usual and the next gone, something in her genes. *I* don't suddenly disappear. She took after her father. To tell the truth, I was glad to be shot of her. There is something about adolescent girls I find intolerable.'

Maurice laughed and Clodagh, catching his eye, smiled.

'What did she do?' Maurice asked.

'Do?'

'Yes.'

'She became a servant.' Clodagh May's voice was chill.

'How did she set about that? I thought they were an obsolete species.' Maurice laughed.

'It's no laughing matter.'

'Of course not, do go on.'

'It began waitressing in the holidays. Well, that's all

right, I suppose, just. Working behind the bar in the pub I didn't like, but it was in her holidays. Then one day she was gone and later I heard she had become a "domestic". I was humiliated. Well, wouldn't you be?'

'I have no children.'

'No. And I suppose you—'

'Would not be humiliated?' Maurice grinned. 'Do go on,' he said, 'please.'

Clodagh May frowned. 'Oh well, to cut a long story, some years later I broke my leg. I needed help in the house. I have a daily but we needed someone living in, and nurses cost the earth when you can get them. So Giles suggested—'

'Giles? How did—'

'He was living here, did I not say? He was working on his book.'

'I did not know he wrote.'

'Of course, brilliant, to think of that talent cut down so young—'

Maurice said, 'Terrible, absolutely terrible,' and wished she would offer him another drink.

She said, 'Shall I go on?'

'Please.'

'Refill my glass. This is bringing it all back. I'm not sure it's good for me. Get yourself a refill, too.'

Maurice said, 'Thank you,' and took both glasses to the drinks table, where he measured an inch into each. 'Do go on,' he said. 'It's cathartic.'

Clodagh took the glass from him. 'So I wrote,' she said, 'told her to come. She came. She did the work. Giles looked after me, of course, but she did the rest and—' Clodagh May sipped her drink.

'And?'

'She behaved like the skivvy she was. God! When I think of it!'

'And?'

'She got him into trouble, didn't she? Got herself

pregnant, had the cheek to say he raped her. But she would say that, wouldn't she?'

'And Giles?' I'm beginning to think I knew this fellow, Maurice thought, enjoying himself. 'And Giles?'

'Darling Giles explained it, I can hear his voice: "Little bit tiddly, that sort of thing? Rather like you and Daniel" – that was naughty of him – "Could happen to anybody." It had. "So what," he said. "You and I will have a baby." And that's what we did, we had Christy.'

'I thought Giles married – I thought—'

'Of *course* they married; I could not have Christy illegitimate. Bad enough that the mother was a servant.'

I am not hearing this. Maurice hugged himself. I love it, I must make her go on; it's beautiful. 'So?' he said.

'So she buggered everything up,' snapped Clodagh May. 'Took Giles off on a honeymoon to Paris. People would have gossiped if they had not, but *then*, would you believe, she takes Giles off to some squalid flat in London and, when my grandson is born, he only comes to his home on visits.'

Maurice ventured, 'Tough,' and then, 'Surprise.'

'Surprise?' Clodagh May, who had kept her voice low, shouted, 'Surprise, you say! The next surprise is she divorces him. What do you say to that?'

Maurice said, 'On what grounds?' hoping for the indictment of smelly feet and parts, or better still adultery, and if adultery who with and in whose bed? He held his breath, guessing.

Clodagh May drew her legs up, to sit contained in her chair. Distancing herself, she said, 'What does it matter?' She stared past her visitor. 'Now I have nothing,' she murmured, 'nothing.'

Maurice glanced uneasily at the toys sitting in their malevolent row. 'You have their grave,' he said.

She said, 'Would you have expected me to have

Giles and Christy freeze-dried?' And presently she said, 'Have you far to go?'

Dismissed, Maurice Benson headed for the main road but, level with the pub and reading an enticing notice, *Open all day*, he stopped and went in. The landlord with whom he had chatted earlier was gone, the customers too. A bored woman polished glasses to the rhythm of piped muzak. Maurice leaned against the bar. She said, 'Whatalyahav?'

'I'd better have something soft, I'm driving.'

'A non-alcoholic beer?'

'That will do, thanks.'

She said, 'You have been drinking shorts with May and Brownlow,' and poured his drink.

Maurice said, 'Somebody been watching me?'

She said, 'This is a small village. You a friend, then?'

Maurice said, 'You could say that.'

'Didn't see you at the funeral.'

Maurice said, 'Couldn't make it,' and sipped his non-alcoholic beer. Then he said, 'Tell me about the widow.'

The woman said, 'You work for the *Sun*?'

'I'm not Press. I was a friend of Giles Piper; tell me about Julia.'

The woman leaned dimpled arms on the bar. 'Julia, she'd gone before I came here, and from what I hear she should never have come back.'

Maurice said, 'Ah,' and hopefully, 'Why?'

'You should ask her yourself if you were a friend of Giles. Got her address?'

Maurice said, 'Yes,' and then, at a venture, 'You didn't like Giles, then?'

She said, 'I didn't say, did I? Some found him devious, can't say I did. Straight to the point, your friend. No messing about, up the girls' knickers. Shouldn't slander the dead, should I? It was a dreadful accident, dreadful.'

Maurice said, 'I heard. Mrs May is taking it hard. Might I offer you a drink?'

She said, 'Thanks, I'll have a shandy.'

Maurice said, 'What was she like as a mother?'

'The girl or her mother?'

'The mother, she didn't strike me as the maternal type. You a mother?'

'Not yet.' The woman eyed Maurice, daring him to suppose she had left procreation too late, and following this train of thought, she said, 'Clodagh May was a teenage bride, to hear her talk, Julia born when she was eighteen.'

Grinning, Maurice said, 'What else is she like?'

'You've met her. Not much money but class, she imagines, and Giles just the same – his grandfather was a Sir, but you'd know that. No money, but to hear them talk little Christy was going to Eton and us wondering who would pay. They were a funny couple!' The woman smiled. 'Thing was, Julia didn't fit.'

'Oh?' Maurice willed her to go on.

'She's divorced your friend, hasn't she? I never saw her when the child was here, it would be with its daddy and Clodagh May. But she came to the funeral. I saw her.' The woman looked past Maurice towards the road he had followed to the cemetery. 'They say in the village that she never stayed with her mother after she and Giles married, even before the divorce; if little Christy visited she'd stay at a farm which does bed and breakfast.'

'Funny.'

'Not really. Before she married, she had not been home for years. It was Giles and Clodagh who'd come to the pub, they were regulars, but one night Clodagh fell over a chair here in the bar.' The woman laughed. 'She broke a leg. I shouldn't laugh, but it seemed funny at the time.'

Maurice Benson said, 'Other people's accidents are.'

The woman said, 'Well,' forgiving herself. 'It was then they sent for the girl to look after her mum and help Giles, who was designing the garden. They could have got help from the village, but Clodagh May's not one to spend on help if she can get it free.'

Maurice said, 'So that was when Giles met her?'

'That's right. She looked after her mother, ran the house and worked with Giles. Did most of the work, according to some. I like flowers but I'm an Interflora lady, I don't get my fingers dirty. But she did.' The woman's gaze flicked past Maurice. 'The poor girl,' she said. 'Another beer?'

Maurice said, 'No thanks. Mrs May talked as though she and Giles—'

'No, no,' said the woman. 'She watched and I dare say Giles watched, too. People say it was mostly Julia did the garden. They say she can make a dead stick grow, pops a seedling in the ground and says, "Grow, you bugger," and it does, knows all sorts about gardens, birds, wildlife, that sort of thing. Green, don't they call it?'

'So as they toiled in the garden, they fell in love?' suggested Maurice. 'An idyll in Eden.'

The woman snorted. 'A bonk in the potting shed, more like! No!' she exclaimed in sudden irritation. 'I feel really sorry for poor Clodagh May, she was passionate about that fellow.' As Maurice opened his mouth to speak, she added, 'I don't know why I'm gossiping with you. If you've got the girl's address, why don't you ring her up, ask her all these questions yourself?'

Pushing himself away from the bar Maurice said, 'I may just do that.' (One could stir things up on the phone perhaps?) And as he opened the door to the road he asked, 'Which fellow was she passionate about?' But the woman had turned her back and switched the muzak up loud.

9

Julia Piper had walked with no aim other than to get away which, since what she hoped to escape was herself, was an exercise in futility. It had been a fine night but now it started to rain. After hours on unforgiving pavements her feet ached and the rain trickled off her hair down her neck. There had been nowhere to rest or shelter; the seats on the Embankment were occupied by sleepers and the doorways of shops crowded with people huddling in cardboard boxes. Walking steadily, avoiding contact, she kept mostly to side-streets. Early in the night she had been narrowly missed by a speeding car. The driver had swerved, hooted, shouted, 'Stupid bitch! Cow!' before driving on.

Crossing Trafalgar Square she sat briefly on the steps of St Martin-in-the-Fields, but moved on at the approach of a policeman to wander across Shaftesbury Avenue into Soho. Now very tired and walking at a snail's pace, she knocked against a man carrying a heavy backpack hurrying along unshaven and angry. He too exclaimed, 'Stupid bitch! Cow!' and she found herself longing for green fields and ruminating cattle, their sweet breath scenting the air as, sitting humped and contented, they chewed the cud. Then ahead she saw steps, an open door, and people going into a church; she followed them in out of the rain.

Moving up the church, she sat on a rush-bottomed chair in a darkish side chapel. The other people kept to the body of the church; she was alone. She stretched her legs and eased her feet. An old man shuffled up, took a candle from a box, stuck it in a holder, fumbled for a match and lit the candle; he mumbled, crossed himself and wandered away. Watching the flame, Julia closed her eyes.

When she woke there was a Mass going on; where she had had the chapel to herself, there were people, six or eight women, several men in City suits, and hurrying in late a middle-aged couple with a little girl. The man sat in front of Julia and gestured to his wife to sit across the aisle with the child. The couple did not look like the child's parents, more like an uncle and aunt; the man kept glancing fussily at his wife while the child, a girl of about ten, fiddled with her plaited hair, looked bored and sniffed. As the sniffs grew louder, the man passed a handkerchief across to the child. Mutinously she wiped her nose and handed the handkerchief back. Julia averted her eyes. Since she could not leave without causing a disturbance, she tried to pay attention to what the priest was doing. She had never been to a Mass and thought she had better copy the man in front, rise and kneel, sit and stand when he did.

She felt terrible after her sleep and could only catch an occasional word, for the priest muttered and his intonation was foreign. Somebody rang a thin-sounding bell and people knelt; the priest held something up and the bell tinkled again. Clearly it was a sacred moment; there was a hush. But the man in front of her was watching the child. He leaned across the aisle and, whispering indignantly to his wife, said, 'She is picking her nose.'

Covering her face with her hands, Julia snorted with laughter and stuck her fingers in her ears until the Mass was over and people were leaving. Watching the couple go out with the child she saw the man speaking angrily to the woman, and wondered whether what he had said was, 'Stupid bitch! Cow!'

The old man's candle was guttering. She got up, took

a fresh one from the box, lit it from the dying taper, breathed in its homely smell then sat down again. Some time later she remembered that she had once, years ago, before she married Giles and the advent of Christy, worked for the fussy couple and been sacked because she never, when she dusted, replaced their collection of ornaments in the correct order. This useless memory reminded her that she should resume work immediately if she wanted to pay the pile of unopened bills scattered among the letters lying on the floor of her flat, and recollecting the unhappy period when she had worked for the middle-aged couple. She remembered, too, that the woman had jealously counted the biscuits she ate with the grudgingly provided mid-morning Nescafé. This in turn made her realize that she was hungry, had eaten little since Mrs Patel's curry.

There was a sandwich bar crowded with jostling office workers in the street. She queued and bought a sandwich and then, since the rain was still drenching down, she returned to the anonymous darkness of the church.

While she had been away several people had come into the side chapel; they knelt or sat as though in anticipation. She chose a chair as far from them as possible and, with her back turned, surreptitiously ate the sandwich; then, appreciating the stillness, sat back and eased the shoes off her aching feet.

Quite close to her was what looked like a sentry-box with a heavy curtain across and she noticed vaguely that people went behind the curtain, reappeared, knelt for a bit, then lit a candle, crossed themselves and went away. She sat mesmerically watching the candles, which flickered when a companion was added to their number. (Christy had loved candles, loved blowing them out and watching her wet her fingers before snuffing the wick.) Soon there would not be room for any more candles, but there was no need to worry, the people had left, she had napped. She yawned and stretched her legs, stiff with fatigue.

When like a Jack-in-a-box the priest appeared from behind the curtain, she was badly startled, realizing that all this time she had been sitting by a Confessional, and that the priest might suspect her of eavesdropping. Overcome with confusion she averted her eyes, but the priest walked past her, leaving her alone.

Her heart was beating with shock; it was time to go. She leaned down to put on her shoes, but her feet had swollen. The shoes would not fit. She almost wept with frustration.

'Perhaps I could help?' The priest was back and standing near her.

'I did not realize it was a Confessional; I can't get my shoes on. I wasn't listening. I'm so sorry. My feet have swollen and will not go into my shoes—'

'No hurry,' he said, 'no hurry at all.' He sat beside her.

'And I ate a sandwich in here. I'm sorry about that.'

'So you ate a sandwich.'

'And I laughed when that awful man went for the child for picking her nose when the bell—'

'At the Elevation of the Host, m-m-m.'

'Oh, curse these shoes. I must go! So you noticed him.'

'Sit quiet a while.'

'I have sat quiet. I've been here hours. I've slept.'

'No harm in that.'

'There *is*. I have to work, pay my bills, pull myself together.'

'It looks to me,' said the priest, 'as though you'd "been together" too long.'

'I'm not together any more,' said Julia. 'I am solo. Giles took Christy in the car when he was banned from driving; they were both killed. I thought it was safe,' she said, her voice rising. 'Thought it was only fair for the child to see his father. Don't you see? I am responsible. If I had been sensible and bloody-minded, Christy would be alive now.'

The priest was silent.

'I am not "together",' Julia went on, 'any more than my feet are together with my shoes.' Still the priest did not speak. 'And don't imagine,' said Julia, who, having started to talk, could not stop, 'that I am sorry about Giles being dead. I am absolutely delighted. He was selfish and violent and cruel and a rotten father. I was divorcing him anyway; he terrified me when he was drunk and I did not like him sober. He smelled and I found it hard to stand up to him, though I did once hit back in desperation and broke his nose; I am proud of that. But usually I cringed and held Christy between us as a shield. I knew, you see, that he was not quite enough of a shit to hit the child. Oh God!' she exclaimed. 'I don't know why I am telling you all this; it is no business of yours. I have no faith, my belief in God is ropey and I am not even a Catholic. This is a Catholic church, isn't it?'

'Yes.'

'I only came in to escape the rain. Oh, blast my swollen feet!' Again she tried to force her feet into recalcitrant shoes. 'They simply won't go.' She shook with frustration.

'We could leave aside your absence of faith,' said the priest, 'move out of here to the presbytery where my housekeeper could give you a cup of tea and a foot bath. That would be a start – the feet and shoes getting together,' he said.

Julia said, 'That sounds like heaven.' Then she said, 'I am sorry. I am drivelling. I'd better shut up,' and blew her nose.

'We could also,' said the priest, 'find you a bed for the night.'

Julia said, 'Oh, thank you, thank you, but no. I have a

perfectly good bed; I must get back, if I can get my shoes on. I am not as destitute as some. You are very kind,' she said. 'Forgive me. I have made use of your church and wasted your time.' She was on her feet now, holding her shoes; she looked at him for the first time. He was middle-aged and grey and tired; he watched her quizzically. She felt it would be a horror to deceive him. Painfully she said, 'There's another thing I should tell you, but I can't. It's not a murder or anything like that, and it might seem a small thing to you, but to me it's the ultimate betrayal.'

He said, 'Let me deal with your feet and your shoes,' and led her towards the door.

Julia thought, I am being a bore, there's a limit to what he can stand. He probably gets all the flotsam of the Government's Victorian values in here; he doesn't need me. I must not impose. She thrust her handkerchief back in her pocket and walked beside him, carrying her shoes. Passing the altar the priest genuflected and she, looking up and seeing the Virgin framed in delicious mother-of-pearl, exclaimed 'How lovely, how surprising. Most Catholic churches in England are hideous.'

He said, 'This is the Bavarian church.' He did not explain, but asked, 'Do you live in London?' distancing her somehow by his question. When she said, 'Yes,' he said, 'I will give you your bus fare.'

And she, distanced, exclaimed, 'Thank you, but I have some money. I had enough to buy a sandwich.'

And he said, 'So you did.'

They were by this time at the door of the presbytery; he unlocked the door, ushered her in and called to his housekeeper. The opportunity to tell him more was over; she bottled it up.

But later, as the bus which would carry her back to the World's End came rushing to a stop, she hesitated in the crush of people climbing on board.

The priest had not flinched at a broken nose; could

71

she not have purged herself of that other infinitely worse burden? Then, as she hesitated and people pushed from behind, the conductor reached down, caught her arm and pulled her into the bus.

10

'I thought I would just look in to see how you are getting on.' Rebecca strode past as Sylvester opened the door. 'I see you've given your door-knocker a polish. Jolly good, it's such a pretty one. I like dolphins; getting quite rare, the dolphin knockers. The Americans bag them all.' She pressed on into the sitting-room. 'I was just passing,' she said, 'on my way.'

'Where to?' Sylvester teased, not expecting an answer. 'Where were you on your way to?'

'Oh!' Rebecca exclaimed, coming to a halt. 'Oh!' Her large eyes probed the room like searchlights. 'A writing table! That's new! It's a beauty, Sylvester.' She stroked the mahogany, slid a drawer open. 'These are quite hard to come by, Sylvester, and it has its original handles, marvellous. And it's in jolly good nick. Lashing out a bit, aren't you?'

'It was my father's, it's been in store. Celia didn't like it.'

Rebecca laughed. 'I don't suppose for one moment she realized what it's worth, or perhaps she thought it was a copy? Or has Andrew Battersby got lots of valuable writing tables?'

'Perhaps he has. Like a drink?'

'Oh, yes please, just a little one. And the chair; that's new, too.'

'Also my father's.'

'It's Chippendale, lovely.' She ran her hand across the back and down the arm.

'Yes.'

'Just look at its legs,' Rebecca crooned. 'My goodness, Sylvester, I wish I had legs like that. Mine are like grand pianos.'

'I wouldn't say that,' said Sylvester, who had often thought so. 'I'll get your drink.' He left his visitor eyeing the room.

Rebecca stopped stroking the chair and looked about her. Something was different apart from the desk and the chair; there was a subtle change since her last visit. The sofa was posed as before and the armchair, the shelves lining the back wall were still stuffed with books and the mantelshelf bare, as was the floor. What was it?

Sylvester came back from the kitchen, carrying a tumbler in each hand. He handed Rebecca hers. 'Do sit down.' He indicated the sofa and sat in the chair by the desk, keeping his back to the window.

Rebecca said, 'Delicious. You know exactly how I like it.'

Sylvester said nothing, crossed his feet at the ankles, sipped his drink.

'If you are refurnishing, you should let me help you,' Rebecca offered. 'I am pretty hot on antiques.' Sylvester thought, she never gives up. 'For starters,' Rebecca went on, 'you will need some rugs. Those Persian rugs were lovely.'

Sylvester said, 'Turkish.'

'Of course, Turkish. Any hope of getting them back? Surely that's the sort of thing Andrew Battersby would have lots of?'

Sylvester said, 'I wouldn't know.'

Rebecca said, 'Well, you must have rugs. You can't live with a bare floor, it's so uncosy. I'll look about. I know a man in Fulham who has an excellent collection at quite moderate prices.'

Sylvester said, 'No.'

'No? But—'

'They are being cleaned.'

'What are being cleaned?'

'My rugs.'

'So you've got some rugs?' Rebecca flushed. 'Your father's?'

'I bought them.'

'Oh, lovely. Persian?'

'No, Kelim.'

'Oh,' said Rebecca, 'Kelim.' She swallowed some of her whisky. He's forgotten how I like it, she thought, this is weak. She looked at Sylvester, sitting with his back to the light in his father's chair with his father's writing table behind him. 'Oh,' she said, 'I'm latching on. Now you have the house to yourself you've started on "the new novel". You are shot of Celia and have time to write. That's it, isn't it? What's the novel about?'

'I am writing the life of Wellington's valet,' Sylvester improvised. (What animal is it, he asked himself, which, when it gets something in its jaws, can't let go?)

'Wellington's valet? I didn't know he had a valet. Well, I suppose he must have. There will be a lot of research, I can help you with that. And if you want typing done, you must come to me,' said Rebecca.

'I shall have a word processor.'

'It will spoil the look of the room. You don't want a word processor, just let me – I would like to help,' Rebecca said bravely.

'I know you would.' Sylvester uncrossed his legs and stood up, holding his empty glass.

Rebecca perforce stood too. 'You have done something to this room,' she said, 'something other than the desk and the chair. What is it?'

Sylvester took her empty glass and stood waiting, a glass in each hand. Then Rebecca exclaimed, 'I know! It smells. It smells of beeswax. It's clean. Look at the floor! It's polished like a mirror. Did you get one of those firms with an electric floor polisher? Really, Sylvester, you should have asked me; some of those firms are daylight robbers. No, don't tell me,' she cried, laughing, 'you did it yourself!'

Sylvester said, 'My cleaning lady did it.'

'Oh!' cried Rebecca joyfully. 'Mrs Andrews. I'm so glad you changed your mind. I told you she would look after you.'

'Not Mrs Andrews.'

'Not Mrs Andrews?' Rebecca's voice rose. 'Who, then? What's she called? What agency did you use? Was it reliable?'

'I didn't use an agency.'

'Sylvester!'

'I advertised in the Corner Shop.'

'You what? You didn't! I thought you were joking.'

'It was a coincidence.' Sylvester was patient. 'I was paying for my papers – by the way, the service includes removal of horrible stinking advertisements from the colour mags – and I placed this advertisement and bingo, that was it.' He laughed. 'Works like a charm. As you see, the place is clean,' he boasted.

'What is the woman called?'

'Mrs Piper.'

'Mrs Piper?'

'Yes.'

'It's a gypsy name. Oh, Sylvester, do be careful. What is she like? It sounds terribly risky.'

'I haven't seen her.'

'What can you mean? You must have seen her, I saw Mrs Andrews for you. What are her references?'

'No references.'

'And you haven't seen her!' Rebecca rolled her magnificent eyes. 'How d'you manage?'

'If she wants anything, floor polish, Ajax, that sort of thing, she leaves a note. I leave the money for it with her money, and that's it.'

'How does she get in?'

'With a key.'

'And who gave her the key? You must have seen her

76

when you gave her the key. Sylvester, you are teasing me.'

'No, I am not. I gave the key to the Corner Shop; they gave it to her.'

'You are winding me up,' said Rebecca, aghast.

'No, I am not.'

'Sylvester, how can you be so trusting? Mark my words, she will steal the spoons.'

'Celia took those.' Sylvester leaned down and pecked Rebecca's cheek. 'Now I must get back to the Valet,' he said gently, while indicating the door with a hand holding an empty glass. 'I must not keep you. You were on your way somewhere.'

'Yes,' said Rebecca courageously. 'I must not dally gossiping. I shall be late.'

Sylvester watched her go and, as he watched, he remembered that the animal who would not let go was supposed to be a pig. Once a pig had something clamped in its jaws, he had read, it chumped whatever it was up.

Perhaps I really could write the life of Wellington's valet, he mused, sitting at his desk. Margaret Forster wrote a splendid life of Elizabeth Barrett-Browning's maid. One would have to do a lot of daunting research, though, because if one did not and got contemporary details wrong, the experts would be down like a ton of bricks. Far better to stick to the novel; he knew all too well the details for that, though how, Sylvester asked himself as he stared blindly out of the window, would he rivet the attention of readers with his humiliating tale? 'Oh, Mother,' he said out loud, 'if you were not dead I would come and complain, grumble that you put the idea in my mind, where it sticks like a burr.'

Remembering his mother, Sylvester stood up and began wandering about the room. 'Write it all down, then I will read it,' she had said. 'Write the absolute truth. It will help you and may make me laugh. You will have worked your pain into fiction. I have always

77

wanted you to be a writer. And don't be discouraged,' she had said when Celia had discouraged. She had enjoyed his only novel, Sylvester remembered, coming to a halt by the bookshelves; it made her laugh and cry. Only she recognized it as the truth, for all writing is in a sense autobiographical.

He eased his only and slender *œuvre* from the shelf, then pushed it disgustedly back. I dedicated it to Celia, he thought, and she mocked it. I should have dedicated it to my mother. Blast Celia, he muttered, how am I to fashion her into fiction? And who, he wondered, would want to read about a man who falls hopelessly in love with another man's wife and she apparently with him, who goes through all the trauma of her divorce (for it is not funny even in these days to be cited as co-respondent), who marries her and then after a short time the wife returns to the first husband, taking with her all her possessions and considerable quantities of loot belonging to husband number two.

'I was fond of those spoons,' Sylvester said out loud. Then realizing that his mother would have found this amusing, he chuckled and said, 'Thanks, Ma, it will be an indulgence to write the truth about Celia. And I will dedicate the novel to you.'

Feeling hungry, he went down to his kitchen and made himself a sandwich of wholemeal bread and cold roast beef bought from a delicatessen on his way home. Ruminating about Celia he spread the beef with mustard, then poured himself a fresh whisky. Sipping it, he looked at the pad used by his cleaning lady to communicate messages. There were two. The first said: *You need more bath soap.* The second read rather bluntly: *Your garden requires TLC.*

Munching his sandwich, Sylvester went back upstairs to look through the french windows and note that the garden did indeed need attention; it was a mess. Among the compound of bits of paper, dead leaves, clumps of dandelion and rotting stalks of last year's annuals perched an odious simpering cupid, imitation Renaissance, its plaster wings discoloured and cracked, its vacuous face smeared with sparrow droppings. There had been angry words when Celia had installed it, tears. She had learned, though, during their brief marriage, that the cupid would not suit Andrew Battersby's Barnes set-up, so left it to linger as she had left the smell of 'Emotion', which the excellent Mrs Piper had by her polishing and scrubbing so successfully eliminated.

'Soon put paid to you,' Sylvester said out loud and, throwing open the french windows, he stepped out, wrenched the simpering cherub from its stand, carried it through the house and dumped it by the dustbin.

Returning to the kitchen, he wrote on the pad: *I would be grateful for any suggestion re TLC for garden.* It was possible, he thought as he finished his sandwich, that worthy Mrs Piper would suggest some honest and able-bodied pensioner or an out-of-work worthy who would take on the garden on a business basis. Between Mrs Piper and the corner shop there probably flourished a grapevine of untapped labour. He would of course pay cash, just as he paid Mrs Piper, so deftly circumventing the Inland Revenue. Indeed, Sylvester thought, it was more than probable that the estimable Mrs Piper had someone in mind: an unemployed husband or son-in-law who would be glad of the job. Why else would she draw attention to the garden's derelict condition?

11

On leaving Sylvester, Rebecca had tried not to feel
rebuffed. The Sylvester she had worked for had
changed. It's all that blasted Celia, she told herself.
Before Celia he relied on me, called me his Reliable
Rebecca. In the office I was known as RR. If I had not
been so reliable, not related Celia's messages so
faithfully, I could have put a stop to that disastrous
marriage. And what a lot of pain that would have
saved. But perhaps not, she thought; it would not
have altered much. She remembered sadly that long-
ago incident when, back in the office after a bibulous
lunch, Sylvester had so nearly kissed her. He had been
on the verge, held back, kept to the verge. At the time
she had told herself he had too much respect, but the
reality was that he shrank from her bossiness. I am too
capable, too reliable, she told herself ruefully, and
bossiness lost me that job; he eased me out. Look at
this afternoon, she thought, he could not wait for me to
leave.

But the habit of guarding Sylvester's interests died
hard and the way he was behaving now he was free of
Celia was dangerously irresponsible. She would just
cast an eye on this corner shop, Rebecca decided, see
what sort of seedy establishment it was that recom-
mended gypsy cleaning women. She quickened her
pace towards the narrow alleyway that led through
the houses at the end of the street into the district
beyond, and Maurice Benson, snooping at the corner
of Sylvester's street, followed her at a distance.

* * *

Not ready to use the telephone number Madge Brownlow had given him, and working on the assumption that Sylvester had made friends with Julia on the train, for why else would he have tried to trip him at Paddington if not to protect the girl, Maurice was waiting for Sylvester to lead him to Julia. If asked why he was interested in either Julia or Sylvester, he would have been hard pressed to say other than that he owed it to toffee-nosed Sylvester to queer his pitch, and that from what he had gathered of Julia she was fair game for a tease. Only if pressed hard would he have admitted to any sexual interest. Now without much enthusiasm he followed Rebecca, in case through her he could find some lead into Sylvester's life.

Rebecca had never used the alleyway before and, finding herself in unfamiliar streets, took a while to locate the corner shop. When she did she was unsure whether she was pleased or sorry. Expecting to find something seedy and louche, she was surprised by Patel's Corner Shop. It was bright, clean and welcoming. Inside the shop divided into two halves, the one for papers, magazines and freezers for fish, meat, fruits and ice-creams, the other for shelves stacked with exotic groceries all imaginatively and agreeably arranged. The whole shop smelled of exciting spices and herbs.

Although it was after normal closing time the shop was full of customers and the owner, for it could be none other with that welcoming smile, stood behind the counter by a gleaming till wearing a spotless high-necked shirt whose whiteness enhanced his brown complexion, black hair and trousers so creased they exaggerated the stick-like quality of his legs. Leaning slightly across the counter, Mr Patel conversed with a customer while all about the shop people heaped their purchases into wire baskets. As they flitted among the beautifully stacked shelves they paused to block other people's way, chat with acquaintances and greet friends. Rebecca was reminded of the atmosphere in the shops of the small market town where she had been brought up, where everyone knew one another at least by sight.

Interrupting Mr Patel's conversation, a woman customer called out, 'Can I pay, Mr Patel? I'm in a rush. My mother-in-law is coming to supper and you know what she's like.' She stood waving a ten-pound note, impatient yet friendly.

'Pay tomorrow,' said Mr Patel, unwilling to stop his chat.

'No, no, no,' the woman protested.

'OK.' Mr Patel called something over his shoulder and resumed his conversation, while through a beaded curtain which reminded Rebecca of shops in Italy came a small woman in a bright sari. She carried on her hip a baby and beside her, gripping her sari, trotted a little boy. She smiled as she took the proffered note and gravely gave change, but shyly she did not speak. The customer, satisfied, cried, 'Thanks, Mrs P, thanks,' and hurried out of the shop. Mrs Patel, observing that her husband remained engrossed in pleasurable conversation, stayed by the till to take money and give change.

Not wishing to be seen loitering, Rebecca took up a wire basket and explored the shop in the hope of finding the notice-board that Sylvester had so riskily used. As she perambulated she eyed the wares with astonishment. There was so much that was strange to her, though obviously not to the clientele, who nudged past her chattering, busily stacking their baskets with esoteric commodities she had never even heard of. Gingerly she helped herself to a jar of chutney, a packet of rice and, a little further along the shelf, a packet of Bombay duck; then at last she found the notice-board and avidly scanned the neatly written cards. The advertisements hardly differed from those in her home town. Accommodation was needed. Beds were for sale, so were cars, a bicycle and a child's buggy. Massage was offered and reflexology; there was even a palmist. The board might have been hanging in a shop in the country. The only difference there might be were fewer homeless puppies, kittens and white rabbits on offer, though, strangely, there was a goat, which must surely, she thought, be a rarity in Chelsea.

Scanning the board, Rebecca felt sharp disappointment; the cards were so respectable, innocent and hopeful, it was impossible to take exception to any of them. She was even tempted to make use of the board herself, should she wish to exchange her typewriter for something more up-to-date. Sighing, she turned away and prepared to pay for her purchases when, moving towards the counter, she became aware of a commotion.

The baby was letting out a series of exhilarating crows and shrieks, jogging and kicking in its mother's arms, fighting to leap or take flight towards a customer who had just come into the shop. Simultaneously the child who had perched on a stool while its mother worked the till, jumped down and rushed round the counter to clutch the newcomer round the knees.

The newcomer, a young woman, crouched down, put her arms around the child, hugged him, then lifted him up and set him on the counter beside his smiling parents. Then she held out her arms and took the baby from its mother and held it close.

Rebecca watched the little group of parents, children, and the young woman who, oblivious of the people in the shop, appeared wrapped in an emotion stronger than that of any normal greeting. The children's parents were smiling and joyful; the mother patted her baby's plump leg, then stroked the woman's hand; she did not speak but her eyes brimmed with feeling. What was going on between the Indian woman and the English girl?

Holding her packet of Bombay duck, Rebecca was conscious of a violence of emotion and an inexplicable rapport between the two; then, aware that she was staring, she forced herself to turn away and pick a jar of curry paste off a shelf while still keeping a surreptitious eye on the group by the counter.

She was no child lover, yet she found herself moved by the two women; there was generosity in the way the Indian gave her baby to be held and a curious tenderness in the other woman's manner of taking the child, holding it close to her face, laying her cheek against the baby's.

Watching her, Rebecca could imagine the silky feel of the child's skin and surprised herself, smiling as it gripped the girl's nose in a plump fist, then encircled her finger in a pudgy grip. But amusement changed to astonishment as she noticed that the baby's mother had begun to weep, huge tears splashing on to the counter.

Now the girl handed the baby back and Rebecca heard her say, 'It's all right, Mrs Patel. Don't cry, please,' while she eased her finger free of the infant's grip, leaned forward and kissed the weeping woman. Then she bent down, kissed the little boy, ruffled his hair and, turning, left the shop. As she left the larger child shouted indignantly and tried to follow but was held by his father, who then shepherded his wife and both children out of sight but wailing loudly through the bead curtain.

'What was all that about?' a man in front of Rebecca, waiting to pay for his basketful of goods, enquired belligerently. 'He's—'

'He wants his friend.' Mr Patel checked the goods and, taking the man's money, gave change.

'Still not with you,' said the man. 'But your kid seems upset,' he persisted. 'Unhappy.'

Standing immediately behind the man, Rebecca felt an urgent wish to kick him. 'Excuse me,' she said, 'you are holding up the queue.'

'But the kid's unhappy,' said the man. 'It's—'

Rebecca said, 'Please move.' She was larger than he was.

He moved. He would not dare accuse the shopkeeper of cruelty and yet, standing aside to let her pay, he lingered. Mr Patel checked Rebecca's purchases, put them in a bag, took her money and gave her change. Then, catching her eye as he handed the money, he said, 'His friend is dead,' in a voice so low she barely heard him.

Rebecca said, 'Dead?' Standing by the counter, her hand holding her change was arrested on its way to her purse as she gazed into Mr Patel's oriental eyes.

'If there's one thing I won't put up with it's the bullying of children,' said the man who had spoken before.

Rebecca said, 'Shut up.'

'Come along, Tim.' A girl Rebecca had not noticed took the man's arm. 'Don't make a nuisance of yourself,' she said, giving his arm a jerk. 'You should not go to the pub before you shop,' she said, leading him away. 'Sorry, Mr Patel,' she called as she pulled him out into the street past Maurice Benson, who was lingering in the doorway.

In the street Tim began to mutter, then yelled, 'Bloody Pakistanis,' and the girl yelled back, 'Mr Patel is Indian and – you – are – a – bloody – racist, you really *are,* it comes out when you're drunk!' And to Maurice Benson's amusement she smacked his face. Then she said, 'Don't you remember? Those two babysat for each other? The Eddisons told us. The Patel kid misses his friend, that child upstairs who drove the Eddisons mad with his noise? You know, the one that was squashed in the accident.'

'Decapitated,' said Tim. 'Oh! Oh *dear!*'

The girl said, 'Yes! The one on the top floor above us.'

Tim said, 'Oh! I get it. Oh my God! Shall I go back and apologize?' He turned on his heel.

The girl said, 'No. Leave it. Come along home.'

Maurice Benson followed them discreetly to note their address, while Rebecca, who had no cause to notice Maurice Benson, headed for the bus stop and home.

12

After his tussle with the cupid Sylvester had lolled gloomily on his sofa. He had not told Rebecca that he would probably be away for a month or even two, if he took a holiday at the end of the business trip proposed by his partner. He was afraid she would volunteer to keep an eye on his house, pay Mrs Piper for him, forward his mail. Worse, she would say he did not need a cleaning lady while he was away and suggest he sack Mrs Piper. 'Then,' he could hear Rebecca's voice saying, 'when you come back I will engage reliable Mrs Andrews for you.'

Can it be, Sylvester asked himself, that I am afraid of Rebecca?

Yes, a bit.

Do I want to go to America for a month? I could ski in Colorado. 'Miss the worst of the winter,' his partner had wheedled. 'Meet new and amusing people, have a complete change, do you good,' John had said in that fruity voice of his, meaning forget your divorce. Sylvester had said he would think about it. Now he sat staring at his father's desk. Was it not time, this piece of furniture suggested, that he snapped out of it and got back to work on the novel whose gestation marriage to Celia had brought to a halt? Had there not been a plan, prior to Celia, to take a year off, let the house to rich Americans, borrow a remote cottage and polish off the next book? There had, but Celia had not cared for the idea. 'Five wasted bloody years,' Sylvester muttered as he reached for his empty glass. Rising, he took a step towards the door and the bottle downstairs; it was still quite difficult to think of Celia without alcoholic fortification. But he paused to answer the telephone, which had begun to purr.

'Yes?' he said. 'Yes, it's me. Hallo? Well no, not yet, I'm thinking about it, mulling it over. Don't harass me – No, I don't mean that, no – Tell you what, I'll let you know tomorrow. Yes, definitely, yes – Yes, I said so, didn't I? Sorry, I'm a bit *distrait* – Yes, yes, of course I will, goodbye.' He replaced the receiver.

There had been a first draft of novel two. Where was it? He put down the empty glass and went back to the writing table. Mrs Piper had polished the outside but she would be shocked by the mess inside, he thought as he pulled out the drawers: old bills, old letters, programmes, snapshots, pencil stubs, exhausted rubber bands. Ancient cheque stubs, rusting paper clips, out-of-date stamps, a plethora of rubbish – all useless. He began to hum. 'Nothing, nothing of interest, let's chuck it away,' and seized with the subtle delight of destruction he began tipping the contents of the drawers into the waste-paper basket. 'No manuscript,' he sang, 'what did I do-oo-oo with it? Did I destroy it? Oh!' he cried in painful recollection. 'I gave it to Celia, to bloody-uddy Celia and she left it behind in our honeymoon hotel. Oho-ho, how could I have forgotten?' he roared. (Celia had detested his singing.) 'She *laughed* at it, la-la-la-laughed,' he sang in a loud bass voice. *'Laughed.'*

He shook the contents of the last drawer over the waste-paper basket. 'And, oh! Here you are laughing, you bitch! Celia posed laughing in the South of France.' He snatched a photograph from the pile of papers and tore it across. 'And there you go,' he sang, dropping the bits into the basket. 'I gave you my heart,' – he was chanting now in recitative – 'and you made it plain that you had little use for it except as a stepping-stone back to boring old, rich old Andrew Battersby and his grand-new-house-No! Let's call it a *mansion* on the edge of Barnes Common. What was a romantic dream for me was merely a temporary perch for you,' Sylvester roared.

'Right,' he said, feeling better. 'I shall leave a note for worthy Mrs Piper and she will expunge all trace of Celia from the drawers of the writing table as she so excellently has from the house.' And he gathered up the trash and carried it to the dustbin. On his way back he decided to buy a fresh stock of writing paper, envelopes and typing paper, folders and biros, and start the new novel.

'*Wellington's Valet*,' he said grimly as he picked up the telephone and dialled his partner. 'When I get back,' he said out loud. 'Hallo, John? You there? I'll go – yes, I said so. Yes – OK. I'll be in tomorrow and we can discuss. Bye.'

Gosh, thought Sylvester, I made up my mind. It was not so difficult. A month in the States, then back refreshed to the office, the desk and the novel. This merits a celebratory drink; there may be life after Celia yet.

In the kitchen, pouring whisky, he whistled cheerfully; tomorrow he would plan his itinerary, buy his ticket, fax all the people he needed to see in New York and on the West Coast; but first, even before he went to the office, he would buy that stationery, make sure there was something to come back to.

The book mocked by Celia had been about Love. It had even begun with a quote from A. N. Wilson: *Falling in love is the greatest imaginative experience of which most human beings are capable.* 'It is also a pitfall,' Sylvester muttered. 'A trap, and not one Celia fell into.' Sipping his whisky he looked out into the area and, observing that the garden cherub had been cleared away, thought sourly that it had been the closest approximation to a child that his ex-wife had been willing to give him. The novel, when he wrote it, would definitely not be about Love.

On leaving the kitchen Sylvester saw, on what he was beginning to think of as Mrs Piper's pad, a message. It read: *About your garden. The work can be done Wednesdays and Fridays at five pounds an hour. Should you care to give* carte blanche *as to plants and planting, work can begin instanter. I would suggest you open account at a garden centre* (here were listed three with telephone numbers) *then dung, compost, shrubs, bulbs, plants, etc. can be ordered at once and work put in train while you are out. J. Piper.* There was a PS which said: *Please state spending limit.*

"*Carte blanche,*' Sylvester murmured, 'put in train ... dung ... compost. This old biddy is what my mother would have called a treasure.' Perhaps, he thought as he went upstairs to change his clothes before going out to dinner, she is not as old as I suppose and the recipient of the five quid an hour is her boyfriend? No, he thought, taking off his trousers, it will be her son-in-law and whichever, he thought, getting into the bath, five quid an hour is peanuts. I must leave her a note. Oh, he thought, I must tell her I am going away and arrange that she gets paid. Of course Rebecca would arrange that for me, he thought as he soaped his feet, but then Rebecca would also know and impose a good gardener and a better garden centre. It was imperative to manage without her. Lying in his bath, Sylvester thought ruefully of his kind, bossy, erstwhile secretary, who had driven the whole office mad with her efficiency and monthly threats of resignation. It had taken all the courage he possessed to take her up on it one day and bid her goodbye. His partner John had been right when he said, 'You should not have said, "But we shall remain friends",' for here she was still bossy, still friendly and out of office hours! Celia would not have made that mistake.

Sylvester stood up in the bath to soap his parts, then, lying back in the water, he remembered his ex-wife's singular lack of interest in the erotic. Not for her was

90

there any delight in sexual juices; she lay back and thought of something, probably Andrew Battersby's income. He had even once, when persuading her of his marital rights, found her lying back and reading a novel straining her eyes sideways, quite a feat when one thought of it.

It had not even been a well-written novel, he remembered, as he stepped out of the bath and reached for his bath towel. He had shrivelled inside her and withdrawn. Withdrawn, too, from their marital bed and without much dignity. There was no other bed in the house, the sofa in the sitting-room being too short for his long legs; he had finished the night dossing down in the bath.

Sylvester did not much enjoy the dinner. His hosts, old friends, steering away from any mention of Celia, had been altogether too tactful. His fellow guests, a merchant banker and his wife, whom he had not previously met, had too obviously been primed as to the break-up. The sixth member of the party was not, as he had expected, an unattached female but his cousin Hamish Grant who, having reached the age of fifty plus neither poor, unattractive nor homosexual but unmarried, was something of an enigma.

However, the food was good, the wine too, his hostess pretty and the conversation an informed mix of politics, travel and opera; Sylvester felt he should have enjoyed himself more than he did. When the party broke up he said he would walk home, it was not far. Hamish suggested that he keep him company for part of the way, so they watched the banker and his wife drive off in their Mercedes and set off walking in the frosty night, side by side, Hamish swinging an umbrella.

Presently Hamish remarked, 'That was a succulent pheasant,' and Sylvester said, 'And a very good claret.' Another hundred yards and Hamish asked, 'You staying on in your little house?' To which Sylvester rather huffily replied, 'I see no reason to move,' and Hamish pleasantly agreed. 'No reason at all. You lived in it long before you married.'

For another couple of hundred yards neither cousin spoke. Then Sylvester, not wishing to appear churlish to his old relation, said in a conversational rush, 'I think of my bit of Chelsea as a village. I have a local woman to clean, at least I suppose her to be local. I advertised in my corner shop; I have a corner shop. The owner greets me by name; I buy my papers there, have an account. If I don't actually know my neighbours, I know them by sight.'

And Hamish, laughing, said, 'Of course! I find the same thing in Kensington. It's all still there if you look. *Napoleon of Notting Hill,* Chesterton,' which pleased Sylvester, who had not thought of Hamish as particularly well read. 'My mother,' Hamish went on, 'sent you a message, by the way. She says come and stay any time, if you want a change of scene or a breath of fresh air, and she will put you to work in the Wood.'

But Sylvester, rearing touchily away, exclaimed, 'Very kind of Aunt Calypso, but I haven't a car at the moment.'

To which Hamish replied equably, 'I suppose Celia took it. You could go by train.'

'It was registered in Celia's name.' Sylvester surprised in himself a vestige of protectiveness, then he said, 'I *did* use the train the other day. I'd been to the country for the weekend. A woman punched the alarm and stopped the train.'

Hamish said, 'I've always wanted to do that, but I never had the nerve—'

'There was a sheep stuck on its back; she wanted to rescue it.'

Hamish asked, 'And did she?'

Sylvester said, 'Yes.'

Hamish exclaimed, 'What a splendid woman!' And

then he said, 'I think our ways part here.' They had reached a street corner.

Sylvester suggested, 'You could come in for a nightcap?' He liked his cousin, whom he had never known well, and did not want to part.

But Hamish said, 'Thank you, I won't. I have to start early, I'm driving to Scotland.' He added, 'Don't forget my mother's invitation,' and Sylvester said, 'Please thank her for me, she is very kind. Tell her I am going to America for a month.'

'During which time I hope your divorce comes through.' Hamish stood leaning towards Sylvester, both hands on the handle of his umbrella. 'You may note,' he said, 'that I do not share my mother's aptitude for tact. I apologize.'

Sylvester said, 'It's all right, actually I am rather relishing my single state. I rather suspect your ma did not much like Celia.'

To which Hamish laughingly replied, 'She detested her, said she was put off when you got engaged to her by the way she could not keep her hands off you. "Kept fingering" was Mama's expression.'

'That did not last,' Sylvester said drily and Hamish said, 'Hah,' and struck the pavement with the ferrule of his umbrella.

The cousins said good night and parted, Hamish swinging briskly towards Kensington, while Sylvester, turning into his cul-de-sac, let himself into his partially empty house where, still congratulating himself on his solitary status, he went contentedly to bed.

But did not sleep, for his mind was enviously full of his cousin Hamish and his bachelor state. Then he remembered the family theory that Hamish's avoidance of marriage was not intentional but due to unrequited love for a woman older than himself, their cousin Sophie, who, when everyone imagined her set as a spinster, had married another cousin, Oliver Ansty. Perhaps Hamish is not the happy soloist he appears, thought Sylvester, turning over in bed appreciating the space. All the same I envy him; he had not had the humiliation of being cuckolded by a woman like Celia. And, thinking of Celia, he turned over so violently that he displaced the duvet, which fell to the floor. Retrieving it, Sylvester remembered his Aunt Calypso's expression as relayed by Hamish, 'kept fingering', and felt quite sick. It was so apt; he could hear his elderly relative's cool voice. Oh, curse Celia, Sylvester grumbled. 'I must get to sleep,' he muttered out loud. Try counting sheep, he exhorted himself, thoroughly awakened by the thought of Celia. How many sheep had been in that field when the girl stopped the train? Why had he not noticed? More to the point, he thought, reverting to his niggling lingering pain, why had he not noticed how quickly, how soon after their marriage, Celia had begun to salvage her burned boat and recapture her first husband? Hamish was right, Sylvester thought. I must stop playing dog in the manger, stop letting her stew from, let's face it, spite, get it over, sign all the papers, hurry the solicitors up – I'll do it tomorrow before I go to the States – then I can go with a clear conscience. Resolution made, Sylvester turned on his side. There was only one sheep in that field, he remembered it now. Just the one sheep and the girl.

13

When the dog saw Julia Piper turn into the street it ran towards her as to a long-lost friend and Julia, who had never before set eyes on the animal, stood stock still, remembering that brief period in her life with Giles which had been one of unadulterated joy.

The dog, an animal of mixed and complex breed, chucked its head under her hand, nudging persuasively with its bony skull, pleading for a caress, all the while chuntering and whimpering in a pleased and conversational manner. It had a roughish coat, dark brown along its spine, fading to ginger and cream flanks. Its intelligent eyes were partly obscured by tufts of hair. It was a large dog and nobody had thought to dock its tail to make it look smart.

The dog in Paris had been similar but with a darker coat; it, too, had a knowing expression, but it had been older, less demonstrative and trustful than the creature whose head she fondled now.

The Paris dog had appeared outside the café where they sat holding hands. It wove its way among the tables carrying its tail high, its flanks brushing against the customers' legs. Making a beeline for Giles, it rested its head on his knee and gazed up into his face. Giles had dropped her hand and stroked the dog, scratched its ribs. She had watched it close its eyes in ecstasy when he patted its flank, and gravely, without snatching, it had accepted a lump of sugar.

The chestnuts were in flower and the sun was shining on that afternoon as it had on previous days. In the parks and gardens there were beds of iris and the air was scented with lilac. In the Luxembourg Gardens the gravel crunched under their feet and water splashed cool in the fountains. The dog, who had followed them, lapped the water, and the water dripped from its furry jaws. Giles put his arm round her shoulders as they walked; when she leaned her head back her neck rested on his bare arm. He carried his jacket and walked in his shirt-sleeves. As she lifted her face to the setting sun, feeling its warmth, Giles had said, 'What about dinner? An early dinner. I am feeling hungry.'

They ate in a restaurant in a quiet courtyard off a side-street where they had eaten the night before and the two nights before that, sitting each time at the same table. They ate fresh asparagus and veal with cream and mushroom sauce, and strawberries dusted with sugar. Giles drank Chardonnay while she drank water. They ordered coffee and Giles drank brandy. She felt supremely happy and secure talking to Giles, watching the people round them, listening to the chatter.

Some time during the evening the dog had left them. Leaving the restaurant, they had strolled down to the Seine to watch the barges and pleasure boats, crane their necks downriver to see the spire of the Sainte Chapelle as they had done the night before and the nights before that. Then, wandering back to their hotel, they stopped at a café and Giles ordered a *fine*. They sat at a table on the pavement watching the strolling crowds. Before he had finished his brandy, a breeze spang up which shook the chestnut trees and the flowers began drifting down to be trodden underfoot on the pavement.

Back in their hotel, high up on the seventh floor, she had undressed and, throwing the window open to the night, had looked across the narrow street and seen, as she had the several nights before, a woman working at a desk in a brightly lit room. 'She's working very late,' she had said to Giles undressing in the room behind her and he, half-undressed in his shirt and boxer shorts, had said roughly, 'It's not late.' Snatching up his trousers, he put them on again and, taking his wallet from where he had laid it, he had made for the door.

Surprised, she had said, 'Where are you going?' Or perhaps she had been too startled to say anything. Anyway, she remembered, standing in the street in London stroking the strange dog, Giles had left the room without answering. 'Vamoosed,' Julia said to the dog, and shivered in recollection of that long and evil night.

She had been too proud to follow and look for him in the cafés and bars they had frequented; she waited standing by the window, watching the woman working at her desk in the room across the street. When at last the woman put away her work and left her office, switching off the light, she had finished undressing and, getting into bed, lain wide-eyed, ears cocked for Giles's return.

But she was asleep when the door burst open and Giles staggered in; he was drunk and the dog was with him.

'It was looking a bit puzzled,' Julia said to the dog in London, 'and I don't know where they had been, but they both smelled terrible and were so wet they might have been swimming in a fountain; there had been a thunderstorm and I had slept through it. They were very good-humoured, I remember that.'

As she walked Julia fished in her bag for her key and, reaching the house where she lived on the top floor, she said to the dog, 'You had better go home now.' Opening the door, she went in and closed it in the dog's face.

Climbing the stairs to her flat, she wished she had not met the dog; it reminded her of the dog in Paris, and being so happy for those few days with Giles.

At first it had been all right when Giles came back;

she had laughed when the dog shook itself and leapt on to the bed with her, rubbing its face on the covers trying to get dry. She had laughed, and Giles had laughed too, lurching about the room half-in, half-out of his trousers, romping with the dog who, playful in the way dogs are when they are wet, rushed about the room jumping on and off the bed, humping its back, tucking its tail between its legs and barking.

The racket they made woke people; somebody sent for the concierge, who came up in the lift and knocked on the door. There was a hissed altercation. '*Alors, Monsieur, que faites-vous? D'où vient cet animal? Sale bête. Vous réveillez les clients. Vous faites un bruit épouvantable.*' And Giles, '*C'est mon ami, mon copain,*' getting back into his trousers, tripping over his shoes, tottering along to the lift with the dog in his arms, chivvied by the concierge, laughing in the lift as it went down, his laugh echoing up the lift shaft. And she had laughed, too; the dog was such a comical and friendly dog. What happened later was no fault of the dog's.

I would rather not be reminded, Julia thought, reaching the top floor and letting herself into her flat. The flat was stuffy; she had been out all day working. She slipped off her shoes and went to open a window and look out along the gardens behind the houses, in one of which was a plane tree which, having shed its leaves, displayed to full advantage its peeling branches and mottled trunk.

There were plane trees too in Paris, and if she looked out of her window which gave on to the street she might see the dog; it might still be there to remind her of Giles's return that morning, minus his canine companion but with a bottle of whisky. Where had he got it at that hour? All those years later she was puzzled; it had never bothered her before, but now it niggled. 'Oh God,' she said out loud, wishing to blot that night and the many similar nights from her mind.

It had been her morning sickness which set him off; he had up until then been kind, made a joke of it. But as she retched at the basin, he had grabbed the toothglass for his whisky and knocked a tooth and hurt himself. Drunk and drinking he had suddenly yelled abuse, calling her a 'stupid bitch, cow'; then he asked nastily why her mother had never taught her to fuck and cursed her when, clumsy from drink, he broke the glass.

Rapidly she had tried to pick up the shards for, lurching about in his socks, he was in danger of cutting his feet. He had forestalled her, scooped up the broken glass and thrown it in her face, cutting her eye, slicing his fingers, splattering blood on the wall.

It was raining in Paris that day when they left and raining in London when they got back. They did not see the dog again; it was not the dog's fault. Now, reminded of those few short days of unadulterated joy, Julia Piper was justly grateful that none of the subsequent years of fear and disgust had managed to obliterate their memory.

14

One reason Maurice Benson's career as a private investigator had been less than successful had been his inconsistent attention-span; it was only when embarked on his career as a twitcher that he was ever to become totally absorbed by the subject he was watching.

On the evening he followed Rebecca from Sylvester's house to Patel's Corner Shop his attention was first deflected by the curious scene between a young woman he thought he recognized and Mrs Patel and then, while he was trying to place her, by the silly and acrimonious argument which broke out between Janet and her lover Tim, Janet maintaining that the Patels originated in Bombay or Bengal and Tim vigorously asserting that the family came from Karachi. Quite how he had become drawn into the dispute Maurice could not later remember – perhaps he had trailed too close on their heels – but with Tim holding his arm and calling him 'squire', and a little later 'mate', he found himself drawn up a street to the right as they left the shop, while Rebecca turned sharp left and was lost.

With Tim holding his left arm and Janet gripping his right he resigned himself to swaying along between his new and argumentative acquaintances; it was possible, he supposed, that they would know more about the young woman he thought he recognized than what he had overheard in the shop. For the present, though, it was not wise to interrupt Tim; he had obviously consumed more alcohol than was good for him and was, with it, aggressive and being made more so by Janet. Maurice did, though, observe and begin to wonder why, as they walked, Janet, who was steering their trio, kept turning right each time they reached a corner; some ten minutes after leaving the Corner Shop it was again in view but from a different angle. Before he could stop himself, Maurice exclaimed, 'We have walked in a circle!' Tim, who had stopped and was rummaging for a key, let out a shout of 'Traitor!' and, breaking loose from Janet, departed at a run.

Janet said, 'Now you've done it. Go after him.'

Maurice said, 'Why?'

Janet said, 'He's doubled back to the pub. I especially didn't pass it. I am not going after him, you must. It's your fault; he was coming home like a lamb.' Then she said, 'What are you waiting for? Go on!'

Maurice, who had experienced this scene with other couples, said, 'All right, but just tell me, was that woman in the shop Julia Piper?'

Janet said, 'Of course. She lives on the top floor. Do hurry, I do not want Tim any drunker.'

Maurice said, 'Thanks. OK. Have you a key?' He noted the number on the street door.

Janet said, 'Of course I have a key. Do look sharp and fetch Tim back.' She added rather reluctantly, 'Please.'

Maurice said, 'OK, number seven, the house with the dog. That your dog?'

Janet, noticing the dog, said, 'Certainly *not*, they shit on the pavements. What's it doing sitting here? The pub,' she said, taking a key from her bag, 'is the Goat, just round the corner. Oh, do buck up!' And she pushed past the dog to put the key in the lock. 'Get out of the way,' she said, aiming a kick at the creature, who snarled and shrank aside but dashed through the door as she opened it.

Maurice said, 'It seems to belong.'

'Probably to someone visiting the Ellisons. Oh,

please hurry and fetch Tim!' Janet shouted. 'He will pay attention to you. He did this once before we set up together; he went off with my brother and my father pried him from the bar. I am sure,' she said, 'you will manage.'

Maurice, thinking he could do with a drink, promised to do his best and set off for the Goat, where Tim was at once visible sitting at a table with what looked like a very large gin or vodka.

Maurice furnished himself with a pint of bitter and, approaching Tim, said, 'Mind if I join you?'

Without looking up Tim said, 'Feel free.'

Maurice sat, swallowed some beer, lit a cigarette. Tim said, 'I suppose Janet sent you.'

Maurice said, 'Spot on.'

Tim said, 'I am sobering up.'

'You could have fooled me,' Maurice said.

Tim said, 'This is water.'

'Water?' Maurice peered into Tim's glass. 'Vodka and lemon.'

'Perrier.'

'Go on—'

'Taste it.'

Maurice dipped a finger, tasted, 'M-m—. Why water?'

'As I said, sobering up. I'm awash.'

Maurice drank some beer before asking, 'Why?'

Tim, who had not noticeably sobered, said, 'That would be telling,' and looked sly.

Maurice inhaled his cigarette and waited. At the bar a group of men were discussing a goat for sale. 'True, there's an advert in Patels.' 'What's a goat doing in London?' 'For sale, d'you say?' 'Yes.' 'My guess is some fool gave a kid a kid.' 'Whatever for?' 'For a pet, stupid.'

'Tell me about Julia Piper.' Maurice leaned towards Tim.

'Top-floor flat.' Tim drank his Perrier.

'Know her well?'

'No. Janet thought she was committing suicide.'

'Suicide?'

'She made Janet drunk; she's not used to it, poor little thing. Could you get me another Perrier or two? Here's the money,' Tim fumbled in his hip pocket. 'I've gotta drink a lotta Perrier.' He belched. 'Excuse—'

Maurice went to the bar, replenished his glass, returned with three bottles of Perrier, put them in front of Tim.

Tim said, 'Thanks. Could you pour? Hands a bit shaky.'

Maurice poured. 'Julia Piper?'

'She shouted at Janet about God. Most odd.'

'God?'

Tim swallowed his Perrier water in large gulps. 'That's a lot better, it's working.' He refilled his glass. 'Tell you something.' He leaned towards Maurice.

Maurice said, 'Yes?'

Tim whispered, 'Want to – but can't when I'm pissed – d'you get me?'

Maurice said, 'Well—'

Tim hissed, 'It's not well. If I can't, she'll despise me. It's bloody humiliating, it's—'

Maurice said, 'Julia Piper?'

Tim said, 'No, no, Janet. What has Julia Piper got to do with it?'

Maurice said, 'I thought we were discussing Julia Piper.'

Tim said, 'No, no, never even spoken to the woman. It's Janet, she's the object of this exercise,' and he drank more Perrier. There was a burst of laughter at the bar and a voice said, 'If the Pakis buy it, they don't butcher kosher.' Another voice jeered, 'You're confused, kosher's for Jews.'

Tim said, 'If Janet were here, she would go up to that lot and make a speech about racism. She's like that, a wonderful girl. You married?'

103

Maurice said, 'No.'

'Girlfriend?'

'No.'

'Boy?'

'No.'

'Thought not. No sex? What d'you do about sex, then?' He was still partially under the liberating influence.

Maurice said, 'Not much.'

Tim said, 'Gosh.' There was a pause while he finished his Perrier, drinking slowly and thoughtfully until the glass was empty. Then he stood up and, turning to Maurice, shook him by the hand and said, smiling, 'All clear now! Time to go home. Thanks a lot. Must rejoin my lovely Janet. A breath of fresh air in the street and hey presto, total recovery. How's that for an advertisement for Perrier water?' And he pushed the door open and was gone.

Maurice Benson said, 'Bugger,' and went to get another beer. He drank it standing at the bar, thinking about Julia Piper. Now he had found her, he was unsure what he wanted to do.

Why not give her a bell? he thought. Perhaps not after all this beer; there was no hurry, better to wait.

15

Dreaming, Julia stretched out an arm and took the receiver off, then, turning over, snuggled back to sleep.

The noise came again and this time she was awake, remembering that Giles, dead, was unlikely to pester her with midnight calls. Lately he had made silent calls, barely breathing, an unnerving alternative to a previous method of threats and abuse. Had her mother been party to that last call? It must have been made from her house. Perhaps not; she was normally in bed by midnight. Giles would have sat up drinking, he was usually drunk when he made the calls. He had had a cold. Hearing him sniff, she had said, 'Blow your nose.' He had laughed. She was glad that his last communication had been a laugh. She had not dared hang up on him as she usually did, for Christy was with him. But that was all; Giles had laughed and hung up.

The noise came again. She jerked awake and lay propped on her elbow; it was repeated. She swung her legs off the bed, switched on the light and, reaching for Christy's whistle, gripped it in her hand.

Wide awake now, she waited, heard a slight thump and a scratching sound; puzzled, she crossed to the door and opened it.

The dog came in quietly.

Stepping backwards, Julia sat down on the divan. The dog laid its head on her knee and she cupped the back of its skull in her hand.

Her clock said three in the morning. The street was quiet; the inhabitants of the other flats slept. She could hear her heart thump and, stroking the dog, feel his heart beating against thin ribs. Beginning to pant, the dog glanced up then looked away; she rose and filled a bowl of water. It drank thirstily. She said, 'You are a stray. I should not feed you,' but she gave it bread and milk, which it ate. Then she said, 'It is too early to do anything about you,' and got back into bed, pulling the duvet up to her chin. The animal stretched out beside the bed with a contented sigh. She said, 'I will take you to the police or the Battersea Dogs' Home.' The dog thumped its tail on the floor. She said, 'You came like a thief, you must belong to somebody,' but it did not respond. She sniffed the palm of her hand for the faint smell of dog and longed for country smells. She said, 'I don't know how you got into the house, and if this is somebody's idea of a joke I don't find it funny. I will get you out of here before I go to work and be rid of you.' But the dog had fallen asleep.

In the morning she overslept and hurried late to her first job in a block of flats near the river, where she cleaned for a woman journalist, took messages on her telephone and left a meal ready to be warmed up in the evening. She did not like the woman, who was sluttish, leaving dirty knickers and tights on the floor for her to wash but, conscious of being a nuisance, paid above the going rate.

She was late, there was no time to take the dog to the police; the police station was out of her way and so, too, was the Battersea Dogs' Home. The dog ran cheerfully beside her through the streets. When she reached the block of flats where the journalist lived on the fifth floor she turned to the dog and, hardening her heart, said as harshly as she could, 'Go home. You do not belong to me.' The dog looked baffled.

In the lift going up she ground her teeth, resolutely refusing responsibility, and when she reached the flat brutally refrained from leaning out of the window to see whether the animal was waiting.

The woman journalist, though personally untidy, liked to find everything just so when she came in from her day. Picking up the woman's clothes, hurling them with bath towels and bed sheets into the washing-machine, smacking clean sheets on to the bed, roughly shaking the duvet, washing the kitchen and bathroom floors, cleaning the bath and hoovering the carpet, venting her rage, Julia assured herself that it was stupid to be sentimental. Left in the street, the dog's chance of survival was greater than if she had taken it to the police. It was a street-wise animal. It must belong to somebody. It would find its way home. Taken in by the police, it would be passed to the Dogs' Home, where nobody would claim it. Had it been a claimable dog, it would have sported a collar; unclaimed it would be destroyed, it being a creature of mixed breed whom nobody would want. It was far better not to interfere. Julia cursed and swore out loud as she cleaned the journalist's flat and allowed the telephone to peal unanswered, knowing that she should answer it. She could not trust herself to be polite or take messages and write them down.

Having finished her desperate cleaning she washed a lettuce, made a sauce for pasta and laid everything ready for an evening meal. Before pocketing the money the woman left ready for her, she took a sheet of writing paper and wrote a note in which she suggested the woman get herself an answerphone, that she was sorry but owing to unforeseen circumstances she would not in future be able to come and clean the flat. This done, she slammed out of the flat and, taking the lift to the ground floor, walked out into the street which she found mercifully free of dogs. But in the street she remembered her unpaid bills and the convenience of working for an employer she hardly ever saw who, though messy and untidy, paid regularly and without fuss. So she turned back and went up in the lift to re-enter the flat and tear up the note she had left on the kitchen table.

On her way back to the street she remembered the smell on the woman's sheets when she had stripped the bed and conjectured that there must be a new lover; and because the smell nudged some part of her brain which had been inattentive as she worked, she worried until she had located the smell and, having found it, was amused. It was the aftershave advertised in the sachets stuck in the *Sunday Times* magazine which Mr Patel sedulously removed for his more discerning customers; and it was to one of these customer's houses she was now on her way, her new invisible employer, Mr Wykes, who left her money ready and notes of polite thanks. And, she thought as she hurried along, there was the garden; there might be a reaction to her hopeful proposal.

A note was propped against an empty milk bottle on Sylvester Wykes's kitchen table. Julia read:

1. Please, Mrs Piper, clean out the drawers of the desk in the sitting-room.

2. Apropos your suggestion re garden, have opened account with Garden Centre you advise. Please tell the man to spend within reason—

Julia let out a sigh of pleasure. Then: 'Within reason?' she whispered. 'Apropos? Man, what man?' The note went on:

3. I shall be away in the US for a month as from Monday; please find cheque to tide you over until I get back plus money for the man.

The man again? She frowned and read on.

4. The answerphone is set, please do not answer the telephone. In case of trouble my office number is 071 100 2157.

5. No need to forward letters, but I will be grateful if you will chuck out junk mail.

The note was signed S. Wykes, with a cheque made out to Mrs Piper stapled to it. She fingered the cheque, puzzling over the amount, which exceeded her needs, then overleaf she noticed a postscript which said: *As I have not had time to get an extra key cut, could you let the man in with your key? Should this be inconvenient, perhaps you could leave your key with the corner shop – they seem obliging – for him to collect there? Sorry about this. In haste. S. Wykes.*

Out loud, Julia said, 'What a trusting old fellow!' and, 'Of course they are obliging!' Upstairs there were signs of departure: cupboards left open, the bed rumpled and unmade, a torn Pan Am label on the floor, damp towels in the bathroom and blobs of shaving cream in the basin. Gathering the sheets from the bed, Julia compared their smell favourably with those of the woman journalist before bundling them with the towels into the washing-machine. While the machine churned she cleaned the drawers of the writing desk with a damp cloth, leaving them ajar, then addressed herself to the rest of the house. It was only when all was in order that she allowed herself to step out through the french windows and view the garden.

She stood for a long time in the gathering dusk before setting off for home via the Corner Shop, where she bought herself a lettuce, some grapes and a steak.

'A steak.' Mr Patel raised his eyebrows. 'Fillet?'

'I am celebrating.' She told him about Sylvester Wykes's garden.

'And I was thinking you had a new boyfriend. The Wykes gentleman asked me to keep the key perhaps. I said of course I would when he came to cancel the papers.'

'He seems to be a very trusting sort of old man.'

'Not so much trusting as not caring, I think.'

'Oh?'

Mr Patel raised both hands, clutching the air. 'A gentleman with nothing to hold,' he said.

'Poor old thing,' Julia said. 'May I see the children?'

She went through the bead curtains to the room beyond, leaving Mr Patel to serve a customer.

Mrs Patel made her tea, which she drank holding the little boy on her knee. He was surprisingly heavy, gripping the front of her shirt with a pudgy hand, wriggling his bottom into a comfortable position on her lap and gazing up with his father's lollipop eyes. 'He is so very like his father,' she said.

'Story!' the child shouted. 'Story!'

Shyly Mrs Patel said something to the effect that Christy, too, had been the spit of his father. Julia knew this was what she said for Mrs Patel had said it often before and Mr Patel had translated. 'That was so,' she agreed, 'and I – but come on, story. Three Bears?'

The Three Bears told with squeaky noises and dangerous growls, she put the child down, kissed the sleeping baby and said she must go. 'Yes, yes,' she said, 'I must,' disentangling her legs from the little boy's grip. 'But I will come again and teach your mum English, it's high time she learned.'

Mrs Patel, who understood perfectly, laughed.

As Julia left the shop, Mr Patel said, 'There was a man asking – I thought new boyfriend perhaps a possibility? But then I thought, No,' and he wagged his head, and since Julia was in a hurry and incurious he did not describe Maurice Benson.

Julia went light-footed along the street; she was hungry and looking forward to her steak, but most of all she cherished the prospect of working in Sylverster Wykes's garden. Fifty yards from home, feeling in her bag for her key, her heart sank: the dog was waiting on the doorstep. Seeing her, it raised itself from its haunches, pricked its ears and wagged its tail.

Resolving to deny it, Julia came to a halt just as the Eddisons, coming out of the house, exclaimed, 'Oh, it's still there,' as they slammed the door shut. 'Shoo! Go away! Kick it or something, Peter.'

'It's a horrible stray,' Angie Eddison addressed Julia.

'The Fellowes say it's been lurking all day. Perhaps one should call the police?'

Remembering occasions when Angie Eddison or perhaps Peter *had* called the police, Julia heard herself say as she inserted her key in the lock, 'I don't think this one will cause a domestic incident.' To the dog she said, 'Come on, then.'

Inside the house she found her knees were shaking and had to sit on the stairs where, as she hugged the dog, she heard Peter Eddison say, 'How bloody rude!' and Angie Eddison, 'Stuck-up bitch, no wonder her husband left her.'

While Julia climbed the stairs to her flat with her new friend, Angie, crossing the street, said, 'Gosh, that woman's a weirdo! Did you see the way she looked at us? She slammed the door in our faces.'

Taking her elbow and hurrying to avoid an oncoming car Peter hazarded, 'It's a communal door.'

'Of course it's a communal door, darling. It's a question of manners. *We* don't slam it.'

Unwisely, and releasing his wife's elbow, Peter said, 'I wouldn't call the way she shut the door a slam.'

'Wouldn't you?' Angie questioned. 'What would you call it?' When Peter did not reply she went on, 'Just when we are spared the shrieks and whistles of her noisy brat, she imports a dog!'

Optimistically Peter suggested, 'It may not bark.'

Angie said, 'Whoever heard of a dog which didn't? I tell you, it will be worse than thumps and bumps and obscene shouts when her ex came visiting; at least he wasn't there all the time.'

Peter said, 'They are both dead.'

Angie replied, 'And the dog is not.' Then she said, 'Do I sniff an accusation of insensitivity? Are you reproaching me?'

Peter said, 'Certainly not,' and Angie said, 'Well, then!'

But later in the pub, as they sat at a table with Janet and Tim Fellowes and some friends of theirs just back from a holiday in Kerala and eager to relate its charms, she reverted to the subject of Julia Piper. 'You should meet this woman in the flat above ours. We hardly know her but she is thick with the family who run our Corner Shop, they come from somewhere like Kerala – Indian sub-continent. The wife can't speak a word of English; *she* was imported. *He's* been here for years—'

'An arranged marriage,' Peter interjected.

'I know, darling, but it works, not like some; the Piper woman's, for instance. That's our neighbour,' she explained to the travellers from Kerala. 'Anyway, what I was leading up to when Peter interrupted was that, although this Indian wife doesn't speak any English, this peculiar woman in the flat above us is great friends with her and their children were, too, until her child was killed in a car crash. But that's another story. What I am really getting at is that it's possible to communicate without words, without knowing the language. I expect you found that in Kerala—'

'They all spoke English in our hotel,' said the husband of the travelled couple. 'But you were saying, they are friends, these two. What has—?'

'They made friends when she was pregnant with the Whistleblower. They went to the antenatal clinic together,' Peter interrupted.

The wife of the couple who had been to Kerala asked, 'Who is the Whistleblower?'

Angie, checked in mid-flow, said, 'How on earth did you know that, Peter?', ignoring her new acquaintance's query.

Peter said, 'A chap told me, oh, ages ago. Because she couldn't speak a word and was unlikely to understand, Mrs Patel was afraid to attend the clinic, so the Piper woman, who was going anyway, took her along.'

Deflated, Angie said, 'Oh, really?' Then, aware this was a social occasion, she laughed and said, 'They must have looked pretty comical toddling off together, bean-pole Piper and tiny Patel, arm in arm I expect like a huge choc-ice.'

At which Janet, who up to now had sat silent, exclaimed, 'That's a thoroughly racist remark,' and Tim, taking fright at this turn in the chat, hastily demanded a full report on their friends' holiday.

16

It was as though someone deciding to till the garden had lost heart before they began. There was a fork, a trowel, a hand fork and a pair of secateurs, all brand-new; and in a paper bag a pair of gardening gloves with the price label still attached.

The earth in the beds round three sides of the oblong was grey and dead. Among residual stalks of last year or the year before's annuals, not even a dandelion showed life. Julia forked the earth, turning it, breaking the gritty clods, digging as deep as she could, bending to extract bits of glass, snippets of Cellophane, rusty nails and plastic flower-pots which some foolish instant gardener had stuck in the borders, pot plant and all, leaving them to do or die, and die they had. Working the sterile earth she considered the glories of compost and farmyard manure and, as she dug, she vowed to rejuvenate this sad little London garden, surprise it, give it a shock.

The beds dug over, she fetched a broom and swept the paving between the beds. She noted with pleasure that it was not, as she had expected, of some cement composition but lovely Delabole slate. Sweeping the debris from the flower-beds into a heap, she shovelled it into a bin-bag. Then, taking the secateurs, she set to work on a wistaria clinging forlornly against the house. While pruning its excess of brittle tendrils with utmost severity, she dreamed of how in the spring the vine would bud and produce exquisite bunches of scented pea rather than waste its energies in a profusion of leaves.

She had left the dog in the street, partly because she hesitated to take it into her employer's house, and perhaps too to see whether it might after all come to its senses and return to where it belonged. Twice as she worked she heard it bark, and at one moment growl loudly and savagely at some person, a man by the sound of his curses, but drowned in her thoughts and plans for the garden she did not pause to see what was up. Wearily at last in the gathering dusk she viewed her *oeuvre*, visualized the garden as it would be when she had planted it, the beds full of scented delights and between the flagstones cushions of aromatic herbs.

The dog barked again, calling her this time with impatient yelps. Reluctantly she went into the house, locked the french windows, put away the tools and, hitching on her coat, went out to the street. She was tired, but felt a lightening of spirit she had not experienced since Christy's death. Gardening was therapeutic, she thought, and of course the dog was company. 'I suppose I shall have to find you a name,' she said to the animal as they set off together along the pavement.

Patel's Corner Shop was still open. The dog waited outside; she went in.

'Dog food?' exclaimed Mr Patel. 'You have a *dog*?'

'I seem to have.'

'A dog! Well, well! Winalot or Chappie?' Mr Patel's rendering of the word Chappie was upbeat and seductive.

'I had better have one of each, please.'

'Do not spoil the brute.' Mr Patel put two tins of dog food into a bag. 'Mrs Patel has taken the children to visit her sister,' he said.

'Oh.' What I would love to put on those poor flower-beds, Julia thought, is some real farmyard manure, and some of the compost we made, Giles and I – but how to get it?

'You are tired? Pot of tea?' Mr Patel broke in on her

thoughts, leaning across the counter radiating affection and sympathy.

'No, thank you, dear Mr Patel.' Should she buy dog biscuits? She looked round the shop. 'You don't happen to know of a van I could hire, or a car?'

'A car? A van?' His voice rose.

'Ours, I mean mine was smashed.' (Oh bloody, bloody Giles.)

'Of course, oh, of course.' She was afraid he would mention Christy, but he said, 'Insurance? They pay up?'

'Not enough.'

'Very bad, very bad.'

'I need to go to the country.' The need grew in urgency as she spoke. 'I want to walk with the dog and I want to fetch real manure, compost.'

'Compost? What is it?'

'Stuff you dig into earth to make things grow, and breed worms.'

'What for?'

'Did I not tell you I am working on Mr Wykes's garden?'

'I think you clean the house,' said Mr Patel.

'But I am working in his garden, too, did I not tell you?'

'You did not.'

'I thought I had.'

'Stick a notice,' suggested Mr Patel, pointing towards his notice-board. 'I will not charge and I will enquire, but this compost, does it smell?'

'Not much, but manure might.'

Mr Patel sighed. 'I will write a notice. Now pot of tea?' he suggested.

Julia shook her head. 'Thank you and bless you, but I must go back and feed my new chum.'

'Pedigree Chum!' Mr Patel exclaimed. 'I have that too, is excellent.'

'Another time.' Julia thanked him and went on her

116

way, the dog trotting beside her. Because it did not occur to her that she might be followed, she failed to notice Maurice Benson who, snooping until she had let herself into the house where she lived on the top floor, retraced his footsteps to the Corner Shop and engaged Mr Patel in conversation and presently, to keep Mr Patel sweet, made one or two purchases.

Perambulating the shop he came to a halt by the notice-board and began reading the cards. As he read Mr Patel came up behind him, opened the case and pinned a new notice on the board. *Wanted to Hire, Car or Van.* Maurice Benson read it, and put two and two together. The telephone number he observed was the same as on several other cards, presumably the number of the shop. Mr Patel would take messages and pass them on to people wise enough to cherish their privacy like Julia Piper. Having selected a few items, Maurice returned to the counter to pay. Mr Patel took his money and gave change. 'I see someone wants to hire a car or van,' Maurice said. 'I'd be interested. I have a car which does not earn its keep.'

Mr Patel said, 'Oh, yes?'

'I'd be ready to rent it, or drive it for that matter for whoever—'

Mr Patel said, 'Oh yes?' again.

'So how do I get in touch?'

'The person is already suited.'

'But I just saw you pin the notice on the board, the person can't be,' said Maurice.

'The person is,' said Mr Patel.

'But I just saw—'

'In India it is custom to keep all notice-boards full. It is old custom, good for custom.'

'Do you mean to tell me that half your notices are bogus?'

'Bogus?'

'Fake.'

Mr Patel laughed, not trusting Maurice Benson.

117

'So no kittens neutered in need of a home?'

'Kittens? Yes, sir, there are kittens, you want a—'

'What about the goat?'

'No goat.' Mr Patel laughed again. 'Is joke. You want Kit-e-kat?'

'No, I do *not*' said Maurice Benson.

Mr Patel watched him leave the shop and, later that evening, when Mrs Patel had returned from visiting her sister, he telephoned Julia Piper and offered her the use of his van.

17

There was no radio in Mr Patel's van; the windscreen wipers creaked across and across, sluicing the rain with a noise both soothing and monotonous.

The dog sat upright and anxious at first, but presently settled to lie across the seat with his jaw pressed warmly on Julia's thigh; with London behind her, her thoughts yet stayed with the little garden so starved of attention and the first aid she planned for it.

She found herself comparing it with the only garden she knew well, her mother's, and the work she and Giles had shared during arduous but agreeable hours of labour.

Long before planting the camellia hedge, the cost of which had so startled the village, there had been the weeding and trenching, raking and levelling of the entire area to Giles's design. She had worked with him willingly, for it took her out of the house and the proximity of Clodagh's constant demands and nit-picking criticism. Even so, propped on a sofa, her broken leg in plaster, Clodagh had overseen their activities shouting suggestions and directions through the open french window, her strong voice carrying, as Giles said, 'as through a loud-hailer', a remark which had made her laugh.

From time to time he would leave her at work to chat with Clodagh or, with the excuse that he had an idea for the book he was writing which must be noted before he forgot it, he would go to his room where once, needing to go to the lavatory and passing his open door, she had seen him asleep, sprawled on his bed, and been too soft-hearted to rouse him, excusing him for he sat up late keeping Clodagh company when she was, she said, in pain and sleepless. At that period she had judged Giles a kind and caring man to be so good to her difficult mother.

Labouring together, they had made the compost heap, a mountain of grass cuttings, weeds, newspaper, kitchen rubbish, tea leaves, autumn leaves, potato peelings, even old socks. Giles tested its degree of fermentation with a long metal stave, saying, 'Next year, when this is properly rotted, we will spread it on the garden. It will be rich and friable. But this year she must buy dung.' Clodagh had cavilled at the cost of farmyard manure and its pungent smell. Was that the time Giles had a row with Clodagh, a row which woke her in the night? Was it that row or another which, erupting again next day, caused Giles to say, 'I could murder the old bitch and bury her in the compost heap'?

She had laughed; one laughed easily when attracted to the person who made the joke. 'When *she* is rotted,' Giles had said, 'mine will be the richest, most friable compost in the county,' rolling the Rs in the word 'friable' so that for days they giggled at the mention of compost. ('Here, put this with the compost;' hoots and toots of silly laughter.) Temporarily then they were united against Clodagh, not only by the irritation caused by her bossiness but by a joke shared. That was before Giles, catching her unaware on the day Clodagh had been taken to the hospital by Madge Brownlow to have her cast removed, had tripped her, forced her to the ground (by the compost heap) and raped her.

Driving through the night in Mr Patel's van, Julia shivered as she remembered the cold ground on her back and retched, her mouth filling with bitter saliva at the recollected taste of Giles's blood when she bit the hand which stifled her screams.

Madge Brownlow, returning with her mother

released from plaster, had turned about and taken Giles to the hospital to have the wound stitched. 'No, I would not recognize the bitch,' Giles had said. 'All I know is that it bit me for no reason.' Clodagh said, 'Make sure he has an anti-tetanus injection, Madge.'

'I must be out of my mind to even dream of it,' Julia said to the dog. 'I can't go back there, however good the compost.' The dog sat up yawning and yowling and peered through the windscreen, for day was breaking; they had come a long way. 'OK,' Julia said. 'You want to pee, I want to pee.' She stopped the van, switched off the engine and, getting out, discovered that the rain had stopped and they were at the top of a hill by a wood in a stretch of country she had never seen, but which reminded her of some place she had fleetingly known a long time ago. And her mother had not been there.

So who had she been with?

A robin sang from the top of a bush, establishing its territory. They jumped a ditch and walked through trees still dripping with rain until they reached a clearing, where she stopped and listened. Far away a cock crowed; in a field by the wood a cow coughed and another tore at the grass with its long harsh tongue. In the wood a startled pheasant cack-cacked.

'What's that?' she had asked.

'Just a pheasant.' He had held her hand. She had had to reach up, her head barely level with the man's knee. 'Come on,' he had said, 'not much further. We are nearly there.'

'Where's there?' she had asked.

And he had answered, 'Home. My home. Your home, now.'

'Goodness, what a funny thing to remember,' Julia said to the dog. 'That was my *father*! It was his home, or had been, but not mine for more than five minutes. Or five days, perhaps? He had run away with me,' she

121

told the dog. 'It was lovely and exciting, frightening, too, but he got bored and sent me back.'

The dog raised front paws against her thigh to stare up at her face. She stroked his head. 'I can't remember it properly,' she said, 'but I am hungry, let's find somewhere to have breakfast.' She turned and went back through the wood and presently, driving on, saw a sign that said: *Bed and Breakfast.* Turning in at a gate, she stopped at a farm where she asked whether she could have the breakfast without the bed? The woman was agreeable and sat her at a table by a window, the dog at her feet, to wait for bacon and eggs, mushroom, tomatoes, toast and coffee.

The woman asked, 'Would your dog like something?'

Julia said he would and the woman said, 'We give ours lights and biscuits, that do?' Later, watching him eat, she said, 'Nice dog, bit of a lurcher. My husband likes lurchers; you wouldn't want to part?'

And Julia exclaimed, 'Oh, no!' When they were alone she said to the dog, 'So that's what you are, a lurcher. I shall have to find you a name now I know what you are.'

Back in the van, feeling a need to tramp across country, she headed west towards Dartmoor humped heavy on the skyline, its sombre autumn colours presaging winter but still streaked orange and rust by dying bracken. Climbing the slopes up narrow twisting lanes she stopped at a high point, parked the van in a disused quarry and, with the dog beside her, set off walking. At first it was enough to breathe the air, watch a cloud's shadow racing along the side of the hills, spot buzzards wheeling, note clumps of gorse in flower, catch the eye of shaggy ponies who looked up snorting as she passed and black-faced sheep who stood their ground to stamp their feet at the dog, and listen to the roar of a river in spate charging towards the pewter-coloured sea in the distance. But watching the dog bouncing and leaping in the bracken, whose colours complemented its coat, she was reminded as she had been earlier in the wood of that half-forgotten incident in her childhood. There had been a dog, a springer spaniel. The man who was her father had said, 'Look how lively he leaps,' as he tried to distract her attention, for she whimpered with fatigue. He had said, too, 'We are nearly there. Oh, do shut up. It won't be long now.'

'Where was "there"?' Julia murmured, racking her brain, until suddenly, watching the lurcher leap, memory clicked into place.

Her father had carried her across a sweep of lawn to a long, low house with a veranda stretching its whole length. Spaced along it were earthenware pots of lilies, whose scent was overpowering in the hot summer air. From the house came an old woman who, although she embraced her father, was not glad to see him. Drawing them into a cool hall, she said, 'What on earth possessed you? You can't possibly manage – it is not fair on the child. You know what you are like. You will never keep it up,' and, 'I, with your father as he is, cannot—' and, 'It is not possible even if I—' and, 'The child looks done in. Give her to Emily who will do what's needed, bath, food, and bed,' and, 'It is not possible, dearest. This is totally idiotic, unthought out, and it puts you in the wrong.'

But the man who was her father used his loud angry voice. 'Rubbish, of course I can manage. I have made up my mind; I've got her, I shall keep her,' and, 'It's not as though that bloody cow wants her, she does not even pretend to *like* the child.'

And the old woman said, 'Don't use expressions like that, Daniel,' and, 'You should have thought of all this years ago before you—'

And he, shouting now, 'Even if you won't help us, I've made up my fucking mind, I shall keep her, I—'

The woman said, 'Darling, this is all bluster,' and, 'And I can't see you managing.'

He said, 'I am keeping her and that's that,' and then, 'I need a drink, where's the whisky?'

'The decanter is where it always is, and I would prefer it if you did not get drunk with your father so ill; dying, actually.'

Another woman had appeared and taken her from him, carried her upstairs; she remembered it now standing high upon the moor, the wind chilling her neck. A day later? A week? Weeks? Certainly there had been time to get to know the house, the walled garden, sleepy cats, delicious-smelling kitchen, stable, garage, cobbled yard. Her father had carried her about (he became irritated matching his pace to hers), shown her things, talked to her. But then he talked less, brushed her off when she climbed on his knee. 'Why don't you run to Emily?' The old man dying upstairs was taking his time. They said, 'Don't make so much noise. He must not be disturbed.'

Out loud, Julia said, 'Why have I never realized? Grandparents? I blotted them out, blotted it all out. Especially I blotted out the day he put me in that car with a strange man and woman, who took me back to Clodagh.' Standing in the icy wind Julia Piper remembered the expression of relief her father could not hide when they parted. He had waved as the car started, waved and walked back to the house.

A pair of buzzards wheeled and shrieked above her, circling on a thermal. 'What a clay-footed world.' Julia addressed the dog, who had ceased his leaping and stood beside her. 'But you are only a lurcher dog, your paws are not made of clay.' And, remembering that last sight of the man who had been her father, she thought, Poor man, he did not have the bottle to hang on to me any more than Giles to disentangle himself from Clodagh. It was impossible, she thought with wry amusement, to call one's husband's mistress 'Mother'.

'Oh!' she exclaimed. 'Enough of that. Let us walk and run,' she said to the dog, 'Leap joyfully. Oh!' she said. 'Joyful, that's a good name. What's it like to have a name and be a lurcher? Come on, Joyful, run.'

About midday, returning to the van, she drove down into a valley, stopped at a pub and ate steak-and-kidney pudding washed down with lager. The helping was so substantial she shared it with Joyful. Not since Christy's birth had she had the chance to tramp across country; while mourning his death and stretching her tired legs, she appreciated this freedom rather guiltily. 'Short legs shackle.' Her father was back; the train of thought begun that morning was not quite over. He was dead, she knew, had been dead for years. She remembered the solicitors' letter for Clodagh, his next of kin. He had not remarried, but alone in some seaside resort – Margate, Frinton, Weston-super-Mare? – he had died intestate, leaving a trail of debts.

To rid herself of memories that were becoming intrusive, Julia tried to think whether there was anything else she should remember before putting him out of her mind once and for all, as she hoped sooner or later to do with Giles. Sitting in the warm pub comfortably replete with steak-and-kidney pudding, memory surprisingly obliged. Two men were playing darts and one let out a whistle which matched the first note of a song her father had sung to her during those first days when he kidnapped her and was not yet finding the situation tedious: *You're the cream of my coffee, You're the lace of my shoe, You will always be My necessity, I'd be lost without you.* She had loved the song, believed it, believed him. Then he became bored. Giles had the same charm, she had believed him also; for a while.

At the bar she asked for her bill. As she paid it, she enquired whether there was a garden centre here-abouts and was told of one at Widdicombe and that St

Bridgit's at Exeter had most things if she was heading back that way. By the time she had visited both the van was packed with delights and she drove up the motorway considering where, at what angle, in which corner she would plant the rosemary, lavender and sweet-scented box. Against which wall she would put the roses, clematis, jasmines and vine. How she would fill the beds with iris, pansies, pinks, mediterranean daisies; where to fit in the primroses, auriculas, stocks, sweet violets and wild strawberry. Which corner would be best filled with lily bulbs, dwarf narcissi, daffodil, crocus and tulips? Where between the flag-stones should she cram in cushions of thyme? But first of all, she thought gleefully, she would trench into the sparse and pitiful London soil the contents of the plastic bags stuffed tight with splendid odoriferous horseshit and equally useful but less pungent mushroom compost.

When all was unloaded she would wash the Patels' van inside and out. 'God knows,' she said out loud to the dog, 'when you and I will crawl into bed, but it's been worth it, even if tomorrow I can hardly keep my eyes open when I am back to Real Life cleaning that journalist's flat.'

Hours later she climbed the stairs to her flat and, stripping off her clothes, got into bed; she was too exhausted to appreciate that somewhere on the hills of Devon she had shed at least part of her grief. And when she was practically asleep, the telephone pealed. Stretching out an arm and taking the receiver, she said, 'Stuff it,' then, turning on her side, slept.

It was only on the following day, when she was filling the journalist's washing-machine with drip-dry bed linen and dirty knickers, that it occurred to her that whoever had disturbed her in the night and been given a rough reception could not be Giles.

18

In his hotel in Los Angeles Sylvester waited for his partner's call from London. As he waited he sifted through letters which had been addressed to him in New York, where business had gone well. He had met old friends, been to parties, shopped for shirts, socks and underpants at Brooks Brothers, before driving up to Vermont to see 'the Colour' and meet an author whose manuscript disappointed (as did 'the Colour'; over when he arrived). Leaving before his mail could catch up with him, he had flown to Los Angeles for a week's work before ten days' holiday in Colorado where the snow was late, the skiing poor and he tired of his own company. Back in Los Angeles, his flight booked for London, bags packed and expecting to be in his office within thirty-six hours, he imagined these much-travelled letters would be of little interest.

Two were from his solicitor detailing the course of his divorce which, according to a fax received that morning, was now a *fait accompli*. Next, a gossipy missive from a colleague noted for irritating sexual and lavatorial jokes: *Rebecca, lovelorn, telephones to enquire about your progress but in reality to ensure that we should not miss the finalizing – what a mirth-provoking expression – of your marital split and to find out whether you have fallen for some randy super American girl or can she still cherish a mite of hope? We in the office all hope for a super sex girl, it would be good for your health.* There was more in similar vein. Sylvester dropped the letter into the trash basket.

The last missive in Rebecca's strong hand began: *Really, Sylvester, you were unwise not to leave your keys with me. Your cleaning woman, if that's what she is, puts out rubbish which smells of horse. I suspect she has allowed squatters in. There was a horrid mongrel on your doorstep yesterday and a scruffy sort of man followed me from your street to the King's Road. The police, of course, won't lift a finger and your answerphone tells me you are 'busy at the moment and will ring back if I leave a message'. I hesitate to worry you when you must be extra low with news of Celia marrying Andrew Battersby when your divorce comes through in January. She has not let the grass grow, has she? The office do not seem to know when you will be back but tell me you have made splendid deals, no surprise there. I hope you have not overworked, it will not assuage your grief. You should take a little holiday, try to forget this sad, sad news. Yours affectionately, Rebecca. PS I see in* The Times *that your aunt has passed away.*

Sylvester was laughing when the call came through from London. He said, 'Hallo, John, see you Friday. My flight is tonight.'

John said, 'Glad I caught you. I want you to go and see Marvin Bratt.'

'Who is Marvin Bratt?'

'Was a Republican Senator. He has a manuscript we must go for. He is in Virginia, you can just pop—'

Sylvester said, 'Oh God! I am hankering for my own bed. I've been away too long—'

John said, 'Don't be such an old woman. Now listen, here's his number. It's near Charlottesville, you'll love it.'

Sylvester said, 'I won't.'

John went on, 'He will ask you to stay. He has a smashing wife and always lays on super girls. You'll love it, have fun. I always do.'

Sylvester said, 'Why don't you go yourself?'

'You're on the spot. I am busy. It's nearly Christmas and one of the children has a birthday.'

Sylvester said, 'What a bore. I shall have to cancel my flight.'

'Weaker men than you have managed that.'

'How long will it take? What's the book about?'

'Holocaust of American Indians. Hot stuff.'

'Fashionable.'

'We need that book, Sylvester.'

'What's he like, this Bratt?'

'Genial man. Looks as if he has mumps, sort of chipmunk face like that general. His wife Elvira is smashing, you'll love her. Have a go.'

'At the wife?'

'The book, you fool—'

'How long will it take?'

'Haven't a clue, but pin him down.'

'I shall have to send money to my cleaning lady. I have overstayed, she—'

'Even that's been managed before now, or shall I ask Rebecca to—'

'God forbid. She pursues me with aunt-like adjurations—'

'Does she? She used to do it to me, it's menopausal.'

'If that's so, it's the longest in history—'

'Yeah, well. Have a good time. Fax me—'

Sylvester said, 'Don't ring off. Can the man write?'

'I've only read his speeches. Not bad. If he can't write, we can tinker. It's the subject matter, his angle—'

'What's he like, apart from mumps?'

'Can't think, really. Oh, he's a health freak, so is Elvira, sex every night and twice at weekends. It's like cleaning their teeth or jogging. You'll have a good time – and by the way the booze flows. You'll have to join in—'

'Sexually?'

'No, drinkwise. Sexually, too, if you want to, I imagine.' John chortled.

Sylvester said, 'Thanks a lot. Just what I need.'

John said, 'Well, it is,' and, 'Fax me.'

Sylvester said, 'Goodbye,' and, sick of snide innuendo, muttered, 'and fuck the lot of you. Fax, my arse.'

On the telephone Marvin Bratt boomed hospitably, 'Come right away. We'll talk business and then have fun. Elvira will have neighbours for dinner. My son and his wife may be here and Sal Schultz, a lovely girl, is our house guest, just divorced. You too, I believe? You'll love Sal. She's a real fun girl, pretty and healthy.'

Sylvester muttered, 'So she's not got AIDS.'

'I didn't catch that?'

'Clearing my throat.'

'So, see you Friday?'

'I must stir my pins.'

'You do that. Ewan and Simon are coming Monday; your partner John seemed keen I see you first.'

'Ewan and Simon of Narrowlane and Jinks?' Sylvester controlled his voice.

Marvin Bratt laughed. 'Got it in one. Coupla snakes in the grass, but they have the money. See you Friday.'

Supposing John was only sending him to see Marvin Bratt so that he could, when Narrowlane and Jinks published the book, say, 'We were offered it but we turned it down, it wasn't right for our list.' Sylvester was several times tempted when changing planes on his journey to Virginia to take the next scheduled flight to Heathrow. But from Heathrow, he thought as he sat in his plane, there was only the taxi drive into London to an empty house. Then, ordering himself a drink he thought, but is it empty? What was it silly old Rebecca had said? And then he remembered her postscript: *I see in* The Times *that your aunt has passed away.* Gosh, he thought, I was fond of Aunt Calypso. I shall miss her. She wasn't that old; she was always kind in an unirritating way. And didn't she recently send a message via Hamish asking me to stay? I must get in touch with Hamish. I'll telephone Hamish, find out about the funeral; I ought to go to it. Oh, he thought, I may have missed it! Damn and blast John for sending me on this idiotic wild-goose chase. Then, he thought as his Scotch began to soothe, I shall not bother with this boring manuscript. Ordering another Scotch, he thought, Serve John right. I will have fun. It's a long time since I had any. I shall do as my host suggests, have fun with this healthy fun girl, if that's what's intended. Let's face it, it's a very long time since I had a healthy therapeutic fuck and no strings attached – better not be.

In this cavalier frame of mind Sylvester arrived to stay with Marvin and Elvira Bratt, cheerful and looking forward to some well-earned pleasure and partially pickled in Scotch.

19

Meeting Julia in Patel's Corner Shop, Janet asked, 'Is that your dog?'

Julia said, 'M-m-m.' Then, since the girl appeared friendly, she said, 'M-m-m,' again, remembering that the girl consorted with the Eddisons who had been disagreeable to Joyful, tried to kick him.

'A letter!' Mr Patel called from his counter. 'For you, Mrs Piper, from the US of A.' He extended his white-shirted arm, a letter pincered between delicate brown fingers.

Julia took the letter. 'Thank you, Mr Patel. Shall I save the stamp for your collection?'

'Please.' Mr Patel's smile was radiant. 'Yes.'

'Fancy having a letter addressed to you here,' exclaimed Janet.

'There is no end to the marvels and resources of Patel's Corner Shop,' said Julia, and exchanged a complicit glance with its owner.

Janet followed her out of the shop. 'So it *is* your dog,' she said, noting the activity of Joyful's tail; he had been waiting outside.

Julia said, 'You could say that.'

'What breed is he?'

'A lurcher.'

Janet said, 'Oh,' and, falling in beside Julia, walked with her. 'I am glad you have got *something*,' she said. When Julia failed to respond she said, 'A dog is a lot easier.'

'Than what?' Julia bristled.

Not as stupid as she was apt to appear, Janet said, 'I

was not going to mention – no – I was looking for something clever to say about spelling backwards: you know, D-O-G as opposed to G-O-D? But now I have lost my thread.'

Vaguely remembering that when they had last spoken she had been somewhat offensive, Julia said nothing in reply.

Made uncomfortable by her silence, Janet ventured, 'Tell me about the Patels, apart from having children in common.' (Should she have mentioned children, having just steered clear?) 'What makes you like them? You obviously do. You seem friends, and it's obvious they are fond of you. Everyone else who goes to the shop is a mere customer.'

Julia said, 'I can talk to Mrs Patel.'

'But she doesn't speak English,' Janet exclaimed.

Julia said, or Janet thought she said, 'That's why.'

They walked on a few paces, Janet's heels tapping, Julia's feet silent; then, relenting, Julia said, 'They have tact and humour; it's the combination.'

Janet, puzzled, said, 'Humour?'

'Several years ago,' Julia said, 'I came along the street and there, chalked on the Patel newspaper board, was: *Huge Maggi Reduction.*'

'Soups?'

'Those, too.'

Janet burst out laughing. 'Oh! I *see.* Witty, understated, *double entendre.* I shan't tell Tim, he's such a Tory.' She added thoughtfully, 'Such a racist.' They had reached their front door. She said, 'I am very glad you have a dog.'

And Julia, dimly remembering their first encounter, said, 'And you have God up your sleeve.' She put her key in the lock, opened the door and vanished up the stairs with Joyful.

Reaching her flat on the top floor, she opened her employer's letter. It read: *Dear Mrs Piper, My business detains me in the States. I do not know when I will be*

133

back but please carry on. I enclose my cheque to cover your work and the hours of the gardener. Should it be insufficient please let me know on my return. Sylvester Wykes. She was putting the envelope safe on the mantelshelf for Mr Patel's stamp collection when the telephone started ringing; she lifted the receiver and said, 'Hallo?'

Whoever it was was in a call box; she could hear traffic. At night when the calls came, there was silence. She relaxed. 'Hallo?' she said again. There was a high-pitched giggle, then a child's voice said, 'Mummy, Mummy,' and, 'Mummy, where are you?' plangent, squeaky. Then an adult laughed.

Sweating, trembling and dizzy, Julia sat down on the divan. Joyful pressed himself against her leg. 'Your mother, Clodagh May, holds you responsible,' said a man's voice, 'and so does her friend Madge. They sit in the parlour – that's what darling Giles called it, isn't it? – and grieve for murdered Giles and murdered Christy. For it was murder, wasn't it, letting him drive? Now don't hang up on me,' said the voice. 'Your mother grieves,' it went on. 'She and Madge tend the grave. It's a nice grave, as graves go; the magpies like it. Do you like magpies, Julia? I watch them and I watch you. Magpies are supposed to be unlucky,' said the voice. 'Giles and little Christy were unlucky, weren't they?'

There was a pause while the man slotted in coins. I should ring the police, Julia thought. They have ways of catching these people. 'You still there?' asked the man. 'I thought so. Do you know,' he said conversationally, 'she has little Christy's toys all there waiting? Those great big toys sit in a row waiting, waiting. Bit creepy, really. Bit over the top, wouldn't you say? But I don't suppose it interests you really, because you are free, aren't you? They are not coming back, darling Giles and little Christy, so you are free for your other – what shall we call them – interests? That the right word?'

Shifting sideways on the divan, the telephone cord at full stretch, Julia sat on something hard and painful. With her free hand she reached into her hip pocket and extracted it, then, putting it to her mouth, she blew with all her strength into the telephone. She was still blowing Christy's whistle into a now silent telephone when Joyful's terrified and lunatic barking made her desist.

20

There is something exhilarating about disaster, Sylvester thought as his plane droned towards Europe. He snuffled with suppressed merriment, outright solitary laughter having earlier in the flight antagonized his neighbour, who assumed him to be drunk.

Remembering his arrival at Marvin Bratt's grandiose establishment, Sylvester snuffled again, for he had immediately wrong-footed by being a head and a half taller than his host who, though perfectly formed, handsome and athletic, was a small man, a condition to which he drew attention by standing a step higher on the porch as they shook hands.

Aware that his height could cause irritation, Sylvester had tried to remedy the situation by moving back and down a step so that his eyes came level with his host's which, china blue in a tanned face, glared out above a luxuriant moustache, aware of his ploy. He had erred again, Sylvester remembered, by voicing an anxiety presently in his mind and asking whether he might put a call through to England, explaining that a favourite aunt had died and that on the various stops of his dog-leg journey he had failed to get in touch with his cousin, only child of the said aunt. He had been surprised when, with un-American lack of generosity, Marvin Bratt said, 'Sure, but make it snappy. First things first; you are here to discuss my book.'

A maid had taken charge of his bags and he followed his host into a book-lined room. 'My library,' Marvin said, then, pointing to a telephone on an outsize desk, added, 'Telephone,' and repeated, 'Make it snappy.'

Made to feel he should apologize for his aunt's inconvenient demise, Sylvester felt damned if he would.

There were two walls of leather-bound books in the library. A third wall was of glass, with a view across a large garden towards a distant swimming-pool circled by magnolia trees, whose glittering leaves reflected along the edges of the water. The fourth wall was plastered with life-sized photographs of what he assumed were Marvin's wife and daughter: both blonde and both beautiful. Under these was the desk, a swivel chair and opposite the desk a deep armchair. Marvin said, 'I'll fix you a drink, you'd like Bourbon,' and moved towards a drinks cabinet.

Sylvester, who disliked Bourbon, and not wanting a drink, said, 'No, no thanks,' and began to dial.

Ignoring him, Marvin poured drinks and said, 'So she's left you some dough, this aunt.'

Sylvester shook his head. The telephone was ringing in England.

'So what's the rush?' Marvin brought a tumbler of Bourbon.

'Hallo,' said Hamish's courteous voice. 'I am sorry I can't come to the phone just now, but if you'll leave a message I will come back to you as soon as possible.' Then it added, 'Wait for the bleep. Quite a lot of idiots don't.'

Sylvester said, 'Curse it, Hamish, I have been trying to reach you ever since I heard of Calypso's death. I am desperately sorry. I am in America, back in London soon and will try again,' and frustratedly rang off.

'You didn't leave your name.' Marvin handed him his drink. 'Siddown.' He indicated the armchair. 'Your aunt,' he said, 'can't run away. Can we now get down to business?'

'Aunt by marriage,' Sylvester muttered and, 'Thanks, but I drank on the plane.' Sinking into the depths of the armchair he balanced the glass on its arm and stared up at row upon row of law books.

Marvin said, 'Why should that stop you?' and sat in the chair behind the desk.

Rearranging his thoughts, for he had expected to like his host, Sylvester said, 'I was not told you were a lawyer – all these books.'

'My father was. I am a politician, now a *writer*. The books give tone.' Marvin stressed the word 'writer'. 'Can we get on now?'

'Please.' (Why am I cast as supplicant? It is he who is trying to sell.) He watched Marvin open a drawer and extract a folder of typescript, place it on the desk and rest his hands on it. He looked happier now that Sylvester was on a lower level. 'I was expecting,' Marvin said, 'that your partner John would come over.'

Sylvester said, 'A child has a birthday, it's nearly Christmas and I am here,' (and will have to do) and though unwilling to kowtow, for decency's sake he added, 'and I am of course extremely interested in your book.' (Some day, who knows, he thought, I might find myself pleading for interest in *Wellington's Valet*.)

Marvin Bratt said, 'I sure hope you are.' When Sylvester said no more he said, 'OK, I shall give you a synopsis, chapter by chapter. You can read it later tonight.'

Sylvester said, 'Certainly.' Sunk below Marvin he had a good view of the moustache, which curtained a tight mouth above a cleft chin. Above the mouth were arranged an arrogant nose, the blue eyes and a bristly head of fair hair. 'That sounds an excellent plan.'

Marvin gulped Bourbon. 'You ain't drinking.'

'I drank on the plane.'

'So?'

'So I'll take my time.'

Marvin said, 'OK, OK.' Then, dropping his voice, he said, 'This book is dynamite.'

And Sylvester said, 'I am waiting.'

For a politician Marvin Bratt had a monotonous

voice; Sylvester's thoughts strayed back to Calypso's death. He should have accepted her invitation, at least rung her up before leaving for America. He jerked back and concentrated.

Marvin Bratt's interpretation of and attitude to the Holocaust of the Native Indian tribes of America was, to say the least, breathtaking. If he was not mishearing, Marvin Bratt approved of the Holocaust, did not think it had been sufficiently thorough and advocated more on similar lines in a campaign which would include Blacks and Hispanics. In fact he planned the elimination from the United States of all peoples who were not white-skinned.

Interrupting, he had asked, 'Jews?'

'Jews in the States are white, right? What we are after is a United States of America which is *white*. Now, where was I? I lost the thread.'

'What about Martin Luther King?'

'A hiccough.'

'Ah.'

'You going to listen?'

'Carry on, please.' The hand which held the unwanted Bourbon had begun to sweat; his shirt stuck to the small of his back. He got up and perambulated the room. 'Don't mind me, I think better on the move.' His throat was dry and without thinking he had sipped the Bourbon. Who was it disliked this stuff as much as he did? Interfering old, well-meaning old Rebecca, retailer of bad news, last seen carping about rugs. (That reminds me, I must collect those Kelims from the cleaners. Could do it on my way in from Heathrow.) Riding the waves of his inspiration Marvin was intoning like a southern preacher, smacking his hand on the manuscript as he made a point. The campaign to purify the nation would take fifty years. No need to rush things, but be thorough.

With his back to Marvin, Sylvester tipped the contents of his glass along the spines of a row of jurisprudence. 'Who carries out this campaign, this policy?' he queried.

'We have a nucleus.'

Sylvester returned to his chair. Should this book be suppressed? Suppression was counter-productive. Could it be published with an introduction? With the right introduction, could the poison in the boil be lanced? At all costs this book must be saved from Narrowlane and Jinks who, with their ultra-right views, would produce it intacta. Marvin Bratt had finished the synopsis. 'Well?'

'As you say: dynamite.'

Marvin Bratt looked pleased.

Searching for words, looking past Marvin's head at the collection of photographs, focusing, he saw that behind the portraits of the blonde women was a vast enlargement, a group photograph. A flock of sheep? Looking closer, they turned out to be tightly packed figures, Ku Klux Klan. 'Oh,' he said, choking with nervous laughter. 'I thought it was a flock of sheep.'

'Sheep?' Marvin was perplexed.

'Behind your wife and daughter.'

'Those ain't sheep.' Marvin rose from his chair.

'Oh no! I see. Your nucleus. Ah.'

'What's funny?'

Unable to take his eyes off the photograph – one hooded figure was much shorter than the others – unable too to choke back his laughter (he had laughed from nerves as children do when an old person falls), Sylvester said, 'I see I was mistaken, I thought they were sheep. Which one is you?'

Marvin Bratt had not deigned to answer except to suggest, 'You need new glasses?'

And Sylvester, unable to restrain himself, had said, 'But to the casual eye, you must admit, you must see the connection.' And then, disgusted and a little frightened by what he had heard, yet craving for the whole he had back-pedalled and excused himself.

140

'Forgive me, I am tired and not making sense. May I read the book alone, go through it thoroughly?' Adding for good measure, for if it had been his work, even *Wellington's Valet*, and Marvin had laughed as he had, he would have snatched back his *oeuvre* and put it under lock and key, 'It is obviously an important book.'

Marvin said, 'Sure,' a trifle suspiciously. 'You shall read it tonight, free of interruption.' Then, switching to the role of charming host which John had described, he had said, 'Now, let's forget business. Come and meet Elvira, my wife, my daughter and Sal, our house guest. There they are by the pool looking beautiful. We want you to have a good time,' he had said as they strolled towards the distant group. 'So often one sees a woman in the distance and she looks a peach and then, close up, she's a hag. That's what's called a disappointing surprise, I promise that won't happen here,' and he laughed as though he had made a witticism.

'It has never happened to me.' He had spoken surlily, still shaken by what he had heard and the photograph of the Ku Klux Klan. To remedy his lack of manners he began to tell Marvin of a woman he had seen from a train window upending a sheep, who had captured his imagination, but might well have disappointed if he had seen her close to.

Marvin, mocking, had said, 'You seem obsessed with sheep. You gotta shrink back home?'

He had then realized the connection: Marvin was getting up his nose in precisely the manner of the interfering fellow who, stinking of alcohol and stale tobacco, had annoyed him on the train. But by then they had reached the group sitting by the pool and he had forgotten the sheep, Marvin's book and the Ku Klux Klan as he took in the sheer force of the three women's beauty.

Elvira Bratt was taller than her husband, golden, lovely and welcoming, as was his daughter, but he knew even before he was introduced to his fellow guest Sal that he would go to bed with her.

It had not really been necessary for Elvira to say by way of introduction, 'This is Sal. You two will have a lot in common. Sal was two-timed by her husband,' or for Sal to squeeze his fingers as they shook hands. 'Hi,' she had said as though sealing an agreement. 'Hi.' And, 'So your wife walked out on you?'

Both of them had said, 'How could she?' and, 'How could he?' in chorus.

Well (he remembered in the plane), well, he had thought, this part of the programme will be easy. This part will be fun, this will counterbalance Bratt's awful book. And he had squeezed her fingers in reply.

'Sylvester's a sheep freak,' Marvin had said, 'fell in love with a sheep from a train window.' He told the story, garbling it. 'He needs treatment.' And Sal, demurely answering for them both, 'We will see what we can do, shall we?'

It had seemed an easy and agreeable assignation at the time.

But he had said, 'Work first,' or words to that effect.

Elvira said, 'Of course, Marvin's book. I hope you can read it tonight? Marvin is anxious you people should like it in Europe. It has a message.'

Sylvester said, hoping he did not sound crass, 'I did notice.' But what he noticed at the time was a livening in his loins from the message he was receiving from his fellow guest such as he had not experienced for a long time.

21

In the plane Sylvester remembered that in his bath before dinner at the Bratts' he had considered prolonging discussion of Marvin's book so that he could stay for two nights, for one tussle with the delectable Sal would only whet an appetite long starved. He recollected too that, soaking in the bath, he had considered and almost decided on inviting Sal to stay in London. He would fly ahead to make a welcome, lay in exotic foods and wine, buy flowers and liven the house which Celia had denuded – he liked it that way but a girl like Sal would not. On his way in from Heathrow he would not only collect the rugs from the cleaners but stop the taxi at Patel's Corner Shop and order the newspapers so that on Sunday morning they could lie in bed and leaf through the papers – or not, according to mood.

At dinner he had sat opposite Sal so that while talking to Elvira and her daughter (whose name momentarily escaped him) it had been possible to exercise eye contact. Droning across the Atlantic he could not remember the conversation except that he had side-stepped giving details of his own divorce but heard full details of Sal's, which were as far as he could now remember pretty mundane. However, the message she transmitted without exactly wording it was another matter entirely.

There had been a lot to drink. Marvin had played the charming host; one forgot the sinister group photograph and appreciated the harmony which obtruded, there was no other word, between Marvin and Elvira and their daughter and son-in-law, all four giving the impression of being contentedly marinated in sexual juices.

After dinner he had excused himself; he must read Marvin's manuscript. He had said, 'See you all tomorrow,' and, 'Good night,' catching Sal's eye: for tomorrow, read tonight.

In the library Marvin handed over the manuscript and walked with him to his room. He had drunk several glasses of water and put his head under the cold tap (I must have been pissed, but quite sober when the manuscript was finished).

The White Continent by Marvin Bratt (it was here at his feet in his briefcase). A complex plan for disentangling genes. A plan to regenerate the White race. (Same old story, different plot.) The White Elite would ship back to their countries of origins all Blacks, Hispanics and Asians who were willing to go. The unwilling would be sterilized so that they could enjoy sex without increasing the coloured population which would, over the years, dwindle to nothing. There must be no repetition of Hitler's mistakes, no violence or unnecessary coercion. Marvin had contingency plans to avoid this, extra finance, a system of benefits for 'tinted peoples'. (There was considerable use of the expression 'tinted'.) This regeneration might take more than one generation, but it would solve the problems of poverty and unemployment and the end result would be a pristine White United States of America. How this was to be achieved was worked out in lengthy and intricate detail, some of it so complicated it would take a genius to unravel.

In the plane Sylvester remembered that when he finished reading he had gone to the bathroom and cleaned his teeth. Then, returning to his room, he read his notes.

Is Marvin Bratt sane? Malevolent? Infantile?

Definitely not for our list, this book.

Dust jacket KKK photograph?

Too downmarket for us?

NB If we don't, Narrowlane and Jinks will.

Publish with Introduction? (Bags I write it.)

Vomit, vomit.

Could it not be rewritten? As joke??

If debunking JC and Virgin M. makes bestseller, why not this?'

Definitely wrong to suppress it, worth the risk?

He had returned the manuscript to its folder, opened the window, looked out at the stars. There was a light in his fellow guest's room; when he knocked on her door she said, 'What took you so long?'

He had mumbled something about Marvin's book. She was very pretty, very sexy.

She had said, 'Boring.'

He had said, 'Have you read it?'

She said, 'He's been talking about it for years, it's kids' stuff. My father's that way too.' She took his hand. 'Want a drink? I've got a bottle here.'

'Ku Klux Klan boring?' He had gaped.

'It's only dressing-up spooky.'

'And *hanging* people.'

'Not often. It's little boys' stuff.' She had shut the door, held his hand. 'Boys only.'

(Anybody with their wits about them would have gone into reverse.)

'What *I* like,' she had said, 'is boys and girls.'

'Oh God,' Sylvester said out loud on the plane.

Their mouths had met in a long preamble. They had stumbled backwards towards the bed. She had said, 'Hey, you're hungry,' and, 'Steady there,' in breathless Marilyn Monroe vein, but helped him out of his trousers with practised hands.

He had said, 'Aaah, don't touch – it's been bloody ages,' grabbing at her while she slithered elflike away, gasped something about 'bathroom' and, 'won't be long'. She had returned, nestled close. 'Didya miss me?' He had sprung away, exclaiming, 'Yuk! Disgusting! You stink!' Made a grab for his trousers, scarcely noticed his humbling detumescence.

As he reached the door she had shouted, '"Emotion" costs two hundred dollars an *ounce*!'

Marvin was in his room reading the notes which he had left by the manuscript. He made no apology for snooping. He had said, 'So you think it would be wrong to suppress my book?'

Dry-throated, Sylvester had said, 'Yes, I do.'

'And you think it will make a *bestseller*?' He had only taken to heart the complimentary bits.

Sylvester managed, 'That is my opinion.'

Marvin replaced the notes by the manuscript. 'I told you it was dynamite.' He had smiled.

There had been some guff about immediacy. A need for urgency, getting in touch with John, with Marvin's agent, catching a plane soonest. Whilst talking he had packed his bags, packed the manuscript. Marvin had not tried to detain him, had not mentioned the fellow house guest. Now on the plane Sylvester laughed out loud.

'Like to share your joke?' He had woken his neighbour.

'I left a pair of Brooks Brothers shorts in a girl's bed.'

'And you find that funny?'

22

'Building up for Christmas?' Angie Eddison overtook Janet. Janet was burdened with carrier bags.

'Sort of.' Janet transferred the heaviest bag from right hand to left.

'You two going away?' Angie enquired.

'We were, but there's been a sort of mix-up.'

'Oh?'

'My mother has had a last-minute, well, she says it's last-minute, invitation to join my aunt on a cruise. And Tim's parents are full up with all his brothers and sisters, husbands and wives and kids, so there's no room for us. We were asked,' said Janet untruthfully, blocking from her mind the letter which had said how welcome she would be 'when married', but that not being married to Tim 'made things difficult'. 'We refused,' she said, 'because we were going, we thought, to my mum, so it's a bit of a mess.'

'Disappointed?' Angie looked appraisingly at Janet. 'It's OK,' she said, 'I've got the key.' They had reached the street door. 'We,' she said, 'never go away. Spending Christmas with relations is hell, guaranteed to make bad blood, herding together and overeating, not to speak of drink.' She put the key in the lock. 'Why don't you be civilized and do what we do?'

'What's that?' Janet stepped sideways into the hall and put down her bags.

'Keep open house Christmas Eve, Christmas Day and Boxing Day. Lots to eat, lots to drink and lots of music. I can't remember sleeping over the last two

Christmases. You'd be surprised,' she said, 'how many people like us do not go away.'

Janet said, 'It's certainly an idea, I'll put it to Tim.'

'It gets everyone done one remotely owes what the French call *la vaisselle*.'

'That means washing-up.' Janet too understood French.

'Yes, love, and it's slang for our sort of party. My cousin, who worked in the French Embassy in Madrid, said that's what they called their parties for assorted odds and sods.'

'It's an idea,' Janet repeated.

'Sent your Christmas cards yet?'

'No.'

'Well, do what we do, put "Open House, bring a bottle". It's a lot of fun, I assure you.' Angie kicked back to slam the street door shut. 'No need to worry about the music,' she said. 'Peter organizes that.'

'What about the noise if it goes on all night?'

'That's OK. All the old biddies who might complain will have gone away.'

'The Piper woman?' Janet jerked her head upwards.

'She can't complain of noise!'

'It's been very quiet lately,' said Janet.

'It has not,' said Angie. 'She blew that bloody whistle at 2 a.m. the other night. Woke us both up.'

'Shall you invite her?'

Angie said, 'No-one with any nous invites a woman whose partner's a drunk.'

'But he's dead,' said Janet.

Angie said, 'They came once in the early days. He was belligerent, bopped someone on the nose, nobody we cared about luckily, but Peter said we mustn't ask them again. They were contrary to the Christmas spirit.'

'D'you ever speak to her?' Janet asked.

'I say hallo if I meet her on the stairs.'

Janet said, 'Oh.'

148

'She doesn't speak to people.' Angie was defensive. 'Unless you count the Patels at the shop,' she said, laughing.

'And *she* doesn't speak English.' Janet laughed too.

'So will you join our Christmas bash?'

'I'll see what Tim thinks,' said Janet. 'I rather warm to the idea.' Then, halfway inside her door, she said, 'What do you do about church?'

Angie said, 'What?'

'You know, Midnight Mass or Christmas morning, all that.'

'My *dear*,' said Angie, 'that's part of the avoidance, one of the things we seek refuge from. Don't tell me you and Tim want to go to church?'

'No, no,' Janet exclaimed. 'It's just that it's one of the things one's always done. Not to go seems funny.'

'No funnier than when you stop needing them to live without nappies,' said Angie briskly.

'Gosh. I'd never thought of it that way.' Janet was admiring.

'Nothing to stop you halfway through the party nipping off to the Brompton Oratory or wherever,' said Angie, 'and come back shriven to Heavy Metal.'

Janet said, 'Gosh,' again and, 'Do we have Heavy Metal?'

'Among other things. It rejuvenates people when their libidos get slack.'

'Oh.'

'We have other stuff, too, smoochy tunes like stand up and hug.'

'What's that?'

'Thirties stuff, Noël Coward, all that. We even have waltzes, if Peter feels like it.'

'How do we manage between your flat and ours?'

'There are the stairs, there are the landings; we use all the space we can get. It'll be useful, too,' said Angie, 'to have your loo as well as ours.'

Quailing but hooked, Janet said, 'Of course.' She

unlocked her door and bundled her shopping inside. Angie's voice from halfway up the stairs called, 'Peter has a chum who plays the saxophone. He's coming—'

Maurice Benson stood by the bar watching his fellow customers. No lover of Christmas, he supposed he should be grateful, in the noisy pub, for what he hoped was a temporary deafness which deadened taped carols and raucous conversation. 'I wish I could get away,' he said to anyone who would listen. 'I hate this time of year.'

'Lonely?' enquired the barman. 'Got no-one to go and visit? No old biddy to give you Christmas lunch and be grateful to you?'

'Not really, no.' Benson reviewed his sparse and inhospitable acquaintance. Then, 'Hold it!' he exclaimed. 'I just might have. Where's your phone?'

The man gestured through the bar. 'At the back. You got change?'

'Thanks, yes.' Benson riffled through his pocketbook and made his way to the telephone. 'I rang you a few days ago,' he said when Madge Brownlow answered, 'and you were out.'

'Who's that? Who's that speaking? Do I know you?'

'I'm the twitcher, friend of Giles Piper. You kindly gave me tea and Julia's number.'

'I rather regretted that. We are not in touch.'

'So I gathered.'

'You are the man who likes magpies. What d'you want? After you'd gone Clodagh wondered what you were after, since we couldn't put you in touch with—'

'Giles?' Maurice Benson leaned against the wall.

'Are you ringing from a pub? I hear pub noises.'

Maurice said, 'Actually, yes.'

'Giles used to ring from pubs.'

'I suppose he would have.'

'There's been a blitz on the magpies. Somebody shot

them, said he did it in the spirit of Christmas.' Madge Brownlow laughed harshly.

'I am more interested in rare birds,' said Maurice ingratiatingly. 'I was thinking of coming your way.'

'Really?' There was no welcome in Madge's tone.

'Got some news of Julia which might be of interest.'

'I doubt that,' said Madge Brownlow. Then, 'What is it?'

'She tried, no, succeeded in deafening me.'

'How comical.' Madge Brownlow laughed.

'Glad you think so,' said Maurice. 'I—'

'Tell you what.' Madge Brownlow's voice changed. 'If you really are interested in rare birds, I can show you where a pair of ospreys come every year on their migratory route.'

'Where's that?' Maurice stopped lounging against the wall. 'I know they stop off at Slapton Ley,' he said.

'This is a lake in Somerset, Julia's secret. Nobody knows except the people she worked for. I only found out by chance.'

'You read her diary,' said Maurice.

Madge giggled and said, 'Interested?'

'Very. I was planning to come your way,' Maurice said. 'Could I drop in?'

'When would that be?'

'Now, next few days.'

'Not over Christmas. Clodagh wants a quiet time with her memories—'

'Christy's toys?' He remembered the row on the sofa.

'And the photographs, and the grave.'

'Not very jolly for you, but what about this lake? Should I ask Julia myself?' Maurice teased.

'Julia would never tell you,' said Madge.

'Ah,' said Maurice. 'Ah—'

'Come later on,' said Madge firmly. 'And if I think it's the right thing to do I'll take you there. Goodbye,' and she rang off.

Maurice said, 'Bloody inhospitable old bitch,' and

returned to the bar. He was ordering himself another beer when Peter Eddison and Tim Fellowes caught sight of him and, since they were feeling convivial, invited him to join the Christmas party.

23

It took an effort of will for Julia Piper to help with the magazines. It being Christmas Eve, both Patels were busy in the shop. As in previous years they would keep working until the last late customer was served before packing their children into the van and driving across London to spend Christmas with Mr Patel's extended family. Julia knew that an hour spent unpacking and sorting the New Year magazines would save the weary Patels that much time. In previous years, when she had volunteered to do the job, Christy had been company for his friend who now played alone, tottering around her, his minute feet thrust into the shoes she had tiredly kicked off when coming back from her cleaning jobs earlier in the evening. As he lurched about and fell with shrieks of enchanted amusement, she gritted her teeth against the memory of Christy, who had instigated the game. She tried instead to sympathize with Joyful sitting nervously, uncertain of his role, lifting a whiskery nose out of reach of the baby who, able to crawl but not yet old enough to play the game with the shoes, cherished an ambition to seize and painfully twist his nose. From time to time, as the dog's patience seemed about to break, Julia stopped her work to hug the baby, who fought for freedom, arched his back and slid back on to the floor. His brother, flinging his arms round her neck, goggled up with lucent black eyes demanding her attention also.

'Everything OK?' Mr Patel's head poked round the door and vanished as quickly as it appeared.

'Yes, fine,' Julia shouted. 'Nearly finished.'

'Big party to be in your house tonight—'

'Afraid so—'

'Downstairs people cook big curry with lots of rice, I think.'

'Oh?'

'Upstairs is turkey and plum pudding, Mrs Beeton whoever.'

'Ah.'

'Something called glühwein for the upstairs and white wine and spirits below. Beer, too.'

'I see.'

'I say beer with curry so they buy many cases.'

'Well done.'

'My wife say music begin already. We sell out of lemons but she keep you two.'

'Please thank her.'

'We shut shop now, I think. No more customers.'

'No, sweetheart, do *not* pull his whiskers.' Julia picked the baby off the floor and, wriggling her toes at the older child, waited for him to surrender her shoes. Then, joining the Patels in the shop, she said, 'The magazines are sorted. Do you want help with the smellies on Sunday?'

'Not to bother.' Mr Patel looked weary. Mrs Patel was twisting the door sign which said *Open* on one side and *Closed* on the other; there were smudges of fatigue round her eyes. Julia handed her the baby. 'I hope,' she said, 'that you will get some rest in the bosom of the Patels. Mind you see she rests,' she advised Mr Patel.

Mr Patel laughed. 'Fat chance! But she will be happy.' And then he said, 'And will you be OK?' (How can I help? his eyes asked. This is your first Christmas without your child.)

'I shall be fine.' Julia touched the baby's plump foot.

'And the party? It is in your house.'

'I'll survive, don't worry.'

She stood on the pavement watching the van

diminish down the street. It was freezing and above the glow of London there would be stars. Joyful whimpered beside her. They set off walking towards the sound of jazz; someone was playing the saxophone rather well. Perhaps, Julia thought, I will be tired enough to sleep when I have fed Joyful. I will plug my ears with cotton wool. The street door was open and in the house people shouted from floor to floor. The party had begun.

At the turn of the stairs Julia edged past cartons of beer stacked in toppling piles. There was a heady smell of cooking, loud voices and clatter of pans. On the Eddisons' landing, a middle-aged man with his hair in a pony-tail blew experimental notes on his sax, perrumph, perrumph, and as she sidled past he broke into 'Night and day, you are the one' while Angie, Peter and others in their flat raised their voices. *Tum, tum, tum, tiddly under the sun, Whether near to you or far, We wonder where you are, And call to You-ooo, Night and daaay—*'

'Come in and get drunk,' they shouted. 'Food will be ready soon.'

With his tail between his legs Joyful broke into a run and was scratching at her door when, pushing past people sitting drinking on the stairs, Julia caught up with him, unlocked her door, let him in and, closing it, lessened the noise. 'Poor fellow,' she said, 'poor fellow,' and went to the window, which she had left ajar. Before she closed it, she leaned out to see revellers converging from both ends of the street.

A figure, detaching itself from a group running ahead, shouted, 'We've got a very funny new game, Angie, a new game.'

'What is it?' Angie yelled; she had good lungs.

'Where were you when Kennedy was shot?'

'Doesn't sound very funny to me,' Angie yelled.

'Hilarious after a few drinks. Is that glühwein I sniff? Super.'

Closing the window, Julia said, 'This is going to be a rough night, Joyful. I can stuff my ears with cotton wool; what can I do for you?' Then the saxophone started up again: *I cover the waterfront*— Shivering and whining Joyful raised his nose and warbled.

When the saxophone stopped, Julia heated herself some soup, fed the dog, undressed, had a bath, stuffed her ears with cotton wool and climbed into bed, pulling the duvet over her head. Since she was very tired, she fell asleep, but not for long; somebody with an electric guitar had joined the party and there was dancing.

Towards closing-time the party, which had shown signs of waning, gathered strength from an influx of people from the pubs. On the floor below the Eddisons turned up the volume of music and the whole house shook to the thump of Heavy Metal. Julia sat up in bed. The dog trembled.

The previous Christmas she had spent waitressing in an hotel while Christy and Giles stayed with Clodagh. The two years since she had endured the Eddisons' annual bash had dulled her memory; now, huddled in bed with the dog, she remembered previous parties. The first year had been a relatively mild affair, Christmas Eve only, petering out by two; but by three years ago it had blossomed to full strength, starting on Christmas Eve and lasting over Boxing Day.

Crouching in bed she remembered how Giles, choosing to be in London either because of a tiff with Clodagh or because there was another party he wanted to go to, had returned to the flat drunk but good-tempered and was undressing when the full blast of the Eddisons' party struck. With the sweet reason of the inebriate he had charged downstairs shouting at the Eddisons to 'Pipe down, shut that bloody noise, cool it'. There had been a shouting match, a fight, a reconciliation. He had joined the party and the noise had increased twofold. Next day he had called her a spoilsport and a wimp for not joining in. Why, he had shouted in hungover rage, had she not, if she objected to normal people having fun, taken herself off elsewhere? Imposed herself on friends as dismal and boring as herself? Unaware, it seemed, that their years of marriage had lost her what few friends she had once had. Certainly there were none by that time whom she could knock up at one in the morning. Miraculously Christy, a gifted sleeper, had not woken. But now?

'We need not put up with this,' Julia said to the dog. 'We will go out.' She sprang out of bed, dressed and, locking her door, negotiated her way to the street; elbowing past couples slumped on the stairs or dancing on the landings. The street when she reached it was silent and the air brittle with frost. 'On the other hand,' she said to the dog as they set off walking, 'we have nowhere to go.'

The streets of any large city in the early hours of Christmas morning are pretty deserted; there was no traffic other than an occasional taxi or a cruising police car. Julia felt exposed and alone as she walked, and surprised herself wishing she had bought Joyful a collar and lead so that there could be between them a physical connection tighter than that of his occasional brushing against her legs as they walked. Had she held a lead their connection would be less tenuous, more comforting, and she would not mind the widening gap between them when he paused to lift his leg, nor feel obliged to stoop and touch his rough coat when he caught up.

Leaving Chelsea behind she crossed into Kensington and climbing Campden Hill into Notting Hill came to a stop in Holland Park Avenue where, beginning to tire, she turned about and began to retrace her steps. By this time, she thought, the party would have died down; she could snatch some sleep, feed the dog. It was stupid, she thought, that she had not asked the Patels for a key; they would have given her shelter. But the shop and flat were locked and closed for days. Would it be possible to let herself into the woman journalist's flat? Take refuge there? Nap on the floor? The idea was idiotic; the woman was unpredictable, might come back any time. 'No,' she said out loud to the dog, 'I must stick it out in my own place. There will be a lull in the party, they can't keep it up. I am being ridiculous.'

Turning presently into her own street her spirit lifted. Three minicabs were leaving the kerb; voices within shouted goodbyes. But Angie Eddison on the doorstep waved and yelled, 'See you soon then for the turkey and plum pud. Peter will have mixed a fresh lot of booze. See you!' Julia watched her go back into the house, leaving the door hospitably open. There were lights in all the windows but the music was less loud; she slipped quickly in, followed by the dog.

The Fellowes' flat door was open; somebody groaned and was sick. Janet's voice cried, 'Oh God, oh God.' She pushed the light switch for the stairs but the lights had failed; the stairwell was dark, lit only by a shaft of light from the Eddisons' door. She climbed up cautiously. A couple deep in talk were propped against the wall on the Eddisons' landing drinking coffee; they did not look up as Julia stepped over their outstretched legs. When the top light switch too failed to respond she fumbled in the dark for her key, and was feeling for her keyhole when a man detached himself from the floor and clutched her, dragging her close into the area of his breath, a mix of alcohol and tobacco.

'Gotcha, Julia Piper.' He held her. 'I have waited long.'

'Gerroff.' She kicked out and drove her elbow into his stomach.

'Now, now. Ouch! You deafened – Ouch! Christ! A fucking dog! Call it off—' Then she was in through the door and slamming it shut, with Joyful whining and growling, his hair risen stiff along his back, listening to steps stumbling down the stairs and a yell. 'I'll be back.'

Opening a tin of dog food, her hand trembled and was cut by sharp tin. Holding the bleeding wound under the cold tap steadied her. 'Any sensible person would go to her neighbours for help,' she said out loud, 'but I can't.'

She watched the dog eat, gulping his food, upset, growling. She sat on the divan and watched the door, listened.

Much later she made herself some coffee, forced herself to eat, then left the house. It was lunchtime; the party was gathering momentum, swinging into a new phase, using its second wind. Someone cried, 'Where were *you* when Kennedy was assassinated?'

Come unto Me all ye that travail and are heavy laden, and I will give you rest. The notice was printed in black letters on a red background. She had passed the church before, or was this a similar church with the same notice? She kept walking to keep warm. Earlier in the day crowds of people had erupted from the Brompton Oratory, streaming out from morning Mass, fanning down the steps to make their way home for Christmas lunch. There had been no notice outside the Oratory; she had climbed the steps and almost reached the doors before losing her nerve and doubling back past the V & A (firmly closed) to trudge up Exhibition Road to the Park and there find a seat, sit, and rest her feet. But not for long; it was too cold. Better to keep moving. Circling back past the Albert Hall and down a flight of steps, she sighted another church and remembered the church where she had sat in the warmth of candles and eaten a sandwich and the priest had not minded. Where was it? She could not place it, except that the bus ride back was a long one, but perhaps this would do? She pushed at the door and almost immediately was sitting gleefully in warm and agreeable chiaroscuro with Joyful leaning against her leg.

But a tall verger in a black cassock loomed near. 'This is a church,' he mouthed over loose double chins. 'You cannot bring a dog in here.' He had a long thin nose.

'He is quiet and good, as you see. He is doing no harm.' Julia did not take to the verger.

'That is not a Guide Dog,' the man said. 'There are of course exceptions for Guide Dogs.'

'He is without sin.' Julia counted the verger's chins – one, two and a half.

'And without a collar, you must take it out.'

'What about the notices which say: "Come unto Me all that travail and are heavy laden?"' Julia prevaricated, still seated.

'You will not find those sort of notices outside this church.' She had offended him.

'Why not?'

'That is for other denominations. Are you going to remove the animal?' He swayed impatiently in his cassock, bony knees poking hillocks in the serge.

She said again, 'He is without sin,' and sat tight in her exhaustion.

The verger said, 'So you say,' and, raising his voice, 'I know your sort. *Out*!'

'And what sort is that?' Her fatigue induced resistance.

'The sort which cracks cheap jokes about G-O-D and D-O-G. I say O-U-T, out!'

Getting to her feet, Julia said 'Oh dear, you reduce me to my last resort.'

The verger said angrily, 'Do not threaten me with cheap suicide. *Out*!' and followed them to the church door, which he closed behind her.

24

Sylvester waited for his bags by the carousel. His journey had been dogged by delays and cancelled flights. He was weary. His legs ached from sitting cramped in crowded aircraft; he was in need of sleep and had indigestion. A fellow passenger standing near exclaimed, 'Happy Christmas!' in tones of exasperation and the girl yawning beside him said wearily, 'I believe it's Boxing Day or maybe it's Sunday. Oh! There's our case, catch it before it escapes, here!' and, leaning forward so that a curtain of hair shielded her cheek, grabbed. Watching and yawning too, Sylvester saw that her hair was naturally fair, not the extreme blonde the Bratt women favoured. Their heads, bleached almost white, had resembled silkworms' cocoons. What had possessed him to make a pass at that girl? Not only did she stink like Celia, she had this unnatural hair. He leaned forward to catch one of his bags as it filtered by and noticed disgustedly that in his haste on leaving the Bratts he had shut it carelessly and nipped the fellow to the underpants left in Sal's bed in the zip. 'I bet they're torn as well as dirty,' he said out loud. 'Brooks Brothers' best!' The girl in the act of capturing luggage – she was nippier than her companion – looked at him curiously. She was rather plain, he thought, and forgot her immediately as he wrestled with the zip and pushed the offending undergarment inside, noticing as he did so that it was indeed irrevocably torn.

Wheeling his luggage towards the exit, he decided to have no more dealings with Bratt, to let his partner

John deal with the man. Yet, he thought as he hailed a taxi, it would be a pleasure to write an introduction.

'Is it Christmas Day or Boxing Day?' he asked the driver as he got into the cab.

'It's Sunday, innit?' The driver was burly and dark but not what Bratt would have called 'tinted'.

'I want to stop at a carpet shop in Chiswick.' Sylvester leaned forward and spoke through the glass behind the man's head. 'It's more or less on the way.'

'Be shut, wonnit?' The driver swung out on to the M4 and trod on the accelerator.

'The owner lives above the shop, it's worth a try,' Sylvester shouted.

'Suit yourself,' the driver answered indifferently.

Still vaguely haunted by Marvin Bratt, Sylvester asked, 'Do you believe in social engineering?'

'What's that, then?'

'Holocaust of Red Indians.'

'Don't know nothing about that.'

'Or the Jewish Holocaust,' Sylvester persisted.

'That's history, innit? Like the Crusades. You want to read H. G. Wells,' said the driver, 'get a sense of proportion.'

'Do you listen to Alistair Cooke? He says taxi drivers know everything.'

The driver laughed. 'Not everything. Where's this carpet shop, then?'

Sylvester told him.

'It'll be shut,' said the driver and switched on his radio, distancing himself from his fare.

Sylvester pulled down the window and let the icy air rush in; it pleased him, as did a lowering sky presaging rain. He was glad to be home.

Bowling up the almost empty motorway he remembered other returns. When they were first married Celia had volunteered to meet him, then not turned up. He had worried, fearing she might be ill, have had an accident, and finally he had rung up. Answering the

162

phone, she expressed surprise. 'Oh, you've arrived! No, I did not feel like coming, it's such a rotten day. I imagined you'd take a taxi.' On another occasion he had taken a taxi and returned to an empty house. She had gone to a party. With Andrew Battersby, he later discovered. *Thank you for not smoking.* Sylvester read the notice. 'And thank you for leaving me,' he said out loud, looking forward to an empty house and his own space.

They left the motorway. The driver slowed. 'This the street, then?'

'Yes, thanks. That shop on the left which says Oriental Carpets.'

'Closed,' said the driver, stopping outside.

Sylvester got out, rang the bell and waited. When the owner of the shop opened the door and invited him in, he said, 'Do you mind waiting?' and the driver, shrugging, said, 'You can't win 'em all,' and almost smiled.

'I have not packed them, I want you to see how they have cleaned well. You will have a cup of coffee?' The dealer drew him inside. 'Sit down, please.' He offered a chair. 'My wife brings coffee.'

Sylvester watched the man spread the rugs. 'Are these mine?' He was delighted by the subtle faded colours. 'I had forgotten how lovely they are. They will turn my house into a palace. Is this your wife?' He shook hands and accepted coffee. 'And your daughter?' A little girl stood by his knee; she was beautifully 'tinted', as were her parents. She thrust a toy into his hand. 'For you,' she shouted. 'You!'

Sylvester said, 'Oh, but I—' holding his cup in one hand, the toy in the other.

'You must keep it or she will be insulted,' said the child's father. 'She has many others.'

'And I have none. Thank you very much.'

The child, satisfied, ran out of the room. Sylvester finished his coffee. The dealer rolled up the rugs and carried them to the taxi.

'I know I'm pushing my luck,' said Sylvester, 'but there's a shop called Patel's Corner Shop quite near me; it just might be open. Please stop there.'

'That'll be the lot, then?' asked the driver.

Sylvester said, 'Yes.' He felt very happy. He would order the papers, get a carton of milk – there was only dried milk in the cupboard – hole up and sleep off his jet lag. He hummed as they drove through the late-evening streets, noticing Christmas trees alight in ground-floor windows and holly wreaths hanging on doors. But Patel's Corner Shop was closed and dark when they arrived. His driver was almost sympathetic. 'You can't win 'em all,' he said again. 'Back into the King's Road and second on the left, innit?'

Sylvester said, 'Yes,' and was soon standing on his doorstep with the rugs and his bags round his feet, watching the taxi drive away while he fumbled for his key.

The dolphin knocker was brightly polished and the paintwork gleaming; he turned the key. He was enormously tired, aching for sleep. He put the rolled rugs beside his bags and, shutting the door, listened gratefully to the silence.

From the sitting-room came a rustling sound.

A dog crouched by the sofa; it swept its tail to and fro across the parquet. On the sofa there was a woman asleep.

Overwhelmed by fatigue and surprise, Sylvester sat in the armchair.

The dog rose, came towards him, sniffed his trousers. Sylvester whispered, 'It's all right.' The dog repositioned itself by the sofa. Sylvester stretched his legs, leaned back, tried to think, heard the rustle of the dog's tail. Hadn't Rebecca said something in her letter?

25

When Joyful barked Sylvester jerked awake with a grunt and the woman on the sofa telescoped her legs to her chin and stared speechless across her knees.

Sylvester said, 'My God. I fell asleep. Who are you?' His heart was thudding.

It was still quite dark; the clatter of the letter-box as the postman pushed in mail ceased and the hair along the dog's back subsided. Sylvester repeated, 'Who are you?'

The woman sprang to her feet. Putting the sofa between them, she said, 'How did you get in?'

He could see that she was afraid. He said, 'I let myself in with my key. I live here.'

'*What?*'

'I live here. This is my house.'

Her face was paper white. 'Can you prove it?' She was quite a tall girl, wearing jeans and a heavy sweater under a black coat.

Irritably Sylvester said, 'Of course I can prove it.'

'*How?*' The dog moved to stand between them. She repeated, 'How?' and glanced towards the telephone. The dog, infected by her fear, growled.

Sylvester said, 'The letters which have just come through the box will be addressed to me; my name is Sylvester Wykes.'

She said, 'I don't believe you. Don't move. My dog—'

'I hate to undeceive you,' Sylvester said, 'but your dog wagged his tail when I came in. Why don't you go and look at the letters? I won't move. Go on.'

She hesitated, then edged warily out of the room. Sylvester called after her, 'Don't run away.'

She came back with the letters and handed them to him. She said, 'Are you his son?'

'Whose son?'

'Sylvester Wykes's.'

'*I* am Sylvester Wykes. Who may you be?' His startled heart had settled down; he was intrigued.

'I thought he was quite old.' She spoke as of some character in the past. 'Quite an old man,' she said.

Irritably Sylvester said, 'I've got jet lag and I feel bloody old, but I am not all that ancient. You still have not told me who *you* are.'

'Julia Piper.'

'My cleaning lady? Gosh!' He was taken aback. Breaking into laughter, he said, 'I visualized you as on the old side, too. But tell me, do you work over Christmas?'

Julia said, 'I was taking refuge. Don't worry, I'll go now. I'm sorry I—'

He could see embarrassment flood her face pink. He said, 'Please don't go. Please stay. Have some breakfast,' he said, 'I'm starving. There's food in the house. There should be bread in the freezer, and butter; there's marmalade and coffee and dried milk, we can manage.' And as she still appeared poised for flight, he repeated, 'Please.'

At her feet the dog sat back and began to scratch, its leg thumping on the bare floor. Sylvester said, 'I brought rugs from the cleaners; I left them in the hall with my luggage when I came in. I saw you, I sat down for a moment and fell asleep. I'll take my stuff upstairs. Tell you what, why don't you go and put the kettle on while I do that? I trust you not to scarper,' he said cheerfully.

Half-reassured, Julia said, 'All right.'

Carrying his bags upstairs Sylvester wished that he had watched her instead of dozing off; asleep she would not have looked so wary or so defensive. What was she defensive about? What was she doing here? It was odd. Hadn't Rebecca written something about squatters? Was she a squatter? Far too young to be a cleaning lady. Perhaps she just knew the cleaning lady's name and was using it? He put his bags down in the bedroom and looked about for signs of illicit occupation.

Spotless room, faint smell of brasso and floor polish, his father's silver brushes gleaming on the dressing table. Clean sheets on bed. Bathroom spotless also. Fresh towels on towel rail, bath and basin gleaming and dry as a bone, new unused cake of soap. What's going on? He opened the bathroom window and looked out. 'Good God! What's happened to the garden?'

Running down the stairs two at a time, arriving abruptly in the kitchen, startling the dog, he shouted, 'What's happened to the garden?'

Backed against the stove, a coffee grinder in her hand, Julia said defensively, 'You arranged – we arranged – I thought it—'

'God! I'd forgotten. Quite forgotten. Hi! Don't look like that. Don't! It's bloody marvellous. It's lovely. There's a snowdrop out, a Christmas rose, winter jasmine. It's a work of genius! Who did you get to do it? It's wonderful.'

'I did it.'

'You?'

'Yes.'

'Oh.'

They stood appraising each other across the room. Julia smiled faintly.

It occurred to Sylvester that it was years, if ever, since he had had such an agreeable homecoming. He said, 'Would your genius stretch to making us both breakfast? And your dog? What's his name?'

'Joyful.'

'Apt.'

'Coffee?' She held up the grinder. Sylvester nodded. She pressed her thumb on the button and the kitchen filled with its screech.

When the noise stopped Sylvester said, 'Explanations later.' Julia nodded. He said, 'Toast isn't going to be enough. There should be sardines in the store cupboard; let's have sardines on toast, I'm starving. I bet you are, too.'

Laying the table, finding marmalade, fishing butter from the freezer, watching her make coffee, toast bread, spread sardines and put them under the grill, Sylvester refrained from asking questions. People who are frightened are likely to lie. The girl was nervous; he would wait. Waiting, he sat at the kitchen table and, searching for something innocuous, said, 'On my way in from Heathrow I collected some rugs I bought before I went to America; will you help me arrange them in the sitting-room after breakfast?'

Her eye on the sardines under the grill, she nodded.

'The dealer lives above his shop. It seems to be Bank Holiday, so I was lucky to find him in.'

'Very.'

'I had planned to stop at the corner-shop and buy milk and order the papers, but I had no luck there,' Sylvester said.

'The Patels have gone to spend Christmas with his family.'

'The Patels? Oh, of course, you know them. Stupid of me. He is our go-between! Forgive me, I am still only half awake.'

Julia said, 'Coffee,' and set the pot in front of him. 'Thank you for sending that cheque from America, but it is far too much.'

Sylvester said, 'I did not know how long I'd still be away. I had to go and stay with a weird character. I did not want you inconvenienced.'

Julia said, 'Thank you,' again.

Sylvester poured coffee into their cups and mixed in dried milk; he gulped his coffee scalding hot. He said, 'Delicious, revivifying. You make good coffee.'

'It is your coffee.' She was still uptight. 'Why didn't you ring the police when you came in and saw me?' she asked.

'You did not look very dangerous.'

She said, 'I might have had an accomplice.'

'In my jet-lagged state that did not occur to me. Besides,' said Sylvester, 'Joyful here wagged his tail.'

Julia said, 'So you say,' and drank her coffee glancing covertly at her employer who was not, as she had imagined, an old or middle-aged bachelor, probably homosexual, but young with hetero airs.

Sylvester ate his sardines and progressed to toast and marmalade and more coffee. He said, 'You suggested you were taking refuge?'

Julia said, 'Both lots of people in the flats below me throw a party which goes on all through Christmas. It's noisy and I—'

'Couldn't stand it?'

'No.'

'Ah.'

'I could stuff my ears with cotton wool, but not his.' She glanced at the dog, asleep, nose and paws twitching in a dream. 'He howled,' she said.

'But you could—'

'If the Patels had not been away I might have gone there, but—'

'No-one else?' Sylvester pried.

'No,' she said, averting her eyes.

'So, um—'

'I had walked about – er – sat in the Park, that sort of thing, but—'

'Found it a bit chilly?'

'I tried going back but, well, it was worse. A man from the party was lurking on my landing – I live at the top. He tried to grab—'

169

'And?'

'Nothing, really. He was drunk. It wasn't that, of course.'

'Yes?'

'I recognized his voice. I've been getting calls.'

'Heavy breather? Obscene?'

'They were to me. It used to be my ex-husband, he did it a lot, but he's dead. Then this started and the last time he—' She closed her eyes and breathed deeply. 'He pretended to be a child,' she said, shocking her listener by the misery in her voice.

Sylvester said, 'So?'

'So I went out again. I tried sitting in a church. I mean, nothing else is open over Christmas, is it?'

'I suppose not.'

'No.' She paused, looking away from him through the area window.

'How was the church?' (What a surreal conversation.)

'The verger said Joyful was not a Guide Dog, so—'

'So, out?'

'I suppose it's the rule.' Julia spoke quickly now. 'A rule for dogs. London isn't Italy, I've seen horses in church in Italy—'

'Before the Palio in Siena?'

'Yes. But this church was C of E, rather posh, and although there *is* a church which I am pretty sure would have let us sit and rest our feet, I cannot for the life of me remember where it is or how to get there. I was there once before; the priest was kind, lovely, although I couldn't tell him the worst thing—' Julia stopped, distressed. 'I am boring you,' she said. 'I should leave,' she said stiffly. 'I do apologize, the party may be over. I should never have—'

Sylvester said, 'Oh, shut up! Don't be a fool. I am so glad you did, you are more than welcome,' he said expansively. 'I am really pleased. It's a nice surprise. Stay and help me with the rugs. Have a bath—' Julia laughed. 'You have to tell me what you have planned in the garden. You can't possibly go until you've done that,' he said almost angrily. 'Besides,' he said, '*I* want a bath. I never feel I'm really home until I've had a bath. I will have a bath, then we will spread the rugs and you'll show me round the garden, right?'

Julia said, 'All right. I will just let Joyful out for a pee.'

'But don't run away? Swear?'

'I'll come back and wash the breakfast things.'

Sylvester went upstairs whistling.

In the bath, in the luxury of his own surroundings, he nearly fell asleep again but was nudged by the thought that he must rouse himself to open his mail, listen to a month's accumulation of messages on his answerphone and telephone his office; but before all that he wanted to arrange his new rugs and explore the garden which this extraordinary cleaning lady had created. Surging out of the water he wondered whether she really was what she said, and not some weird sort of joke? Her story was improbable. Wandering about the streets? Sitting in the Park? Trying to take refuge in a church? Pull the other one. He towelled briskly. She would have disappeared when he got back downstairs, pinched the spoons as likely as not, or would have if Celia had not done that already. He pulled on jeans and a sweater and took the stairs two at a time.

'Thought you might have hopped it, like Celia,' he said, arriving in the kitchen.

'Who is Celia?' She had cleared the breakfast debris and was sweeping the floor.

'My wife. Ex-wife, actually.'

'Oh.'

'Tell you about her some time. No, why should I? You wouldn't be interested. Now, will you show me round the garden? I want to inspect it properly, be told what you've planted. The only thing my ex ever

171

planted were things in their pots which she forgot to water, and a ghastly cherub.'

Julia laughed; laughter transformed her face (laughter transforms most faces). Sylvester said, 'Right, then, let's inspect,' and led the way upstairs, picking up the jacket he had discarded when he came in the night before and putting it on. 'Will you be warm enough?'

She said, 'Yes,' indicating that her sweater was thick.

Sylvester said, 'This garden was OK in my mother's day, but nothing has flourished lately except weeds.'

Julia murmured something which ended in 'shit'.

'What?'

'It needed feeding. I gave it compost and dung.'

'Horse?' Had not Rebecca written something about horse manure?

'Actually yes, and mushroom compost.'

Sylvester opened the french windows and stepped out. Julia watched him perambulate, stooping to read labels she had left on the climbers, fumbling in his pocket for his glasses to read name-tags blurred by rain, murmuring the Latin, muttering to himself as he bent to touch a Christmas rose and lay a hand palm down on the earth. 'You have brought a sad corpse to life,' he said, 're-created a garden. And what is so wonderful is that everything you have planted which can smell, will.'

'You noticed.' She was delighted.

'I noticed all right. How can I thank you? Where did you learn?'

'My mother had a garden. I worked in that.'

'Is she dead?' He was sympathetic. 'You must miss—'

'No, no, not dead—' She appeared to recoil from something. 'And in one or two jobs I had, I worked in the garden as well as the house.'

'Jobs?' She had planted a flowering box; he stooped to sniff. Pure honey.

She said, 'Cleaning jobs.'

'Oh?'

'I have no qualifications,' she said stiffly.

'It's a long time since I smelled a flowering box,' he said. 'Did you find this in the garden centre?'

'Actually I did not use the two I suggested, I found everything I wanted in the country. I hope you don't mind.'

'Why should I mind?'

'I had borrowed Mr Patel's van and gone for a walk. I felt desperate for the country.'

'I know the feeling. Did the dung come from the country?'

'Yes. I scrubbed the van thoroughly afterwards.'

Sylvester smiled. 'Gosh,' he said, turning back to the house, 'you have given the wistaria a shock.'

'It needed it.'

'And you have given me rather a shock, too,' Sylvester said, 'I'd forgotten about the garden. How can I thank you?'

'But I have *loved* doing it, it's saved—'

'Yes?'

'Nothing.'

'Shall you help me decide where to put my new rugs and then have a celebratory drink?' (Why was she so reserved? He did not know how best to express his pleasure, was afraid too much enthusiasm might daunt her. Perhaps she would unravel a bit when she'd had a drink?) 'Come on,' he said, 'let's do the rugs.' They went back into the house.

'I thought one in front of the fire.' He brought in the bundle of rugs. 'And one along the bookshelf. What about the others? Come on,' he said, 'it's you who are going to sweep them. How should they go?'

She did not answer but helped him try the rugs in various positions. Joyful stood watching from the hall.

Julia said, 'You should have one by the desk, it's lovely.'

'I was considering sitting at that desk and writing a novel.'

Julia said, 'What's the title?'

'*Wellington's Valet.*'

'That could be fascinating.' She was serious.

'My ex found the idea antipathetic.'

Julia said, 'The last rug would look good by the door.'

'So it would. You have a good eye.' (And, too, ask no questions.)

They spread the rug. Sylvester stood back to view the effect. Screwing up his eyes, fumbling for a handkerchief to stave off a sneeze, his hand encountered an alien object. It was the toy given him by the carpet dealer's child. It was soft and fleecy. Smiling, he turned it this way and that. He said, 'Oh, look. It's made of real fleece, a lamb, neat!' He held it out for Julia to see.

She drew in her breath. 'Christy.' Her face drained of colour, her mouth became an ugly square; tears splashed from her eyes.

Shocked, Sylvester stared, then with a leap of recognition he exclaimed, 'It's the Sheep Girl!' and, stepping across the rug they had just laid, took her in his arms.

26

Julia's head was bowed; her hands held the toy fisted against her chest. With arms encircling her Sylvester looked down on her head and, while appreciating the colour of her hair (almost black), registered concern at the torrent of tears presently soaking the front of his jersey.

He had seen girls cry, of course, but not like this. Celia had wept copiously from rage and thrown things. He had seen his mother in distress but this was something altogether new; by giving her the toy he had triggered some unbearable, desperate emotion.

'Emotion', he thought. Thank God this girl doesn't use it. She smells nice actually, rather like hay. That was a near miss with whatever her name was in America. Thank heaven I caught hold of this girl and did not hesitate. If I had hesitated she would have been out of the door in a flash and lost, as she was that first time. She hasn't registered that I recognized her. She was muttering something, some name? I am quite happy to stand like this holding her, Sylvester thought, looking over Julia's head at the dog who, catching his eye, wagged its tail.

What was the name which was sparked off by the toy? Christy? Something like that. A child? *Her* child? Oh my God! Whatever you do, Sylvester adjured himself, don't interrupt, don't speak, let her weep.

So he stood holding her, Julia wept and Joyful lowered himself into a crouching position with his nose on his paws. After a while Sylvester thought, I wonder what messages there are on my answerphone?

And what, if anything, is in all my letters? And, it really is lovely what she has done to the garden; what a remarkable girl. And the house! I don't ever remember coming home to a house so free of debris and dust; Celia could be a slut. The rugs look lovely. They give the room balance. Celia is welcome to the old lot, one had a bit of moth; I wonder whether she's noticed, or Andrew Battersby? I must not ask but when this girl stopped the train and upended the sheep she looked as desperate as she did just now when I handed her the toy. Perhaps there *is* a connection? I wonder whether she ever heard from British Rail? I wish my mind was not so full of trivia. I wish I knew what to do. He was still standing with his arms round Julia when the telephone pealed and his answerphone voice replied, 'Please leave a message after the tone.' Then: 'It really is very tiresome of you, Sylvester,' said Rebecca's voice, 'not to let me know when to expect you back. I could easily have stocked you up with groceries and put milk in your fridge. Christmas this year is so badly arranged, the shops are shut for four whole days. I am aggrieved, Sylvester. I could have helped. It will be your own fault if you come home to powdered milk only.' *Malgré lui*, Sylvester shook with laughter.

In a hoarse voice Julia said, 'She has telephoned several times when I've been working, but you said not to answer.'

Sylvester said, 'My former secretary. She means well.'

Julia was still weeping; her eyes were swollen, her nose red, her cheeks drained of colour. Relaxing his hold a little, Sylvester manoeuvred her to sit on the sofa. Sitting beside her, an arm still holding her, he presently said, 'Suppose I make us a pot of tea?' and, 'A gulp of whisky would do no harm,' and, 'Your head must be aching. Aspirin?'

Wiping tears with her hand, Julia said, 'So sorry. A kitchen towel?'

Sylvester said, 'Loo paper's softer,' and went to get some, noting as he went that she still clutched the toy which now was as saturated as his jersey.

Waiting for the kettle to boil he wished he was not so jet-lagged; at the best of times it was a nuisance but now he was aware that should he put a foot wrong, or utter an inept remark, all would be lost. 'All *what* would be lost?' he asked out loud. 'All what, for Christ's sake?' He put cups on a tray and filled the teapot; fatigue made him clumsy. 'Whisky,' he reminded himself and balanced glasses and bottle among the cups.

Julia sat where he had left her, one hand holding the roll of lavatory paper, the other the toy. Her tears had stopped. He put a small table by the sofa and poured tea. Celia had despised the table, he remembered with amusement; if she had not, one would have had to put the tray on the floor. He poured tea. 'Sugar?' 'No thanks.' 'Milk?' 'Please.' 'Drink this first.' He measured a tot of whisky and handed it to her. 'Come on, drink it.' Obediently she swallowed. 'Now drink your tea.' He gave her her cup and, pouring himself a generous dollop of whisky, sat back in the armchair to watch her gulp tea and replace the cup rattling in its saucer.

She said, 'Perhaps you had better listen to your messages. There may be something urgent.'

Appreciating this effort towards normality, Sylvester said, 'Why not?' It was not possible to ask questions and awkward to sit in silence. He found a pencil and pad and brought the telephone close. 'I have been away for weeks, but everyone knows. I hardly think there will be anything urgent,' he said, pressing the button.

She still kept a hold on the toy but had drunk her tea; he crossed his legs and lay back in the armchair to listen to various messages from friends, invitations to dinner which he noted on the pad, a message about books he had ordered from his bookshop, please

177

collect, a request from his solicitor to call if he had not received a letter dated such-and-such and sent to New York, some messages of Christmas cheer and, interspersed among these, Rebecca's crisp accents. 'There is something odd going on in your house, Sylvester, which I don't like – there's a dog on your doorstep.' 'I feel very doubtful about your cleaning woman, she puts out suspect rubbish, it smells of horse. You should have stuck to Mrs Andrews.' 'I have seen a seedy-looking man hanging about who may be a squatter or a thief sussing you out. Of course I waited until he moved off.' 'I have been thinking, Sylvester, that you should have an alarm fitted even if Celia has removed everything of value. If only you'd left me the key—'

'And so on and so on.' Sylvester chuckled. 'She has a heart of gold, a mania for interference and not enough to do,' he said to Julia, who did not appear to be listening. 'She would like to run my life,' he said, gulping his whisky, 'but there *is* something that's important, if only I could remember. She wrote to me; what the hell was it? Something to do with a death? It'll come back in a moment.' He switched the answerphone off. 'What is it,' he leaned forward to look at Julia, 'that that toy reminds you of?' One should never, he howled inwardly, drink on a jet-lagged stomach.

'My child had one like it,' Julia said quietly. 'It was his favourite toy, that and his whistle. He was never parted from it; Mrs Patel gave it to him when he was a baby. I have never seen another. Its coat is real fleece. He had it with him when Giles took him to stay with Clodagh, it would have been in the car when they were killed.'

Sylvester felt his throat go dry.

'I found his whistle!' Julia said. 'It had lodged behind a radiator. I have that. Giles was driving when they were killed; I imagined that since he'd lost his

178

licence Clodagh would drive, but he was driving. I should have realized that since she loved Giles, she would let him drive if he wanted. She loved him so much and she adored Christy. She blames me for not being there to do the driving; I always drove after Christy was born, it was safer. She blames me. I blame myself. I know it's illogical because I was *not* there, I was *not* wanted. Giles visited Clodagh alone and sometimes I let him take Christy. It seemed only fair, Clodagh loved him and it would have been unkind to keep him away. But she did not want me, it was Giles she wanted, and Christy.'

Julia paused to blow her nose on a handful of Andrex.

'After the divorce,' she said, 'she wanted them more than ever. She is possessive. She bought Christy toys, life-size things which frightened him; what he liked was his lamb, and the whistle. I suppose the size of the toys represented the size of her love? But life is not like that. I was stupid to let him go. I tried to be fair. I was stupid, too, about Clodagh. I did not take in that she was in love, I thought she was old. I did not suss the situation. I thought she was being kind and helpful to a younger man and that I meant something, I did not grasp the situation. To be honest, I did not want to. Then, later, I thought there's such a thing as the benefit of the doubt; all that! I did not *want* to face up to Giles and Clodagh as a unit, which later included Christy but not me. Clodagh is ten years older than Giles and Giles was ten years older than me, so why not? Why shouldn't they?' She drew in her breath. 'Clodagh holds me responsible,' she went on, 'she told me so at the funeral. She – oh well, that's how it is, she calls me a murderer.' Sylvester drew breath audibly. Julia said, 'I know she does. One of the things my phantom telephoner calls me is "murderer"; when he did it last, I managed to blow Christy's whistle down the phone—'

Sylvester gulped some cold tea. 'Why did you marry—'

'He raped me. He said it was love. We were working in Clodagh's garden. I wanted it to be love. He could be delightful, very attractive and funny. I did not know then about him and Clodagh. I hoped it would work when Clodagh insisted we marry – I found I was pregnant. It did work for a while, but then—'

Sylvester, who had been holding his breath, breathed. 'Then?'

Julia said, 'I don't suppose it's ever happened to you, but quite soon when I married Giles I knew when he was making love to me that he was thinking of Clodagh, that she was the real thing, not me.'

In the silence Joyful whimpered in his sleep. Julia said, 'I'm terribly sorry to rabbit on like this. I do apologize.'

Sylvester said, 'Who is Clodagh?'

Julia said, 'My mother. Didn't I say?'

27

Sylvester's mind seethed with questions, none of which he felt it safe to ask.

Julia blew her nose on lavatory paper and tossed the used tissue into the waste-paper basket. She said, 'I have embarrassed you. I'd better go.'

'No,' he said, almost shouting. '*No*.'

They fell silent and Joyful, changing his position, stretched, his claws clicking on the parquet floor.

Glancing up, Sylvester said, 'My ex-wife Celia had an ornamental French clock with an irritating tick, which she posed on the mantelshelf. Pose was a word she liked to use. "Let us pose this here," she would say. When she left me, she took it and a lot of things with her. Now I enjoy the space.'

Not answering directly, Julia said, 'What about the rest of your messages? You switched the thing off.'

Switched it off and invaded her privacy, thought Sylvester. 'Right,' he said. 'Good idea.' He pressed the button and picked up pad and pencil. If I do this, he thought, it will give us a breather to collect our wits, and listened to three more routine messages before switching off. 'That seems to be the lot,' he said, but immediately the telephone began to peal. He picked up the receiver and said, 'Hallo?'

'What's this about my death?' enquired a woman's voice. 'It's not the kind of joke you usually make. You have thoroughly upset Hamish with your messages of condolence: please construe.'

'Oh my God!' exclaimed Sylvester. 'That's what I was trying to remember. Rebecca wrote me in America that she had read of your death in *The Times*. I tried and tried to reach Hamish to tell him how sorry – What?' He held the receiver away from his ear. 'Yes, that's the one, she was my sec – Oh, Calypso, I'm so *relieved* – What? – Yes, of course I have other aunts – Oh, really? – That one? – But she's been senile for years, one could only be pleased, well, relieved for her – No, no, you sprang to mind because you are my best aunt, my favourite – No, she did not mention your name, she just wrote "aunt" and I sprang to the conclusion – Yes, please forgive me and apologize to Hamish – You will? Oh good, that's a relief, and Calypso, thank you, you've done something wonderful, you've cheered . . . Oh, she's rung off.' He held the receiver for a moment, then replaced it gently and with a sense of joy watched Julia laugh. She had a merry laugh.

'How,' she asked, still laughing, 'did that happen? What made you think your aunt was dead?'

With embellishments he explained Rebecca's letter. 'Rebecca is the one who thinks you are a squatter. She is the one whose messages you have just heard, she condoled in a postscript – I remember it now.'

Julia said, 'I wonder who the seedy-looking man can be?'

'What seedy man?'

'The one she saw lurking in the street when she spotted Joyful on your doorstep.'

'What was he doing there?' Sylvester glanced at the sleeping animal.

'Waiting. I do not bring him in when I am working. Last night when I took refuge was the first time I let him come in with me.'

'He is more than welcome,' said Sylvester, 'any time.'

Julia frowned. 'Once or twice when I was in here I heard him bark, and a man swear at him. That might have been—'

'More likely Rebecca's fertile imagination, she invented Calypso's death. It comes back to me – "your aunt has passed away". She can equally have invented a seedy man.'

'An aunt did die.' Julia grinned.

'I see you are able to quibble.' He was delighted to see her more cheerful. 'Tell me,' he leaned towards her, 'did British Rail ever make trouble?'

'British Rail?' she asked in puzzlement.

'When you stopped the train to save a sheep which was stuck on its back.'

'What do you know about that?' Julia stared at him.

'I was on the train. I watched you. I wanted to help but I hesitated and did nothing. Was there a fuss?'

Julia said, 'Oh?' Then, 'No, nothing. I think the guard must have fixed it; he was kind. How odd, I had quite forgotten.'

'I wondered,' Sylvester blundered on, 'whether your action then had anything to do with that toy? You looked then, with that sheep, just as you did just now when I gave you the toy.' Distraught, he thought; she was distraught.

Julia looked down at the toy. 'It's wet,' she said, 'soaked.' She put the toy down. 'Yes,' she said, 'it's probable.'

Sylvester said, 'Go on, please tell me.'

Julia looked out at the garden; he should have a bird bath, she thought. That would round off the garden, make it complete. She said, 'I had been to their funeral. Giles and Christy's. My – Clodagh has them buried in her village cemetery. I don't feel Christy is there, and I don't care about Giles. I was on my way back to London; I would not go into her house. She was glad when I left, I could see that. She made a big thing of the funeral, she and her friend Madge; it was their "do", nothing really to do with me. I was not exactly compos. Yes, the sheep did trigger a connection with Christy. If I could help the sheep, it helped Christy.

Something of that sort? Nothing logical. I was on a "high".'

'Of grief?'

'Yes.'

He remembered her grief; he had just seen it again. 'I should not ask all these questions,' he apologized, wanting to ask more, feeling compelled.

'It doesn't matter.' She looked down at the toy, not touching it.

Sylvester reached for the whisky, poured for them both, handed Julia her glass. 'What did you do when you got back?' She had disappeared in the crowd. He had wanted to follow, had not.

She sipped her whisky. 'I cleared all their things out of the flat. I felt mad. I thought I must rid myself of all of it – I did that – scrubbed the place – couldn't talk to anyone – there was no-one – I got some vodka, thought I'd get drunk. A girl from another flat came noseying. I gave her a fright, I think, and she was the one who drank the vodka. I walked in the rain – miles and miles – fell asleep in a church somewhere and the priest – I wanted to talk but there is, there was something I could not, cannot tell, I—'

On the doorstep Rebecca pressed her thumb on the bell.

Sylvester exclaimed, 'Bloody hell!' and, glass in hand, went to open the door.

'I had a feeling you might be back.' Rebecca stood robustly on her high heels.

(This may be the most important moment of my life and she interrupts.)

'Rebecca! What brings you here?'

'Milk!' Rebecca extended a pint carton. 'I was passing on my way out to lunch and it occurred to me that I have plenty and that should you be back I could spare you a pint. Am I not clever?'

'——'

'Aren't you going to ask me in?' Rebecca swayed

inwards. 'We are letting a lot of cold air into your warm hall. I won't stay long, I know what you are like when you are jet-lagged. I just came to see whether you are OK.'

'Thanks, I am.'

'My God, Sylvester! There's a dog behind you!'

'Yes.'

'What's it doing here?'

Joyful advanced, interested but doubtful.

'It's welcome.'

'Are you hinting that I am not? Where on earth did it spring from?'

'He belongs to Mrs Piper.'

'Mrs Piper?'

'Mrs Piper.'

Rebecca mouthed, 'Your cleaning lady? What is she doing working on a Bank Holiday?' she whispered.

'Actually, we were having a drink. Would you join us?'

'No thanks. It's too early. It's not my drinking time.'

Sylvester said, 'It's still American drinking time.'

'I've seen that creature lurking on your doorstep, it growled at me. What time is it in America?'

Sylvester tossed the contents of his glass down his throat. 'Come in,' he said recklessly, 'come in and see what Mrs Piper has done to the garden, it's a miracle. Mrs Piper,' he said, leading the way, 'this is my former secretary, Rebecca. Mrs Piper, Rebecca; Rebecca, Mrs Piper.'

'How do you do?' Julia stood up, extended her hand.

Rebecca shook it. 'Bitter cold day.' She eyed Julia. 'I was just passing,' she said. 'I brought Mr Wykes some milk.'

Julia smiled.

'Come on, Rebecca, have a drink.' Sylvester replenished his glass. 'Look at the garden.' He waved his arm. 'Miraculoso. I think I am a bit pissed.'

'You should not drink with jet lag.' Rebecca moved

185

to look out. 'Goodness!' She stared at the garden. 'What happened to Celia's cherub?'

'Went out with the rubbish. Soon after Celia.'

'As I too must. Nice to have met you.' Rebecca swivelled her glance from the garden to Julia. 'I will be in touch,' she said to Sylvester who, following her to the door, wheedled, 'You sure you won't have a drink?'

'Quite sure.' Rebecca opened the street door. 'See you soon,' she said, stepping out.

Sylvester shouted after her, 'Thanks for the milk,' and, returning to the sitting-room, collapsed laughing into his armchair. 'Where were we?'

But Julia said, 'Tell me about the cupid,' and he knew that Rebecca had robbed him of her confidence. The opportunity was lost.

'The cupid?'

'Oh! The cupid,' Sylvester cried bitterly. 'Celia's cupid! It was horrible, a horrible plaster thing. I can't think where she found it, can't imagine. Anyway, she plonked it in the middle of the garden – she was always going to do something about the garden and never did – then someone whose taste she respected looked at it. I know! It was Calypso, the aunt who is not dead, and from her expression – her expression only, mind, Calypso would be too tactful to voice a derogatory opinion for fear of hurting Celia's feelings, unaware at that period that Celia's feelings are cast-iron – Celia twigged that she had boobed, bought a bit of loathsome kitsch, lost interest in the garden – not that she ever had much – so there it sat. And when she left me to remarry her first husband, Andrew Battersby, she left it behind but took everything else of the remotest value and I was inspired to root it up and put it in the dustbin. I say, Julia Piper, I am talking too much, it's the whisky, but old Rebecca's reaction to Celia's cupid brings it all back. I told you, didn't I, how I watched her load a taxi

186

with the TVs and that she even took my new kettle?'

'No,' said Julia. 'Tell me.'

Sylvester thought, I don't want to talk about Celia, that is over. I want more about her mother; what an appalling unimaginable situation that must have been. I want to know what she could not tell the priest.

Holding his empty glass near his face, he leaned towards Julia on the sofa. She met his eye; there was no way she was going to answer questions. She had become wary; her moment of weakness was past. She had composed herself. She looked less blotchy, she was very nearly smiling. She said, 'Your new kettle? Your wife?'

Frustrated, he sighed into his empty glass, which responded with a whisper like summer sea rustling up the beach. He said, 'We were married about five years; when we met Celia had just discovered her husband was having an affair. We met at a party. I was at a loose end; had not, come to think of it, been tied. There was that instant rapport that one mistakes for love which actually is no more than animal sex – I should know, I have just had a dose in the States, but that's another story. She moved in here. Everyone warned me it would not work, which naturally egged me on. We married as soon as she divorced. She was very, very pretty, blonde, well-dressed but not, I was to discover, at all sexy, not spontaneously so. I do think, don't you, that it's important to get along in bed?' (I should not say that, should I? Will she tell me how it was with that bastard Giles?)

Sylvester waited for Julia to do more than give a slight nod, whose meaning was impossible to construe.

He went on, 'She wanted rich people for friends, travel to fashionable places, smart clothes, all the tinsel. She could not stand me wanting to write. I am lazy and easily discouraged, she soon choked that. She filled the house with expensive china ornaments, with

187

white televisions. Oh!' Sylvester cried. 'Why am I *boring* you with all this?'

'You loved her.' Julia looked out at the garden.

'No, I did *not*!' Sylvester shouted and then, as she did not respond, 'Of course I loved her but I do-not-love-her-now.' (Now, perhaps, we can get back to the Giles/Clodagh complex?)

But apparently sensing his train of thought, Julia said, 'And the kettle?' and he, caught in the snare of half-forgotten pain, told how he had watched, hidden by the pillar-box, as Celia piled the last of her loot into a taxi, elaborating, listing the items, the parcels, the carrier bags, the televisions, even the new kettle, while he waited like a timid fool until she drove away before venturing back to his house, hoping she would laugh for the situation had been absurd. 'Even then,' he said, 'she left traces.'

Julia said, 'Oh?', not laughing as he had hoped she would.

'She used a scent called "Emotion". I had grown to hate it. The house reeked of it after her raid—'

Julia smiled and he thought, she is loosening up, perhaps now I can lead back, but ready for him she said, 'You mentioned another story?' so that he gave in.

'That was humiliating, too,' and as wittily as possible he told of his visit to the Bratts and the débâcle with the blonde who, too, smelled of 'Emotion'. But although she smiled, she failed to laugh even at the loss of the new Brooks Brothers' underpants.

'You do not seem to find my adventure comical,' he said.

'I think Celia hurt you more than you let on.'

'God, no! I am delighted. Ask Rebecca, ask anyone who knows me. I am well rid of her. I – what makes you think I am hurt?' he said indignantly.

'Takes one to know one,' said Julia coolly. 'You are close to tears.'

'It's the alcohol!' Sylvester raised his voice. 'Damn you,' he exclaimed, 'you've set me off.' And through his tears he cried, 'Of course I loved her, of course she hurt me.' He snatched the roll of lavatory paper Julia no longer needed, tore off a handful and blew his nose. 'But I am all right now,' he said, chucking the used paper towards the waste-paper basket. 'My pain is nothing compared to yours! I wish that shit Giles were alive so that I could kill him. I am appalled by what he did to you, and as for your mother—' Then, observing Julia wince, he stopped. He had gone too far.

'It seems to me,' Julia steered him away, 'that she emasculated you.'

'Who?'

'Celia.'

'Not permanently,' Sylvester cried, alarmed. 'And although I shed a tear for her, it is retrospective, I assure you, in a sense painless.' Observing Julia relax, he thought, if I tread warily we can get back to her story. But Julia was standing up, running her hand through her hair, looking round for the dog.

'I should be on my way,' she said. 'I have to work tomorrow. Thank you so much for letting me shelter, the party should be over now,' pulling her sweater down over her hips, distancing herself.

Sylvester said, 'Must you go?'

She said, 'I must.'

He said, 'I will walk you home.'

28

She has lovely long legs, Sylvester thought, matching his stride to Julia's. Celia had stepped fast but unevenly, heels clacking on the pavement. Passing the pillar-box from behind which he had watched his ex-wife's depredations, Julia shortened her stride as Joyful lifted a leg.

'I found Celia's thoroughness somehow admirable,' he said. 'I could have stopped her taking so much but it would have been dog in the mangerish. In a way,' he said, 'she did me a good turn.'

Julia did not answer but stepped off the pavement and crossed the street, the dog pacing close to her knee. Was she listening to what he said? Could she possibly be interested in what Celia had taken? All the things they had bought together? Things which, had she left them, would have reminded him of times past, happy and sad. How could she be? I did love Celia, he thought, and I was jealous. I was hurt and very, very angry.

'But not any more,' he said out loud and Julia nodded as though she understood, squeezing sideways between tightly parked cars on to the opposite pavement.

'One thing I must replace is a car. I am presently carless. Have you got a car?' he asked. 'Celia took it,' he said. Julia did not answer.

Fool, he thought. Car smash. Child and ex-husband killed. Idiot! But I will get a car and take her to the country. She likes the country, I know that much. The car must be roomy for those legs, and there is the dog to consider. There must be room for him.

'Rebecca will want to advise me,' he said, 'she's a know-all.' Julia laughed. So she had been listening. 'She has a golden heart and not enough to do,' he said. 'When she worked in our office, we devoted much time to finding people whose lives needed reorganizing. Lately she has been under the misapprehension that mine is in need.'

Julia said, 'Yes.' They had reached the alleyway leading out of his cul-de-sac and walked through it in Indian file, Julia leading. 'It is difficult to keep Rebecca at arm's length without hurting her feelings,' Sylvester said.

Julia said, 'I imagine.'

What rubbish I am talking. I wish I could tell her something of interest, tell her about Bratt for instance, and the Ku Klux Klan, he thought, drawing abreast as they emerged from the alleyway. I wonder how she would react if I told her Celia has even taken the mattress off my bed and that I am glad the new one is pristine, impersonal, only slept on by me! 'Rebecca does not know about that,' he said out loud.

Julia said, 'What?'

He told her about the mattress. She said, 'Of course that would help.'

'When I bought it the shop said it only needs turning occasionally,' Sylvester said. 'So when you come tomorrow—'

'I shan't come tomorrow.'

'What?' He stood still. 'Not coming?' Had she thought he was propositioning her?

'It's not my day,' she said.

'Your day?'

'I shall come Tuesdays and Fridays now the garden is in order.'

'But you will come?'

'Yes.'

'But the other days? Mondays, Wednesdays and Thursdays?' Could he perhaps invite her to lunch?

'I have other jobs,' she said.

'Oh,' he said. 'Must you?'

She nodded.

'Doing what?' he pried.

'Cleaning people's flats.'

'But—' he said. 'Why?'

'Mrs Patel at the corner-shop cared for Christy with her little boy while I worked – I still work.'

'But is that—'

'It's not *all* I can do,' she said, 'but the hours suit. I don't like offices or having to be with people, having to talk.'

Half-understanding, Sylvester said, 'I see,' and they walked on for a bit not talking. But then curiosity bubbled again and he asked, 'Did you have *any* happy times with your ex, your Giles? I ask, because I did with Celia. It would not be fair to pretend I had not.'

She said, 'Not enough,' and, 'He was not mine.' They were turning a street corner. She exclaimed, 'Oh, God! The party is still raging,' dismayed.

They stood looking along the street. Sylvester said, 'Is this where you live?'

'Yes, number seven.' She stood, irresolute.

The door of number seven was open. Music flowed from upstairs windows, two people danced on the pavement, another pair swayed in the road to the strains of *Non, je ne regrette rien*. Several more sat on the doorstep, glass in hand, singing. Inside the house a hubbub of voices was punctuated by shrieks of laughter and occasional recrimination.

Sylvester said, 'You'd think they'd be cold,' feeling cold himself. 'You can't go back into that, that lot are high on drink and probably drugs, come back with me,' but Julia said, 'I must. Joyful is starving and his food is in my flat.'

Crossly Sylvester said, 'Surely we can find him something to eat in my house?'

She said, 'Your cupboard is bare. Oh my!' as a man,

propelled violently from behind, was precipitated down the steps watched by Peter Eddison. 'That's my neighbour in the flat below,' she said. 'His wife's been known to send for the police.'

'That party's growing rough.' Sylvester was worried.

'The dancers in the road are not disturbed,' she said. 'Last year they had bagpipes and danced reels; that *was* noisy.'

Sylvester said, 'I've an idea. Let's find a taxi and take Joyful to a restaurant,' hoping to lure her, but she said, 'No, I will not be daunted. I live here. There are tins of his food in my flat. I must get to them. I refuse to be pusillanimous,' she said as a window on the second floor flew open and someone with a shout of 'Fuck the washing-up!' hurled a trayful of crockery to crash into the area.

Sylvester said, 'Gosh!', impressed. 'Wow!'

'I must say goodbye,' Julia said, 'and thank you very much for being so kind. I hope you will get some rest and sleep off your jet lag. I really am sorry,' she said, 'to have been such an inconvenient surprise.' She spoke hurriedly and shivered in the frosty air.

Sylvester raised his voice. 'Oh, do shut up! If you insist on going in there, I will come with you, at least see you get to your flat safely. There is no way,' he said loudly, 'that I will let you go alone.'

Julia said, 'It's only a party, I've survived others. I should not have made a fuss. No need,' she said, her voice rising, 'to be gallant.'

Offended, Sylvester cried, 'Ho! Really! If I had not arrived back in the middle of the night you would have gone on sheltering in my house, dog food or not, I bet. You would have waited there until tomorrow.'

Julia said, 'Well, I'm not waiting now,' and set off at a run towards the steps of number seven.

Sylvester and Joyful ran after her, side-stepping the dancing couples just as someone switched the music from Piaf to Rock.

Bounding up the steps, Julia elbowed swiftly through a group of people ebbing in and out of the ground-floor flat. Sylvester, following, glanced from the doorstep into the area where a bulky couple clutching each other tightly were beginning to rock, and hurried after Julia through a din of talk and smell of food, alcohol and tobacco. Joyful pressed close to Julia's heels, but Sylvester could not keep up. There were people sitting and standing all the way up the stairs and dancing on the landings. Some of them were friendly and offered him drinks or cigarettes as his legs became entangled with theirs, so that he paused to apologize. They said, 'What's the hurry?' He said, 'What indeed?' Julia could not escape; he would meet up with her at the top, no need to rush. Panting, he paused to look out of a landing window, get a gasp of fresh air.

Under his feet he felt the house vibrate and wondered how anyone could bear to stay in it. Why had the police not put a stop to the noise? Julia and the dog would go mad, he thought, as he watched a man in a long brown overcoat and black felt hat dancing with two skinny girls in tight black leggings, admiring their high spirits and cheerful abandon. Were it not for Julia, he would be tempted to join them, their dancing was infectious. He was tempted but he turned from the window to continue up the stairs, squeezing past people gathered thick and sprawling on the last flight. 'What's the hurry, you hasty man?' A girl circled his ankle with strong long fingers, digging in her nails. 'Excuse me, I have to get past. Could you move your legs?' He jerked his leg free and, inserting his feet between unknown thighs, clutching the banister, feeling his way, he moved on up. 'Why,' he shouted as he trod on a hand and its owner yelped, 'is there no light?'

'Bulb's gone,' said a voice. 'Careful where you put your feet.'

Sylvester said, 'Sorry,' and moved on to reach the top landing where in almost total darkness he nearly lost his balance as a man thrust past him, making his way down amid squeals of protest. There was a fuggy smell of marijuana; he could discern two or three people lolling against the wall, relaxed and peaceful. Finding what he supposed was Julia's door, he knocked and knocked again. From inside the dog barked. 'Won't let you in,' said a girl leaning against the wall. 'Wouldn't open up to her other friend. She don't seem sociable, no party spirit,' she remarked amiably.

Sylvester felt for the keyhole and shouted, 'It's me. Let me in.' The dog barked frantically. He listened, then shouted again, 'Let me in.'

'No.' Julia's voice was hoarse. 'Go away.'

'I guess she means go away means go away,' said the girl sitting against the wall. 'As I say, she wouldn't let the other man in, so why you? I mean, what makes you different?'

Sylvester knelt and felt along the bottom of the door; there was, as he hoped, a gap. 'Joyful,' he called. 'You there, Joyful? It's me,' and he blew through the gap between the door and floor. From inside the dog snuffled in recognition. 'Tell her to let me in,' Sylvester shouted, 'there's a good dog.'

When the door opened suddenly Sylvester was on all fours. Julia said, 'You do look peculiar.' She had an empty tin in her hand, its jagged lid threatening his face. 'Come in quickly,' she said, 'I thought you were—' and stopped, her voice unsteady.

'Who?' Sylvester scrambled to his feet. 'That's a nasty weapon. Were you going to use it?'

'Yes.' She stepped back as he closed the door.

'Why? What have I done?'

'Not you, him. He tried to get in, he's – I—'

'What? Did he attack you?' He could see she was shaken. 'Who was it?'

'I recognized – I thought I recognized him. Is he out there?'

'Only some people lolling about. There's a girl, I don't think—'

'Large? Broad? Bulky? Is he there?' Her voice rose.

'Nobody like that,' Sylvester said quietly, 'and give me that.' He took the tin from her and, remembering the person who had pushed past him on the stairs, he said, 'Whoever it was isn't here now.'

'You sure?'

'Yes.'

'It was, I am almost sure it was the man who has been telephoning me. I know the voice.'

Below them someone upped the volume of music. Sylvester raised his voice. 'You can't possibly stay here,' he shouted.

'I must.'

'Don't argue,' he yelled, 'you are coming back with me. Now come on, get the bloody dog food and let's get out of here.'

But Julia demurred, not wishing to be bossed about, thinking that she had had enough of Sylvester, that she had not expected to meet him. That now she had met him he was not the nice old homosexual she had visualized who would wear a Panama hat and sit in the garden she had recreated, but a stranger who was taking something from her, had taken something from her, and that she was not prepared to give more. And what's more, she noted, he was raiding her kitchen, stuffing tins of Joyful's food into a carrier bag and preparing to leave, even shouting above the sound of rock, 'Got your key?' Shutting the window, bundling her into her coat and propelling her out of the flat, locking the door, her door, behind them, and fighting their way down the stairs and out into the street.

'Whew!' he exclaimed as they crossed the pavement. 'Whew, that's better! Good God! What are *you* doing here?' he said to Rebecca who, tall and stately, was

196

dancing free and easy, swinging her hips, stamping her high heels in unison with an unknown man. 'God Almighty, what are you doing here?' Sylvester repeated.

'Might ask you the same question.' Rebecca did not stop dancing. 'What's up with your cleaning lady?' For Julia had taken to her heels and was racing down the street. 'Oh, he'll catch her all right,' she said to her partner, 'he ran at university. Now come on, pay attention to the rhythm, they are playing a rumba.'

29

Rebecca had enjoyed her lunch, enjoyed the food, enjoyed the wine and, above all, she had enjoyed regaling her hosts with the description of how, from the kindness of her heart, she had brought a carton of milk to a former colleague in case he, arriving off a flight from the States on Bank Holiday morning with all the shops and supermarkets as closed as limpets – even Patel's Corner Shop, a super shop she had recently discovered which never ever seemed to close (aren't the Asians wonderful?) – was milkless, to find him milkless certainly, but with a dog in the house which was a surprise and, wait for it, an even greater surprise, 'a strange woman', and guess who the strange woman was? His cleaning lady!! Not the respectable Mrs Andrews with impeccable references she had taken the trouble to find for him when his wife left, but a gypsy girl with *no* references but apparently a dog!

She had told the tale wittily, taken care to describe the girl as 'interesting' and the dog, the sort attached by a bit of string, no proper lead. A New Age Traveller's dog? Everyone had laughed over the dog and had been particularly amused by the thought of a cleaning lady visible on a Bank Holiday. They had laughed, too, at her description of Sylvester in the office during the period she had worked for him; his entrapment and subsequent desertion by Celia. Several of them knew Celia or imagined they did, and nearly all of them knew of Andrew Battersby and Andrew Battersby's wealth.

'You should have put a stop to it, Rebecca,' they said,

'saved the poor bloke, he sounds desperately naïve.' 'Why didn't you marry him yourself, Rebecca?' 'If you had married him you would have had a legal position, been able to protect him,' they said affectionately, aware of their friend's character. But, 'Oh, my dears, he isn't my type,' she had cried, laughing, 'he is tall and stringy, he doesn't smoke, he is too good-mannered and polite. And anyway he's far too young.'

'No, no, he would not suit,' her hostess told the table at large. 'What Rebecca likes is a mature man, a bit of a brute who enjoys a strong woman, a tweedy sort of man. Am I not right, Rebecca? They were all such wimps in that office,' she said. 'Small wonder you left. There's a limit to what we can do for the weaker sex,' she joked. 'Rebecca's glass is empty,' she said to her husband, who was the sort of man Rebecca would have liked if she had not nobbled him first. So her host refilled her glass, and Rebecca appreciated her hostess's twinge of jealousy and later, when she was leaving and her host suggested driving her home, she declined the offer, saying she preferred to walk. This was absolutely true; the poor fellow had been too thoroughly tamed to be interesting. It was in this contented mood that, rounding a corner in the Chelsea streets, she came upon the Fellowes' and Eddisons' street party and got involved.

Nobody later could remember who had set a calypso tape on the player, but two people present, who lived in Peckham and had spent holidays in the West Indies, finding it enjoyable, turned up the sound. This increase in volume coincided with Rebecca's arrival and the passage through the street of a car whose passengers of Jamaican and African origin, seeing a party and hearing the music, not unnaturally stopped their car, scrambled out and joined in the dancing.

Rebecca, drawing close to watch and admire the grace, dexterity and sweet humour of the new arrivals, found herself clapping her hands and jigging; and before long, as people flowed out of the house infected by the catchy rhythm, discovered that she had acquired a partner. 'You a friend of the Eddisons and Fellowes?' he asked, dancing rather clumsily, a thick-set fellow in a Barbour.

'Who?'

'People giving the party.'

'Never heard of them. I was just passing.' Rebecca kept her eye on a particular Jamaican who with extraordinary grace was dancing near by. He was, she thought, with his long legs and arms, snapping fingers and flashing teeth, a creature of remarkable beauty. An Ace, she thought catching his eyes, exchanging a smile, an absolute Ace.

'Like a drink?' suggested the man in the Barbour. 'This is hard work.'

'Not at the moment, I drank at lunch.' (Rather a lot; this is just what I need.) 'What did you say their names are? Will they mind me joining in?'

'No, no, everyone does, hardly know them myself. It's a sort of free-for-all, a Christmas and Bank Holiday sort of thing, a junket.'

'What lovely hospitable people they must be.'

'What's your name?' her new friend asked.

'Rebecca.'

'You have lovely eyes, Rebecca.' He danced closer.

Here we go, thought Rebecca. 'What's yours?'

'Maurice, Maurice Benson. I am waiting to see a woman who lives in the top flat. She locked me out.'

Rebecca said, 'Really?', unsurprised.

'I like your legs,' said Maurice Benson.

'Aren't you awfully hot dancing in that jacket?'

Maurice said, 'This is thirsty work, let's get a drink, I am gasping,' and, 'Everyone goes inside when they're thirsty,' and, 'Look, they are going in,' nodding towards the Jamaicans.

Rebecca said, 'All right,' and they followed the man she had been watching as he went into the house with his friends, turning into Tim Fellowes' flat where there was the roaring noise of drinking people. 'You look much too hot in that awful garment,' Rebecca needled. 'Why don't you take it off? You will need it when you are cooling down. I make these interesting suggestions out of sheer habit,' she said. 'I am a bossy lady.'

Maurice Benson's reply was lost in a sudden uproar of confused shouts, scuffling, stamping of feet in the room ahead of them. The Ace Jamaican was shouting, 'Cool it, man, cool it!' He was laughing, but above his laughter Tim Fellowes screamed, 'Who invited you? Who let you in? Get out of my house! Get out, get out! Get back to your trees in Bongo Bongo.'

Rebecca, shocked and craning her neck, cried, 'What on earth's going on?' as she watched the Ace dancer, pressured back by the small infuriated man, good-humouredly warding off his flailing fists, stepping back on to the toes of his friends who, not as good-humoured as he, urged him forward, not back, with a certain belligerence.

'Stop him!' Rebecca ordered Benson. 'Stop that little squirt.'

But Janet, Tim's lover, appearing from nowhere, even smaller than Tim, struck him a crack from behind with a vase, felling him to his knees. As he clutched his head she kicked him in the back, shouting, 'You racist! You disgusting racist! He is only like this when he's drunk, come in, please come in, you are so so welcome.' But the Ace dancer replied, polite though retreating, that he thought perhaps not and, accompanied by his friends, evaporated from the party.

Rebecca said, 'What a splendid girl,' and to Benson, 'Why didn't you *do* something?' He said, 'It's not my scene, lady. Oh thanks, cheers,' as a girl pressed a glass into his hand, saying 'All over, better now,' as though it were he who had caused the fracas and received a blow on the head.

But Rebecca said to the girl, 'He doesn't need that,'

and, taking the drink from Benson, set it aside. Catching him by the hand she drew him back into the street to resume their dance, and it was then as they danced that Sylvester coming out of the house with Julia recognized Rebecca and exclaimed in surprise.

Watching Sylvester race after Julia, Benson exclaimed, 'That's the girl I want to see,' and made as though he would follow, but Rebecca held him back, saying, 'It can't be, she's a gypsy sort of person and that is a friend of mine.' To which Benson retorted, 'She's no gypsy, I know her mother. She is said to have murdered her husband.'

Rebecca said, 'It's impossible, she's his cleaning lady,' which made Benson laugh. And then, because he was tired by the dancing and regretting the drink she had so arbitrarily snatched from him, yet liking Rebecca, he suggested they repair to the pub where in a more comfy atmosphere he would tell her all he knew.

Very anxious to hear Benson's story, but thinking it possible Sylvester might also be in the pub, Rebecca had a better idea. Why not move on to her flat, which was only two streets away? There it would be warmer, more comfortable, more private. Benson agreed. As they made their way through the darkening streets he decided to play down his interest in Julia, not tell his new friend about the phone calls, work the conversation round to his life as a twitcher. And Rebecca, walking beside him, planned to strip him of that awful Barbour jacket which smelled of stale tobacco and alcohol and give him instead a lovely herring-bone tweed which had been left behind by her last – quite a long time ago – lover. This man would look almost presentable in her former lover's tweed, she decided, not nearly so seedy. And, conscious that she was already weasling into his life, she burst out laughing so that Benson eyed her with alarm.

30

Sprinting his fastest, Sylvester managed to catch up with Julia. 'I nearly lost out,' he gasped. 'You are going the wrong way, you should have turned left.' He caught her by the arm, turning her about. 'It's only a minute from here if we go this way.'

Julia said nothing.

'What an extraordinary thing to see old Rebecca dancing in the street. What a spectacle! If I had not seen it, I would not have believed it.' He guided Julia by the elbow. 'I wonder who the bloke she was dancing with could be. He did not look her sort exactly.'

Julia muttered, 'How do you know what her sort is?' And freed her elbow.

Sylvester said, 'What?'

'That is the man who was trying to break into my flat.' Julia's voice rose in pain. 'The man I deafened with Christy's whistle. The man who calls me a murderer, and pretends to speak in a child's voice.'

'Hold on,' Sylvester said, recapturing her elbow, 'hold on. I recognize him now. He was in the train when you stopped it. I took agin him, didn't like his attitude; it was sort of prurient. He wanted to meet you, to speak to you, ask questions. Then he tripped and fell over at Paddington, so I assumed he'd lost you. Here we are,' he said, fumbling for his key, 'and just in time, here comes the rain. That will put a stop to the dancing.'

Julia said, 'Then I can go back,' but Sylvester shouted, '*No*,' pushing her ahead of him into the hall.

'Do quit being silly. The dancing may stop, but the binge inside won't. What an amazing thing,' he said, slamming the door shut and guiding her to the sofa. 'If I put all these connections and meetings into my novel, nobody would believe it. Too contrived, they'd say. Things like that do not happen in real life. It's a rotten, rotten book.'

'But they do,' Julia said wearily. She looked drained, worse than when he had first seen her in the morning. 'You could fit it all into *Wellington's Valet*,' she said.

'You remember the title!' He was enchanted. 'It doesn't have to be called *Wellington's Valet*, that's a title I snatched from the air to annoy Rebecca, stop her prying. I have not even written the first paragraph,' he confessed.

Julia said, 'But you will,' letting her head fall back against the cushions.

'Will you promise to stay where you are for a few minutes?' He stood over her.

She said. 'All right.' She was still muffled into her overcoat; the dog sat close to her feet. He switched on the fire and drew the curtains, shutting out the rain. The street lamps were on; it was growing dark. He felt a renewal of fatigue and very, very hungry as he went downstairs to his kitchen. Rebecca still exerted her governessy influence, he observed, searching through his cupboards: milk was not the only sustenance she provided; months ago, insinuating herself into the house, she had brought and cooked him a delicious pasta. 'Aha! Here we are, half the packet of pasta, a jar of delicious sauce, parmesan cheese, olive oil, let's see what I can do.' Filling a saucepan with water and setting it to boil, he speculated as to what delicious dish Rebecca would cook to ensnare her latest *trouvaille*? 'I bet she feeds him steak,' he said out loud. Uncorking a bottle of wine, he wished her luck.

Julia managed a little pasta but left her wine. She sat half listening as Sylvester told her of a strange adventure with the Ku Klux Klan, three dizzying blondes and a book which might or might not be published. Soon she must step out in the rain and battle back to her flat. She stifled a jaw-breaking yawn, overwhelmed by huge fatigue. 'I'm awfully sorry,' she interrupted him, 'but I had better go now. I have to work tomorrow. The pasta was, er, is delicious. I can't thank you enough but I really should get some sleep. You must be exhausted, too, after your long journey. I have imposed enough.'

But having eaten his pasta and drunk more than his share of wine on top of various whiskies during the day, Sylvester was imbued with a fresh spurt of energy. He knew it would not last for he too was exhausted, but not too exhausted to conquer his natural hesitancy. If Julia was too tired to take in his polite prattle, he hoped and guessed that if he acted fast enough she would be too weary to put up much fight. So here goes, he adjured himself, and said, 'There is no way you are going back to that orgy. You are going to sleep here.'

Julia said, 'What? I can't.'

But Sylvester said, 'Don't argue. Come along. When I say sleep, I mean sleep, "sleep perchance to dream", nothing more. Here we go,' he said, propelling her up the stairs, pushing and pulling. 'Take off your clothes,' he said as they reached the bedroom. 'I will just rearrange these,' he said, dividing the pillows from the heap of four which made reading in bed such an indulgence into two lots of two. 'You can sleep in this, it will come down to your knees, perfectly decent.' He snatched a shirt from a drawer. 'Get into that. While you undress I'll let your dog out for a pee. Would you like a bath? You wouldn't? Well, get cracking, come on, come on,' he bullied, taking her sweater and pulling it over her head. 'Get on with it,' he said, drawing the curtains and shutting out the night. 'When I bring your dog back, I want to find you in the bed, got it?' And, accompanied by Joyful, he left the room.

Five minutes later, for Joyful was not a dog to dally in torrential rain, he was back, locking the front door and taking the telephone off the hook while Joyful scampered back up the stairs.

Seeing him pull off his sweater, kick off his shoes and unzip his fly, Julia in the bed mouthed, 'Where?', coiling her body to spring. 'Whe—'

Sylvester said, 'Where do you expect me to sleep? I am too long for the sofa and the bath is purgatory. *All right, all right,* I am not going to touch you, wouldn't dream of it. I am dead to the world, knackered. If you fear rape,' he said, lifting the duvet and joining her in the bed, 'Joyful can lie between us like a bolster.' And, laying his head on the pillows, he rejoiced to feel the bed shake with her laughter.

31

Squashed among commuters in the tube Sylvester considered the last week, a week spent discussing Bratt's manuscript. All in his office were agreed that the book was badly written and its content foul. Though one editor was doubtful, two were in favour of buying the manuscript and one, a senior member of the firm, was of the firm opinion that properly presented and cleverly marketed the book, for its content alone, was a potential bestseller. All agreed the book needed a preface and, though interest was expressed in his notes, these were soon forgotten as colleagues tossed ideas back and forth among themselves as to how to market, what jacket to choose, and how to manage the publicity. Haste, according to the senior editor, was of the essence. The book was topical, even more topical than most of its kind. It was essential, he suggested with apparent afterthought, that Narrowlane and Jinks should not get hold of it and someone had better travel to the States as soon as possible to sew up a contract. Pressed against alien backs in the tube Sylvester now remembered that Jinks, of Narrowlane and Jinks, had once had an affair with the senior editor's daughter and had not, it was said, behaved well.

It had then been proposed that since he had been first to read the manuscript and had already met Bratt, he should visit again as soon as possible and, if all went well, have a part after all in the preface; and, if necessary, rewrite the whole book. Forgetting his original opinion of Bratt's manuscript, Sylvester had cried off. He had only visited Bratt, he explained, because John could not, it being so near Christmas, a child having a birthday and so on. He too must refuse because he was biased; he disliked the book intensely and its author more. He would find himself incapable of being objective. Someone had said, 'Fair enough, we will think again,' but Sylvester had been unable to leave well alone, as he would tell Julia. He had gone on to say that there was too much ingrained racism in society and that this would be fostered by Bratt's book, however cleverly presented.

'There will always be readers who will rejoice in the book, agree with Bratt's views. It might even start a new cult,' he had said, 'and in my opinion no respectable publishing house should touch it.'

Nobody had laughed, he would tell Julia when he got home, one or two had pretended to agree; nobody had called him pompous to his face. The prime reason, he must tell her, for his refusal was his annoyance at finding his original impression of Bratt's *oeuvre* so exactly coincided with that of the oldest editor, whom he had long considered past it and ripe for retirement. This, he hoped, would amuse Julia, she being a girl to whom he could tell everything; he knew, too, that she would instinctively feel about Bratt's book as he did.

But she would not be there to tell, he remembered with shock; the house when he got back would be empty, as it had been that morning ten days ago when he woke to find no trace other than a dent in the pillow.

'Christ!' he exclaimed as the train strained to a stop. 'I am going mad!' And, pushing his way to the doors, he got out to walk down Sloane Street to Partridges and buy himself something for a solitary supper.

Halfway along Sloane Street he had a better idea; he would cut through side-streets to Patel's Corner Shop, renew his order for newspapers and buy his supper there. There might be a clue. He quickened his step.

Patel's Corner Shop was busy. Arming himself with a wire basket he prowled along the shelves, glancing at his fellow shoppers. Julia's flat was only a street away; did any of these people know her? Had some of them been at that ghastly party? He recognized no-one. Morosely he chose a steak, changed his mind, took two. One could go in the freezer. The lettuces were crisp, he put one in the basket. He chose fruit, oranges, Cox's Orange Pippins, bananas, and sighting mangoes found them irresistible and picked out two. On to the cheese section for a fruity little goat cheese and a hunk of Stilton before running his eye over the notice-board.

Siamese kitten for sale, neutered.

Mountain bike.

Acupuncture.

Philosophy student in need of accommodation.

Aromatherapy.

Half-grown goat.

Volvo Estate car (Yes, I want a car but shall treat myself to a new one and enjoy its smell.)

Reflexology.

Maps of Yugoslavia urgently wanted.

'Sir?' He had arrived at the counter. Mr Patel smiled.

'Oh, ah, yes, thanks.' Sylvester unloaded his basket while Mr Patel worked the till. 'Before I forget, I want to renew my order for newspapers.'

'Mr Wykes, certainly.'

'You remember my name?' He was gratified.

'The *Observer, The Sunday Times*, no smellies, *Independent*?'

'Right, and oh, just a minute, I think I'll have a couple of tins of dog food.' He must not lose hope, it was still possible he would entice her for a meal; it would be polite to feed the dog. He liked the dog.

'Chappie?' Mr Patel made dog food so friendly, so intimate. 'On the shelf there, sir.' He packed the purchases in a strong paper bag with *Patel's Corner*

Shop and *Recycled* printed on its sides. 'Coffee?' he suggested. 'Beans?'

'Oh yes, thanks for reminding me. A half of Kenyan and half of Colombian, please.'

Mr Patel weighed coffee beans, sealed them into a paper bag.

'Is it the same goat?' Sylvester nodded towards the board.

'Is imaginary.' Mr Patel lowered his eyes. 'Your dog like Chappie?'

'He might as well be imaginary too.'

Mr Patel named the sum of Sylvester's purchases. The moment had come to ask about Julia, but he had prepared no question, was at a loss how to start. Could he say he had been to the house where she lived, had rung the bell, a woman from another flat had opened the door and said, 'She's out. Saw her go. No, don't know her. Why don't you telephone or write?' and practically slammed the door? He cleared his throat. 'I wanted to ask—' But behind him, impatient to pay and be on her way, a woman poked him in the back with her loaded basket. He paid, pocketed his change and, cursing his lack of courage, left.

That bloody woman had robbed him of his chance. Mr Patel did know Julia, it was Patel's notice-board which had found him Julia. It would surely be possible to leave a message; could he do it tomorrow? He could write, but write what, exactly? He could stay home from work, lie in wait, catch her when she came to clean. But did she come? Had she been? Houses could stay clean, couldn't they? If she *was* coming as usual, she left no trace. If she were going to come, would she have left his bed so secretly and vanished without a sound? Had he been *snoring* when she woke?

'Oh God!' Sylvester exclaimed. He had not thought of this before. 'Snoring! God!'

'Only me,' said Hamish Grant as they collided. 'Your mortal cousin, not the Almighty. I don't snore.'

Sylvester said, 'Oh! Hamish! What are you doing here?' rather aggressively.

'Just passing. Wondered whether you'd join me for a bite of dinner. Could put you in the picture about my parent's non-demise and non-funeral.' Hamish grinned.

'Put my foot in it there,' Sylvester admitted. 'I have some fillet steak in this bag.' He held up the Patel's Corner Shop bag. 'And salad, cheese, fruit, coffee. I'm on my own, come and share.'

Hamish said, 'Thanks, love to. How was America? Been back long?' He sounded quite friendly.

'Ten days, and if you are not careful I will tell you all about it. But first, how is your mother, my favourite aunt?'

'Worried that you may have lost your marbles.'

'So she sent you to enquire?'

'Thought of it myself. No need to be huffy. Finding myself in this area and having heard a rumour that your firm is doing a book on Marvin Bratt; there was that, too.'

'News travels fast,' said Sylvester. 'It's not *about*, it's *by*. Who told you?'

'I know Narrowlane,' said Hamish evasively.

'Not Jinks?'

'Same thing.'

'So, finding yourself "just passing" in this area, you came to snoop?'

'Snoop's a harsh word,' said Hamish. They reached Sylvester's door. 'You might need a long spoon,' he said gently.

'The thought had crossed my mind.' Sylvester unlocked his door. 'Come along in. Actually,' he said, leading the way into the house, 'I have refused to have anything to do with it. The man is a stinker and what's more he can't write.'

Hamish said, 'That's all right, then. Good Lord! Somebody has been at your garden. Can I look?' He peered through the french windows at the garden, partly visible by the light from the sitting-room.

'Somebody has.' Sylvester drew the curtains. Should he tell his cousin about Julia? Ask his advice? Better not; he was not a gossip, but he had, had he not, picked up the scent on Bratt. 'I'll tell you all about Bratt,' he said. 'Let's eat in the kitchen. Come and talk to me while I cook, help yourself to a drink.'

Hamish said, 'OK, but first I must look at the garden. I remember it was lovely in your mother's day.' He drew back the curtains and let himself out.

Irritated, Sylvester went down to the kitchen, where he put down his shopping and reached for the pad on which, before he went to America, he had found requests and messages from Mrs Piper. The pad was, as it had been for all the days since his return, blank.

'Who did you find to do your garden?' Hamish clattered down the stairs. 'Someone with real imagination and nous. It can't have been you, you know hardly anything about gardens. I need help with mine. Who was it? Will you give me the man's address?'

'I was going to tell you about Bratt.'

'OK, but—'

'Could you uncork this?' Sylvester handed Hamish a bottle of wine and a corkscrew. 'And how do you like your steak?'

'Rare. Shall I lay the table?' Hamish was easily deflected. 'I met Bratt once,' he said. 'Made my hair stand on end, belongs to some cult.'

Sylvester said, 'Ku Klux Klan,' and they discussed Bratt while he grilled the steaks and made a salad dressing.

It was later, when they had reached the cheese and uncorked a second bottle, that Hamish, letting his eye rove around the room, let it rest on Sylvester's shopping. 'I did not know you had a dog,' he said, staring at the tins of Chappie. Sylvester, his tongue loosened by wine, replied, 'I haven't, it's Julia's.'

And Hamish said, 'Julia?'

'My cleaning lady, Mrs Piper. She did the garden.'

'Really?'

'Yes.'

'Wonderful. Would she do mine? Where can I find her?'

'You'd be cleverer than me!' Sylvester exclaimed. 'I have been looking for ten days. She is not where she's supposed to be. I don't want to intrude, I've thought of leaving a note, but would it get delivered? It's a delicate situation. I don't even know if she still comes in to clean, she leaves no trace, it's— Oh dear!'

'Dog hair?'

'She leaves, left it outside.'

'Telephone?'

'It transpires she is ex-directory.'

'Really?'

'Yes.'

'So how do you normally communicate? I leave notes for my lady.'

'So did I! We used that pad. It's been blank ever since – er – well—'

'Er, well what?'

'I can't tell you.'

'Come on, Sylvester.'

'No.'

Hamish raised his eyebrows. 'Is it important?'

'Vital.'

'Oh,' said Hamish. 'I see,' he said, unseeing. 'Hasn't she got a family? I'm almost part of my lady's family, sort of honorary.'

'No.'

'How d'you find her in the first place? Agency?'

'No.'

'What then?'

'I advertised in the corner shop.'

'So you ask the shop. It's simple.'

'I get the impression they wouldn't tell me. I haven't the nerve.'

Hamish laughed. 'Why on earth not?'

'It's a feeling.'

Hamish said, 'Let me think.' Leaning back, he closed his eyes. 'Why not wait in on her day and catch her then?' He was amused.

'I've thought of that, but we are fearfully busy. I can't spare the time.'

'And you say it's important?'

'Yes, *yes*. And I do know where she lives. I went there, I rang a bell at the street door and a woman from another flat came to the door and was bloody rude—'

Hamish said, 'Suppose you tell me what you are really on about. Why not begin at the beginning?'

Sylvester said, 'Oh, all right.' And, gulping down some wine, told his cousin how, returning from America, he had found Julia asleep on his sofa, still wearing her overcoat, taking refuge from a noisy orgy in the flats where she lived and that she turned out to be someone he had once seen leaping out of a train to rescue a sheep.

Hamish said, 'Didn't you tell me about her? Last time we met? We'd been dining—'

'I may have.'

'And what else happened?'

'Nothing.'

Hamish sniffed. Sylvester refilled their glasses, glancing sidelong at his cousin, who said, 'Why are you so evasive?'

'I am not.'

'Not?'

'It's a delicate situation,' Sylvester muttered uncomfortably.

'Why is it delicate?'

'She's a wounded person; her husband and child were killed in an accident.'

'Ah.'

'Have some more cheese.' Sylvester pushed the cheese across the table. Hamish cut himself a sliver, popped it in his mouth.

'You too are wounded,' he said, munching. 'Your ex-wife Celia – she is ex by now, I hope? – pretty well shredded your self-confidence.'

'I wouldn't say that.' Sylvester was irritated that his cousin should have had that impression. 'Any slight nicks in my *amour propre* are long since healed,' he said.

Unimpressed, Hamish said, 'Good.'

Sylvester said, 'I'll make some coffee,' and proceeded to do so, reminded painfully of Julia by the coffee grinder's screech.

An hour later, bidding his cousin goodbye, Hamish standing on the doorstep buttoning his overcoat said, 'You are in love with this girl.'

And Sylvester replied, 'I want to find out whether I am.'

'You said she has a dog?' Hamish cogitated.

'Yes.'

Hamish said, '*Cherchez le chien*,' and laughed as he walked away.

32

'It is something you should know.' Rebecca sat on the sofa holding her drink while Sylvester lolled in the armchair, his legs crossed at the ankles. He had just got back from work when Rebecca rang the bell. 'What neat timing,' he had ungraciously said on opening the door to her uninvited presence. 'Want a drink?'

She had accepted a vodka and tonic, which she now sipped. 'Aren't you having a drink?'

'No.'

'I am drinking alone?'

'Yes.' He eased off his shoes, letting them thud on to the rug. His socks, she observed, were pink of the variety once called shocking. 'Lovely rugs.' She examined the rugs. 'Kelims, I think you said.'

'Yes.'

'Did you get those socks in America?'

'Did you come to discuss my socks?' Aware of sounding disagreeable – Rebecca was after all an old associate, friend, he supposed – Sylvester said, 'Sorry, Rebecca, a shop on Fifth Avenue. They also had electric blue. I resisted those.'

Rebecca gulped down some vodka. Drinking alone put her at a disadvantage; it was not easy to get started. 'Is that smart new Renault outside yours?' she asked.

'Yes, Rebecca, it is, how observant you are. I bought it in London and the socks in New York. Anything else? Did you not say there was something I should know?'

How to begin? It had seemed so simple, but here on his sofa she felt daunted. Had she thought it properly through? She raised her glass, sipped. Would he want to know where she had gained her information and who from? He would. They had known each other a long time, years, but was he the sort to wake in his own bed as she had the other day in hers, to find a strange face on the pillow? She doubted it. She must manage without giving details. 'It's nothing much.' She swallowed some vodka. 'Just something I heard about your cleaning woman,' she said; and because for some silly reason she felt nervous with Sylvester sitting there in his socks, not drinking but watching, she added, 'I was just passing,' which they both knew to be untrue since to reach Sylvester's door entailed, for her, quite a detour.

Sylvester grinned. 'Yes?'

'A person I met told me some oddish things about her.'

'Such as?'

'It may be exaggerated gossip.' As seen from Sylvester's sofa, the probity of her visit was becoming obfusc.

'Would that person be the man I saw you dancing with the other day? In the street—'

'What's wrong with dancing in the street?' Rebecca bristled.

'Did I say so? Even hint?'

'No – but—'

'I thought you were having a lovely time with a bit of Rough Trade. You looked positively frisky.'

'Sylvester! Frisky! Honestly!'

'It's not an insult, of course not! So what piece of news, what spicy titbit did this piece of Rough Trade impart?' Sylvester wheedled.

'His name is Benson, Maurice Benson.' Rebecca disliked Sylvester's description, it was too apt.

When she takes offence, Sylvester thought, she looks positively masculine. A moustache formed like the horns of a water buffalo would suit her. 'I know his

217

name,' he said, 'and he calls himself a twitcher. What did he have to say about Mrs Piper? He smells terrible – of stale tobacco and beer.' Rebecca tightened her lips; she liked the way Benson smelled. 'Did he tell you that he spies on Mrs Piper, and for some reason spies on me?' Sylvester asked. 'Is that the "something" I should know? Did he tell you that he rings her up in the middle of the night and makes threatening calls? Did he tell you that? Did he happen to tell you that Mrs Piper's ex-husband and child were recently killed in a car crash?'

Rebecca said, 'No,' whispering it. 'No.'

'I believe you've been to bed with him,' Sylvester teased.

Rebecca exclaimed, 'What!', flushing up brightly.

'So what did he tell you?' (Perhaps I went too far; she is blinking back a tear.)

'What he told me – oh— He followed her out of interest. Yes, something to do with birds? Went to see her mother who is called Clodagh May and lives in Devon— He had seen her, your Mrs Piper, doing something peculiar which interested him. He is interested in people as well as birds but birds are his passion. He did say, yes, he did, that he had teased her a little about something he knew.'

'He makes obscene calls.'

'Oh, Sylvester, really! I've had obscene calls, you know the kind of thing, heavy breathing and what colour knickers are you wearing? Maurice Benson wouldn't do that.'

'You have?' Sylvester was briefly deflected; for Rebecca to receive obscene calls hardly tallied with the imaginary moustache. 'Knickers?'

'Yes, and the other one is the splendid length of the caller's penis.'

'What do you say to that?'

'Either one hangs up, or one says, "Is that all? Only ten inches? Pitiful".'

218

'Gosh! But back to your Benson, what germs of information did he impart?' Sylvester was unrelenting. 'Did he tell you he accuses her of murdering her child?'

'No, he did not. I am sure he would not.' She was shocked. 'He knows she knows some secret lake ospreys visit when they are migrating and wants to know where it is so that he can log it, the osprey, in the book he keeps as a twitcher. Obviously that is why he has rung her up. Of course it is. But one funny thing he did say is that she tried to deafen him with a whistle.'

'I don't know about the osprey,' Sylvester said, 'but the whistle's true and serves him bloody right. The fellow took you for a ride, Rebecca.' Not for anything would he let her divine his rage. 'I hope you enjoyed it,' he said. 'You look like you need a refill, let me take your glass.'

Rebecca said, 'No, thank you, Sylvester. I must go.' She heaved herself up from the sofa. 'I've got a date,' she said.

At the street door Sylvester pecked her cheek. 'You slept with that hunk,' he said.

Rebecca said, 'Don't be ridiculous!' and slapped the bonnet of his new car as she walked past.

33

When Sylvester recognized Joyful sitting on a doorstep in Notting Hill he nearly caused an accident. The driver of the car which barely avoided shunting him blew her horn, rolled down her window, yelled, 'Male driver!', and making the 'V' sign pulled out to pass. Parking by the steps on which the dog sat, Sylvester's heart beat fast; the hand which pulled on the brake was sweaty. He pressed the button, rolled down his window and uttered the animal's name in a conspiratorial croak. 'Joyful?' Joyful raised the head which was propped on his paws and, meeting Sylvester's eye, flattened his ears in recognition.

When Julia emerged from the house an hour later, clicking the door shut, hitching her bag on to her shoulder, she looked worriedly up and down the pavement.

Sylvester opened the car window a little way. 'He is here. I have kidnapped him.' Joyful thrust a whiskery nose through the gap.

'What the *hell* do you think you're doing? Let him out at once.' Her face whitened in fear then, recognizing Sylvester, she said, 'What are you doing here?'

'And you?' He held on to the dog, lowered the window a little further.

'I have a job here, please let him out—'

'Get in with us.' Sylvester opened the car door. 'Please.'

'Why should I?' She stood her ground; various pedestrians side-stepped to get by.

'Please.' He held the door open with one hand,

keeping a grip on the dog with the other. 'This would be much easier to manage if he had a collar,' he said.

Julia said, 'He has never had a collar. Please let him go.'

'Please get in.'

A woman pushing a twin buggy laden with bald babies brushed past Julia; under their Cellophane hood the babies wailed. Julia got into the car. Sylvester pulled the door shut. Joyful thrust his muzzle into her face. Sylvester said, 'Fasten your seat-belt,' started the car and pulled away from the kerb. 'We are going for a jaunt in the country,' he said.

Julia fastened her seat-belt in silence.

Heading down Holland Park Avenue towards Shepherd's Bush, Sylvester said, 'I am so glad to have found you. I have been trawling the streets, getting funny looks from people who mistake me for a kerb-crawler. It's quite embarrassing.'

Julia's profile was stern; she kept her mouth shut, breathing through her nose, her arm round the dog who sat upright between them.

They joined the traffic streaming towards Chiswick on to the motorway. Sylvester said, 'My cousin Hamish, whom you have yet to meet, is so impressed by what you have done to the garden that he wonders whether you would consider helping him with his?' Julia did not reply. Sylvester said, 'Oh well. We were discussing gardens and he wanted to get in touch with you, and I, feeling a fool, had to admit that I was finding it difficult, in fact impossible to contact you. He went into a long boring spiel about how *he* contacts *his* cleaning lady, none of it relevant. I did say that before I went to America you left notes on a pad about soap and things like that. By the way, I have to ask you, have you been coming in to clean?'

Julia said, 'Yes,' her eyes on the road ahead.

Sylvester said, 'I wondered, because although I have

221

left your money for you, as I did before I went away, you have not taken it.'

Julia said, 'You sent me a cheque from America. It was too much, I told you.'

'So *that's* it. I thought the house was keeping rather too clean to be managing on its own and that it couldn't be the fairies.' Julia made no reply. Sylvester ploughed on. 'Hamish asked how I had come across you in the first place – Oh, by the way, his mother is my aunt Calypso who is not dead and who has not had a funeral—'

Julia said, 'Oh, that clarifies him.'

Sylvester said. 'Yes. Where was I? Ah yes, looking for you. Hamish suggested I telephone, as if I hadn't tried. You appear to be ex-directory. I have also been to your flat and rung bells, got short shrift from your boorish neighbours. You seem never to be in. He next asked how I came to find you in the first place and I told him the notice-board in the corner shop, so he said, or I think he said, "Try there". I had, of course.'

Beside him Julia's mouth twitched into a smile; was this the moment when he could comment on her profile, tell her it was lovely? Not yet. He was driving fast now, spinning down the motorway, pleased with the new car, enjoying the feel of it. Soon they would be in open country.

'I tried to find some trace of you in the corner shop,' he said. 'I get my papers there, shop there, too. It's a splendid shop, I like the owner. I like the way he takes the trouble to remove the stinks from the colour mags. I particularly enjoy his notice-board. There is an advertisement for what appears to be a non-existent goat; before I went to the States it was plain "Goat", but now it's become a "Young Goat", it's imaginary, he says.'

Julia said, 'He reads *Alice Through the Looking Glass*. Next week it may be a kid.'

Sylvester said, 'Thank you,' grateful that at last she

222

had spoken. 'Were you by any chance in the shop, behind the scenes perhaps, when I went to enquire after you but lost my nerve?'

Julia said, 'No.'

'But you might have been? He is your friend?'

Julia said, 'He thought it possible that you were the man who—'

'The obscene caller?' Sylvester took offence. 'God-dammit, how could he?'

'He wasn't sure.' Julia began to laugh. 'He was being careful, that's all. His wife is super-protective. She loved Christy, you see – she is afraid for me.'

'Why should I hurt you?'

Julia did not answer for a bit, then she said, 'You could have left a message with the Patels.'

Saying what? Sylvester wondered what sort of message. What he had to say could not be contained in a message, nor could what he had to say be said driving down the motorway at eighty-five miles an hour. 'In the end,' he said, 'I remembered something my cousin said about finding the dog. I have searched Chelsea, Fulham, Kensington and Pimlico and bingo, this afternoon there he was on a doorstep. I remembered too that you had said he barked at your tormentor. He did not bark at me, did you, boy?' Sylvester took a hand off the wheel and stroked Joyful's head. 'So I found you at last,' he said.

Julia leaned back in her seat and he realized that she had been tense but was becoming less so.

Outside the light was fading into winter dark. He switched on the car lights.

'Are you warm enough?'

'Yes thank you.'

'Rebecca, when she discovered that you were working for me, said you must be a gypsy, that Piper is a gypsy name,' he said.

'It is, sometimes. There are Pipers in Devon who are gypsies.'

223

Later he said, 'When you stopped the train and saved the sheep it seemed to be on its own. Where do you suppose the rest of the flock had got to?'

Julia said, 'I suppose they had moved up the hill. To another field, perhaps? Why do you ask? I had not thought of it until now. Why are you so interested?'

'I can't tell you at eighty-five miles an hour.'

Julia crossed her legs and the dog, tired of staring at the road, slumped against her, nestling to sleep.

Sylvester could not for the moment voice the only words that mattered, but sensed that it would be politic to keep talking. 'I wondered when I tried to find you at your flat,' he said, 'whether if you were in you would threaten me again with a jagged tin of Chappie?'

Julia said, 'It was Winalot, actually. I mistook you for that man who has been bothering me.'

'He complains that you deafened him.'

'How do you know?' She stiffened, drawing her knees up, sitting up straight.

'Rebecca picked him up or she him; they were among the dancers at the street party. He was on the train, as I was, when you stopped it. I remember him. I suspect he followed you, I don't know why, but that's what I think.'

'He accuses me of murder—'

'According to Rebecca that's a mild tease.'

'Is he insane?'

'He has been to see your mother.'

'Good God, why?'

'I rather gather your behaviour with the sheep roused his curiosity, in fact I know it did. On the train I thought he might be some low form of press reporter; I took a dislike to him. I could see it was reciprocated.'

Julia said, 'M-m-m. What else?'

'He kept boasting about being a bird-watcher, a twitcher, and thought there might be a story.'

'But why should he torment me?'

'Ospreys? Do you know something about ospreys? A secret lake? Migratory flights? Mean anything?'

'Yes. Oh! He must have met Madge as well as my – as well as Clodagh.'

'And?'

'She is the only person I told about the ospreys. It's not such a big secret. Ospreys come every year to a lake near some people I worked for in Somerset. We watched them, they were wonderful.'

To keep her talking, Sylvester said, 'Were you there long?'

'A year or two. It was before, before a lot of things. I was happy. They said come back when I had to go and help when Clodagh broke her leg, come back when it's mended.'

'Why didn't you?'

'Giles. Giles was there with Clodagh.'

'So you fell in love.' Sylvester was surprised by his jealousy, at the bile in his voice.

Julia snapped, 'I got pregnant. I married. I had Christy, I—' Her voice rose in pain. 'He—'

'And it's no business of mine?'

'Of course not,' she shouted.

But it is, Sylvester thought, everything about her is my business. And now I've hurt her, brought up the child. Oh bugger, what shall I say next? 'I suspect,' he said, 'that Rebecca has been to bed with your heavy breather.'

Julia said, 'Goodness!' in genuine astonishment. 'Whatever next!' Relaxing her tense legs, stretching them out, she crossed them at the ankles. 'It would take the pressure off you,' she said, 'but does she know what she's taking on?'

Sylvester said, 'She's a tough lady. I daresay she will manage.'

And Julia said, 'If I tell you where the ospreys are, you could give their whereabouts to her to give him.'

Sylvester said, 'That would be generous, but I will

keep the information up my sleeve in case the old girl needs help,' and drove on for some miles without speaking, but curiosity, that insistent emotion, got the better of his silence and he asked, 'Were there *any* happy times with Giles?'

'Yes,' Julia said, 'a few. And you with Celia? Were there happy times with Celia?' she asked brightly.

'Quite a lot actually,' Sylvester confessed, 'but they sort of diminished.' Then, because he desperately wanted to cross-question her and felt it was too soon, he said, 'I'll tell you all about her over dinner.'

Julia said, 'Oh, are we going to have dinner?'

And he said, 'That is the idea, dinner and then a walk for Joyful,' and then, his mind reverting to Maurice Benson, 'I think that oaf tormented you because he thought you were weak. I could see from the train that you were in distress and he could, too. It's the bully in the playground syndrome.'

He was pleased when she said, 'Let's leave him to your Rebecca friend. The only time I saw him properly, he had a bit of watercress stuck in his teeth. If your friend saw that, she would tell him; I refrained.'

'Soon,' Sylvester said, 'we will leave the main road and drive along a lane which meanders down a valley beside a chalk stream. There will be a village pub which will give us dinner. This will do,' he said, slowing the car. 'Let's try this.' He drove now along a road twisting along a valley bottom.

Julia opened her window. 'There *is* a stream.' The dog stood up and, lurching across her lap, snuffled at the window.

Sylvester said, 'Didn't I say?' and presently stopped by a pub in a village street with the stream running along its length. They got out and stood on a foot-bridge while Joyful drank from the stream, then Sylvester pushed open the pub door, led Julia in, and asked whether they could eat.

It was a quiet pub; a few people murmured round

the bar and a small group sat by an open fire. They were shown to a table in a darkish corner where they sat and ordered their meal. There was not much choice.

Sylvester was anxious. He said, 'There is not much choice; are you happy with onion soup and grilled Dover sole? Fortunately there is some good wine.'

Julia said, 'Yes, I am,' and, 'It's midwinter. It looks delicious.' She was furiously hungry.

The wine was poured. Sylvester tasted and approved; Julia drank. 'Lovely.' Joyful wandered away to sit by the fire.

It had been relatively easy to talk in the car. Sitting in the dark without eye contact had been a help, he had gauged her mood by whether she relaxed her legs or drew them tensely up. Now, catching her eye across the table, he was tongue-tied.

She said, 'When did you find this lovely pub?'

'I guessed it would be here.' It had been a gamble, the sort of chance one would take as a matter of course in France. He had taken a risk and it had come off.

'So you've never been here before?'

'Never.' He would have liked to say he had brought her here, taken the gamble, so that there would be no memories to butt in, so that the experience would be theirs alone, but he could not, any more than he had been able to say what he wanted at eighty-five miles an hour.

The waitress brought their soup. Julia said, 'Oh, looks delicious,' and picked up her spoon.

Joyful, who had been roasting himself by the fire, came back to them panting and overheated, and cast himself down to lie heavily across Sylvester's feet.

Julia said, 'He likes you.'

'Where did he come from? A really good lurcher is hard to find.'

Julia said, 'He found me,' and described her meeting with the dog and her attempt at rejection and how, when she rejected him, she felt guilt and distress so that when he persisted she had given in and shared an extravagant fillet steak bought to celebrate the prospect of bringing the garden back to life. 'I felt,' she said, 'that he knew he belonged to me and I to him.'

I wish you would reach the same realization about me, Sylvester thought, watching her spoon in soup. He said, 'He must have had an owner,' and was amused when she said, 'He has one now,' and, catching his eye, 'I am not in the business of looking into his past.'

So they finished their soup.

'Tell me about the Patels.' Sylvester poured wine into her half-empty glass.

'They are my friends.'

'And?'

She drank some wine. 'I was pregnant. I shopped at their shop. One day Mr Patel asked me to help his wife, who was shy and afraid of going to the ante-natal clinic. She couldn't speak English. So I took her along with me. She is a lovely person, we made friends. They are good to me, she's had another baby but our – our children were the same age.'

'Christy.'

'Yes.' Julia sipped her wine, looked away from him. A log fell over and the fire, flaring up, lit her face. There was pain in her eyes. She said, 'She *can* speak a bit of English now, she seldom does but she understands all right.'

'Tell me about your jobs.'

'I work where you found us this afternoon two days a week for a man who is a car dealer. I don't meet him; he's at work. I work, too, for a woman journalist, same thing, same arrangement. There have been other people. Now there is you and your garden. I manage. When Christy was alive Mrs Patel minded him for me – it pays the bills.'

'Didn't your husband pay the bills?'

'Erratically.'

The waitress took away the soup plates, brought their Dover soles. 'Everything all right?'

'Thank you. Yes.' What should he ask her now?

'I thought you were going to tell me all about Celia over dinner,' Julia said, picking up her knife and fork.

34

Sylvester was amused by the way Julia tricked him into talking about himself. Eating their Dover sole, delicious, as were the accompanying chips and watercress salad, she had listened attentively. On through out-of-season strawberries and cream and a most excellent Stilton, which he ate with Bath Oliver biscuits and she merely tasted to keep him company, to their final black coffees, she had listened and munched and, should he flag, murmured a question to set him off again.

Although they shared the bottle evenly, his tongue had wagged while hers stayed mute. Paying the bill while she went to the lavatory, Sylvester was lost in admiration. He had given her a run-down of his life to date. Infancy, school, father's death, university, travels, choice of jobs, change of jobs, first love (in Paris, excellent for his French), second loves (Munich and Vienna, brushing up his German), his mother's death, London life, the meeting with Celia (*coup de foudre* fizzling like a second-rate firework but try, try and make it work). He had even told her what book Celia was reading during their last conjugal conjunction – not Barbara Cartland, but as near as dammit. On to Celia's departure, his mortification, hurt and relief.

'The dinner was delicious, thank you very much.'

He calculated the tip, doubled it and went to stand by the fire to await her reappearance.

He had not yet told her his tastes in music, art, theatre, film or literature but that would come; he jiggled the change in his trouser pocket; nor had he told her what he had not been able to tell her coming down the motorway.

Where the hell was she? She was taking a helluva long time over a pee. She had taken the dog with her. Had she scarpered? Christ Almighty!

She had taken her coat when she left the table. He had heard departing customers start up their cars; she could have cadged a lift, done a runner? Oh, dear God! All through the meal I burbled on about myself, my boring ineffectual life, when I should have been enchanting her with fascinating plans for our future. Oh God, what a fool! I should have found out whether she's been to Venice. Would she prefer to explore Italy or France, or rather go to Peru? Has she seen the Alhambra? Would she prefer the West Indies or Japan? Will she be happy living in my house? Perhaps a cottage in the country? Is she keen on clothes? I've never seen her in anything but that black overcoat and jeans. I don't even know what her legs are like, didn't dare look that night. I'd love to buy her clothes. I'd love to give her things, have her always there to share jokes; and babies, would we dare? 'Oh, dear God!' he said out loud. 'And now she's gone.'

'Sorry to be so long,' Julia said, reappearing. 'The wretch did something he has not done before; he shot off after a cat, disappeared right down the street, didn't come when I whistled.'

'I thought you'd hopped it.' Sylvester helped her into her coat. 'I thought I had bored you into running away.'

In the street the air crackled with frost. Julia turned up her collar; they got into the car. 'I was not bored,' she said.

Driving along the twisting lanes, Sylvester said, 'I talked too much, I apologize. You could not have got a word in edgeways.'

She said, 'I am not used to talking, though I sometimes can with Mrs Patel.'

'Does she understand?'

'Not a lot, but it's good. We laugh a lot.'

'No-one else?'

'A girl from the bottom flat tried to be friendly, but I frightened her. She thought I was plotting to kill myself – this was when they were killed, just after the funeral. Her overture went wrong, she drank all my vodka and I helped her to bed.'

'Not a social success.'

'I could not talk, but longed to. D'you know that state?'

'I do indeed.' I am in it now, Sylvester thought.

'I sheltered from the rain in a church. There was a priest who was kind, terribly kind but I could not tell him the real snag, the real worry.'

The road led them up a hill through a beech wood, the boles of the trees stark in the moonlight. Sylvester said, 'Apropos of nothing, have you thrown away that toy?'

'Oh no! It's not the original, it's not Christy's. Of course I keep it. I did not throw his lamb out. When he was killed, and Giles, I gathered up everything, toys, clothes, books, everything of theirs and got rid of them. I could not bear having them around me. Christy's lamb was with him in the smash. You probably felt the same about Celia's things? Dumb reminders.'

'Not exactly. She took everything except the terrible cupid in the garden. I threw that out.' He was glad she had kept the toy.

Julia said, 'What you need for your garden is an eighteenth-century lead shell for a bird bath.'

Sylvester said, 'Will you help me find one?' Then, 'Suppose we leave the car here and give Joyful his walk?' We leap from subject to subject, he thought, we shrink from vital issues.

They left the car and, climbing up through a belt of trees, dead leaves crunching underfoot, reached open downland.

Julia said, 'When my parents split up I was younger than Christy. My father kidnapped me. I remember a wood like this, holding his hand – reaching up.' A few paces on she said, 'He sent me back in a car with strangers, a man and a woman. It was only a gesture.'

There was a sudden rustling on the edge of the wood and the dog set off in pursuit of a hare. They watched his diminishing shape and listened to his muffled yelps.

Sylvester said, 'Your m— Clodagh must have been immensely relieved to get you back.'

'I don't know about that,' Julia said crisply. 'Clodagh is not the maternal type; children are toys, possesions. What Clodagh likes is a young lover whom she thinks she can manipulate, but who in fact manipulates her. Oh!' she said. 'The hare got away, he is coming back.'

Sylvester took her hand and putting it in his pocket held it there, keeping it warm. 'Go on.'

Julia said, 'I was a mug. I did not know she and Giles were lovers. I was puzzled by her attitude when I found myself pregnant after he had raped me. I was all for an abortion, to get away, to forget the whole thing; her leg was OK by then. But she insisted we marry. I was obtuse, plain bloody stupid, blind, but she wore me down. So I thought, OK, I'd try and make a go of it, Giles could be quite decent, could be, had been attractive and funny. He could laugh. We had laughed together, he made silly jokes about Clodagh – they seemed funny at the time, anyway – so we married, as she insisted. Am I boring you?'

'No. Go on.' They had left the trees and were walking across downland. In the distance there was a stand of trees; everything was very clear by the light of the moon, which cast deep shadows into the valley. It was so quiet Joyful's panting sounded loud, his breath clouding in the freezing air. 'Go on,' Sylvester said.

She took a deep breath. 'We had this lovely honeymoon in Paris. It turned into a nightmare. He compared me with Clodagh I suppose, I suppose he felt trapped.'

'And?'

'Oh, violence, drink, broken glass, all that. And hurtful words, which are so much worse.'

'And you?'

'Trapped, too.'

'Go on.'

'We came back to London to the flat. He came and went. Christy was born. I started work again. Had to. Time passed, as it does. I tried, not hard enough obviously, and little things add up—'

'Such as?'

'He smelled. It's humiliating to recall. Pits, breath, feet. When he drank, he did not wash. I shrank from him, couldn't bring myself to do enough to make the marriage work. It did not really exist except on paper, it never had.'

'But Christy?'

'He existed. I loved him. But then, my God! So did she in her way.'

'Go on.'

'That's what I could not do, go on. I divorced him. I couldn't cite Clodagh and brand my child, and no-one has ever got a divorce because the man smells. So I cited drunkenness and violence, which I could have coped with as thousands and thousands of women do.'

He held her hand deep in his pocket; their feet made a sound like breaking biscuits on the short downland grass. Joyful circled round them, enjoying himself hugely.

'What is it you could not tell the priest who was kind to you?'

'I cannot—'

'You must.'

'No!' Julia shouted. 'No!' Her denial echoed down the valley as she snatched her hand from his and turned away. Sylvester caught her by the shoulders

234

and turned her roughly round. 'You have got to tell me,' he heard himself shouting. He could feel her shoulder-blades through her coat. At any moment she might break away and run as the hare had run, she might escape as the hare had escaped, but he had to persist. 'Tell me.'

'I became violent, too. I lashed out when I should have left him, got out of the flat. I didn't and I broke his nose. I told the priest that—'

'Go on.' He shook her.

'It's irrational, it was an obsession. I *hated* Giles, *hated* him, *hated* him; and Christy I *loved*. But he had Giles's hair, Giles's eyes, Giles's mouth, Giles's expression, his gestures! He was Giles in miniature. The likeness has grown in my mind until it is monstrous and I cannot see my little boy any more.'

Sylvester put his arms around her shoulders and she beat her forehead against his chest. He remembered his own mother holding him when he was little, his legs straddled round her waist too close to see her face as she cuddled him or for her to see his, and holding Julia he searched for words of immediate comfort. Finding none, he found a worry for himself. 'Do you,' he asked, 'look like your – look like your mother?'

'No!' Julia spoke sharply. 'Not in the least.' She fumbled in her pocket for a handkerchief and blew her nose.

'I am glad of that,' Sylvester said, 'and I am glad you broke that bastard's nose. Wouldn't it be – I mean, suppose your little boy looked like Clodagh?'

Julia said, 'Oh, *Sylvester*!' She had not used his name before. 'What a brilliant antidote.'

And presently she said, 'My feet are freezing.'

Sylvester said, 'Let's walk on.'

They had walked much further than either of them realized and reached the strand of trees, walked through to look down into a mysterious valley, standing close together, their sleeves touching, quiet in the windless night. Eventually the dog, feeling the chill, whined. Sylvester pocketed Julia's hand and walked her back to the car. When they reached it she took off her shoes which were wet and leaned back in her seat, wrapping her coat tightly round her. The dog, hopping on to the back seat, stretched out.

Starting the engine Sylvester said, 'If you will let me, I will buy Joyful a collar.'

Amused, she said, 'You are law-abiding.'

'And the bird bath? Will you help me hunt for a bird bath?'

'If you want—'

Angrily he thought, of course I want! I want to collar the dog and collar you! But all he said was, 'Are your feet chilly? If I push this button, it will direct hot air on to them.'

And she murmured, 'Hot air.'

Leaving the lanes he regained the main road and, driving fast, wondered how long it would take to get back to London. The clock on the dashboard was touching midnight.

At least, he thought, there has been a beginning but there may be lots more bogies. I pray she will let me share them. But I have exhausted her, worn her out; she'd been working all day when I found her. I'm sure she had not eaten, she was hungry for that soup. And now she's asleep, the dog too. Yawning, he thought longingly of bed.

'What was it you could not tell me driving at eighty-five miles an hour?'

'I thought you were asleep.'

'What was it?'

'Probably what I am thinking now.'

'Which is?'

'Oh!' He slewed the car into the slow lane. 'OK!' he shouted. 'It's this. I want to wake on Sunday mornings with you beside me in the bed and hear the plop of Sunday papers falling through the letter-box and—'

'And?'

'Not necessarily read them.' He swung the car back into the fast lane.

'Saturday – it's just about Sunday now,' she said.

'What of it?' Was he furious or frightened?

She said, 'You will have to lend me your shirt.'

THE END

A Sensible Life
Mary Wesley

'I LOVED EVERY WORD OF IT'
Christopher Wordsworth, *Guardian*

She was a thin, lonely child with huge eyes and an
extensive vocabulary of French foul language. Amongst
the elegant middle-class British families holidaying in
Dinard in 1926 – leading their privileged lives of secure
routine pleasures – Flora was a ten-year-old misfit.
Ignored by her self-absorbed parents, unloved, and pitied
by the pleasant, stylish people in Brittany that summer,
Flora was – peripherally – included in their gracious
circles. And there, meeting kindly civilised people for the
first time, she fell in love – with Cosmo – with Hubert –
with Felix. It took forty years for the love affairs to be
explored, consummated, and finally resolved.

'IT IS DELICIOUS . . . SHE WRITES WITH THE
KNOWLEDGE AND WISDOM OF SERENE OLD AGE
AND THE EMOTIONAL EXUBERANCE OF GLOWING
YOUNG WOMANHOOD'
Patrick Skene Catling, *Daily Telegraph*

'SUCH GOOD COMPANY THAT IN MORE THAN ONE
SENSE IT'S HARD TO PUT DOWN'
David Hughes, *Mail on Sunday*

'THIS IS A SPLENDID NOVEL; IT IS A DELIGHT TO SEE
WESLEY IN GLORIOUS FORM'
Miranda Seymour, *Evening Standard*

0 552 99393 X

BLACK SWAN

A Dubious Legacy
Mary Wesley

'MARY WESLEY HOLDS YOU BY THE HAND AND YOU
FOLLOW WHEREVER SHE TAKES YOU'
Kate Kellaway, *Observer*

Henry brought his new bride, Margaret, to Cotteshaw in
1944. On the threshold she gave him a black eye and went
straight to bed where she remained, apart from the
occasional malevolent outburst, for the rest of her life.

The two young couples, who encountered her first in
1954, became regular if uneasy house guests over many
years, listening, speculating, keeping a watchful eye on
Margaret's door until finally, piecing together the gossip,
the rumours, the mystery, they found themselves tangled
in the web of Henry's life.

'MARY WESLEY DOES IT AGAIN, ONLY MORE SO;
THIS YEAR'S IS A VINTAGE *CRU* . . . AN EXCELLENT
STORYTELLER AND SURER-FOOTED THAN BEFORE.
SHE MARCHES STRAIGHT INTO HER TALE,
INTRIGUING FROM THE BEGINNING, KEEPING UP A
PACE THAT RARELY SLACKENS'
Literary Review

'WESLEY'S BOOKS ARE A DELIGHT . . . A
BEAUTIFULLY CRAFTED TALE, VERY SEXY, VERY
FUNNY, I JUST DIDN'T WANT IT TO END'
Sunday Times, Perth

'WESLEY BREEZES ALONG WITH CUSTOMARY
GRACE AND NONCHALANCE, SNIPING
MALICIOUSLY AT HER CHARACTERS WHILE GIVING
THEM A MORE OR LESS GOOD TIME'
Financial Times

0 552 99495 2

BLACK SWAN

A SELECTION OF FINE WRITING
AVAILABLE FROM BLACK SWAN

THE PRICES SHOWN BELOW WERE CORRECT AT THE TIME OF GOING TO PRESS. HOWEVER TRANSWORLD PUBLISHERS RESERVE THE RIGHT TO SHOW NEW RETAIL PRICES ON COVERS WHICH MAY DIFFER FROM THOSE PREVIOUSLY ADVERTISED IN THE TEXT OR ELSEWHERE.

All Black Swan Books are available at your bookshop or newsagent, or can be ordered from the following address:

Black Swan Books,
Cash Sales Department
P.O. Box 11, Falmouth, Cornwall TR10 9EN

UK and B.F.P.O. customers please send a cheque or postal order (no currency) and allow £1.00 for postage and packing for the first book plus 50p for the second book and 30p for each additional book to a maximum charge of £3.00 (7 books plus).

Overseas customers, including Eire, please allow £2.00 for postage and packing for the first book plus £1.00 for the second book and 50p for each subsequent title ordered.

NAME (Block Letters) ....

ADDRESS ....

....